Spies and Other Gods

Spies and Other Gods

James Wolff

BASKERVILLE
An imprint of JOHN MURRAY

First published in Great Britain in 2026 by Baskerville
An imprint of John Murray (Publishers)

1

A CIP catalogue record for this title is available from the British Library

Hardback ISBN 9781399826310
Trade Paperback ISBN 9781399826327
ebook ISBN 9781399826334

Typeset in Perpetua by Hewer Text UK Ltd, Edinburgh
Printed and bound in Great Britain by Clays Ltd, Elcograf S.p.A.

John Murray policy is to use papers that are natural, renewable and
recyclable products and made from wood grown in sustainable forests.
The logging and manufacturing processes are expected to conform
to the environmental regulations of the country of origin.

Carmelite House
50 Victoria Embankment
London EC4Y 0DZ

www.johnmurraypress.co.uk

John Murray Press, part of Hodder & Stoughton Limited
An Hachette UK company

The authorised representative in the EEA is Hachette Ireland, 8 Castlecourt
Centre, Dublin 15, D15 XTP3, Ireland (email: info@hbgi.ie)

For J and S

. . . we raised the concern in our 2016–2017 Report that '*if the Agencies intend* [the ISC] *to be used* [as a route for whistle-blowing] *then the current bar on Agency staff being able to commu-nicate with the Committee directly via secure email will need to be removed.*' This has not happened. If the Agencies are serious about their staff being able to approach the ISC Chair, then the bar must be removed.

Intelligence and Security Committee of
Parliament Annual Report 2018–2019

The crowd is untruth.

Søren Kierkegaard

PART ONE

It's every bit as difficult to pick a spy out of a crowd as you would expect. Take that woman across the road, the one in the black coat and red scarf, the one who's let three buses come and go in the last ten minutes. Is she one of us? She's certainly staring at this building with an intensity that suggests something beyond idle curiosity. If she is one of us, why doesn't she just cross the road and come in like anybody else? I suppose it might be first-day nerves, or she could be a visitor – a lawyer, a police officer, a civil servant – although they usually carry a briefcase or folder for their papers, and they tend to have a compliant, institutionalised look about them that's worryingly absent in her.

This woman is the reason there's no collective noun for spies, if she even is a spy, which I'm beginning to doubt. The problem is there's no single distinguishing characteristic shared by everyone who works here, other than an ability to pass unnoticed as we go about our business. 'An order of monks', 'a murmur of nuns' – the best ones speak directly to the core of a group identity, but if that core is unknowable by design then you're left clutching at straws. Ideally it would be something allusive and ambiguous, as in 'a congregation of alligators', or a term that introduces itself as one thing but is secretly another, like 'a circle of friends', which sounds warm and fuzzy unless you're on the outside trying to get in. I suppose that's true of every group. Our power lies in the ability to close ranks and exclude. Groups are all well and good if you're on the inside, but if you're not, if you're out there on your own, don't take it as a threat if I point out that it's only a matter of time before a murder of crows turns in your direction.

She's still there. In normal times I wouldn't give it a second thought. A woman stands looking at a government building – it's hardly enough to bring the police running. But these aren't normal times. I don't want you to get the wrong impression. At this very moment over 535 intelligence operations – a new record – are being run out of this building, both in the UK and overseas, targeting Islamist terrorists, foreign spies, people smugglers, Kremlin apparatchiks, government whistleblowers, Republicans and Loyalists, rogue scientists, a handful of journalists, two MPs and one member of the royal family (not the one you think). The Chinese have recently upgraded their assessment of the combined UK global intelligence capability from 'moderate' to 'significant'. We consistently hit our recruitment targets, staff retention is at an all-time high, projections suggest a small budget surplus and we have already disrupted seven attacks on UK soil this year. Whichever way you look at it, this is an organisation at the top of its game.

Having said all that, having said all that . . .

She's still there, you know. Another bus has come and gone but she's still there.

The thing is, and I'll state it plainly, we are temporarily carrying an unacceptable level of risk arising from one or two significant errors of judgement. I wish it wasn't so. We'll get through it, as we always do, but you'll have to bear with me if I'm a little jittery until that particular case is behind us. It's going to be fine, it really is. I can't imagine why I worried for a moment that a woman at a bus stop might pose any sort of threat to us. In any case, it looks like she's moving on. Thank goodness for that. I don't want to go on about it but there's something about her I really don't like. Call it instinct, call it experience, call it what you want. I'm just thrilled she's not coming in here.

She's coming in here.

~

But who is she coming to see? She's using the visitors' entrance so she's not a member of staff. Security will keep her busy for a good ten minutes. There's two men loitering in the lobby. I would ignore them – it looks as though they're on their way out rather than expecting a visitor – until I hear one of them say:

'I'm not supposed to tell you any of this.'

They're not words you ever want to hear in this place. Secrets are secrets for a reason.

'Go on,' says the other one.

'First day of the course, this is what they do. Someone hands you a screwdriver and says you've got twenty minutes. You're pushed into a pitch-black room. You think: is the screwdriver a weapon? You wave it around, heart racing, can't see or hear anything. Eventually you calm down. You feel your way around the walls, then cross the room with your arms outstretched. There's stuff on the floor. Wood, screws. Those little plastic things. It's a piece of flat-pack furniture. Alright, you think – this is the task: I've got to assemble a piece of furniture in the dark. There's even a sheet of paper, probably the instructions or something.'

'Why's that there?'

'A joke, I suppose. They like a joke. Anyway, you get to work, feeling for the holes and making a guess about what goes where, working as fast as you can. Then the lights go on—'

'What is it?'

'A bed.'

'A bed?' says the other one.

'Well, barely a bed, seeing as how you did such a bad job. Half the slats are missing, it's got three legs, headboard's upside down. This is the kicker, though. Do you know what they tell you then? As an incentive to do better next time?'

'Oh, I know. That's clever. For the rest of the course, it's *your* bed.'

'Worse than that,' he says. 'It's your *instructor's* bed.'

Let's move on.

~

Italics not mine. I should make this clear. Italics theirs. Italics always theirs. Think of me as a pane of glass, nothing more. I might choose where to look, I'll give you that. But what happens out there, the way the world is, that's nothing to do with me. Got it?

~

Two floors up, around the other side of the building, the side facing the Thames. A sign on the door: Media and Communications. This one's a team meeting of some kind.

'How many likes did we get for the post last night?' says the senior officer.

This lot are a good bet because they invite all sorts of people into the building, including journalists, and I wonder if the woman in the red scarf is a journalist. She's got that hungry, burrowing look about her.

'Just over four thousand – a new record. Instagram loves nothing more than letters from children wanting to be spies.'

'We should get the crayons out, start writing them ourselves,' he says. 'What are we doing next?'

'Another one in the Pathways Into Intelligence series. I'm thinking: single mum, left school at fifteen, saw an ad in the local paper, it's a really supportive environment, look what I've ended up doing.'

'Jan's been pestering me to get involved,' he says. 'If you need a photo of your single mum, I mean. One of those moody anonymous ones on the bridge.'

'Please God,' says someone else. 'Not the bridge again. What is it about spies and bridges?'

'Cold War spy swaps?'

'Wasn't it Waterloo Bridge where that bloke got jabbed with a poisoned umbrella?'

'Perhaps a bridge is a kind of no man's land,' says yet another, they're all getting involved now. 'Symbolically, I mean. Suggestive of passing from one state to another, in the way that a spy moves between countries, between identities, between missions, between loyalties even, I suppose, although it might be an etymological stretch, between—'

Alright, that's enough of that. It doesn't sound like they're expecting a visitor. Perhaps it's time to go upstairs.

~

'The fact remains, Sir William, that a complaint has been made from within your organisation, by one of your own officers. We are taking it seriously. We urge you to take it seriously too.'

Two men, no more than five years between them. Suits, of course.

'An *anonymous* complaint.'

'Your point being?'

'That the complainant's wish to remain anonymous raises questions about their credibility,' says Sir William.

'I'm surprised to hear a spy chief express such an opinion.'

'Our sources are not anonymous, Julian. We know exactly who they are. We just don't tell you. It's quite different.'

We're on the top floor, where Sir William Rentoul, the Head of the Service, has his office, along with the rest of the senior leadership team. The official line is that high-level foreign visitors are impressed by the views from up here, and in an organisation dedicated to the application of unseen pressure, that line holds considerable sway. Less frequently mentioned is the report from the Explosive Ordnance Engineering Department at the Ministry of Defence that refers to the 'absorbent quality' of staff on lower floors.

'Nonetheless you must appreciate that some people may prefer to speak from the shadows,' says Julian. 'The new system allows for precisely this – it allows for an internal complainant who fears repercussions to choose anonymity.'

'There would be no repercussions. We welcome whistleblowers.'

'Nobody welcomes whistleblowers, Sir William. That's the point of whistleblowers. Look, it has been a long-standing wish of the Intelligence and Security Committee that your officers should be able to contact us directly if they wish to raise a concern. The journey to this point has been lengthier and more arduous than any one of us anticipated, but we have arrived, as has our very first complaint.'

'Julian—'

'This entire journey will have been utterly pointless if we do not treat that complaint seriously.'

'I am not suggesting that we ignore anything,' says Sir William. 'I am simply introducing the possibility that this complaint may be intended to make mischief. Now, we in the intelligence community have vast experience in the assessment of unsourced information. It's what we do, day in, day out. With the greatest of respect, I worry that your Committee is not qualified to look into this.'

'Surely you're not suggesting that you mark your own homework.'

'Julian, your Committee is made up of politicians. Together you have an important oversight role, yes, but you have no experience of running investigations.'

'The Committee itself would not carry out the investigation.'

'Please elaborate.'

'May I ask Aphra to join us?'

~

Still wearing the red scarf, the woman from the bus stop stands in the open doorway for a moment longer than is necessary, amid the bright piney yellows and oranges of Sir William's outer office. It's not reluctance or hesitation. She tilts forward, dips her nose into the gloom that awaits her as though into a wine glass, breathes deeply of oak, of tobacco, of whisky notes, of the deep dark tannins that come together when serious men say serious things. I don't see her hazel eyes closing but I see them snap open. A long, thin face with one of those strong chin–mouth combinations, pushing outwards, like the beginning of a muzzle, like a telescope.

'Aphra, please, do come and join us,' says Julian Redruth, although it's not his place to invite a guest into someone else's office. He knows it too. It's what they call a micro-aggression. 'May I introduce you to Sir William, the Head of the Service?'

She steps forward, her hand extended.

'It's a pleasure to meet you, Sir William.'

No surname either, from the pair of them. Why not drop the 'sir' too, high-five the man? Sir William Rentoul shakes her hand. It's all information to him. Sir William's an old agent handler, he knows when to assert and when to absorb.

'Please, have a seat,' he says. 'A Scot. Where are you from, Aphra?'

'North of Edinburgh.'

'I understand you're an investigator. Does that mean that you were once a police officer?'

'I was an academic.'

'Oh,' he says, raising his eyebrows towards Julian Redruth to underline his surprise, his amused delight, as though he has been handed an unexpected present. 'An *academic*. What's your area?'

'Formerly, medieval history.'

'Bring us up to the present day, would you?'

'Whatever the Intelligence and Security Committee requires me to look into.'

'Such as?'

'The history of Chinese interference, the impact of new security legislation on employment law, agency expenditure.'

'As a historian—' says Julian Redruth.

'As *an* historian, surely,' says Sir William Rentoul.

'Aphra has been trained in the close study of written texts,' says Julian Redruth. 'With your permission, she will read the file that pertains to the anonymous complaint and summarise the case history, identify gaps and assumptions, interview witnesses, draw conclusions, suggest—'

'Interview witnesses? You slipped that one in there. Many witnesses to interview, are there, in the field of medieval history?' Sir William smiles with a warmth intended to singe their grasping fingers. 'What does that require?' he says. 'A tarot deck? A Ouija board?'

Julian Redruth, formerly a Lancashire village GP, exhales audibly. This relationship between the intelligence agencies and his oversight committee of MPs, assembled weekly up the road in the Palace of Westminster, is one characterised, at least in his experience, by obfuscation, cordiality, delay, opacity and aggression, the latter brought out on special occasions like something lifted carefully from a wooden case and shown to visitors. Put it this way: Julian Redruth never feels that he is on the winning side. He has certainly never achieved the highest purpose for which his committee was established, which is to catch the spies red-handed. The most he has managed is to arrive on the scene in time to detect the toxic whiff of something that has recently moved on. As a result, his reports are marked increasingly by such phrases as 'the Committee was disappointed to learn' and 'it is a matter of some regret' and 'despite numerous requests for'. This language is proof of his failure. No one cares about his regret or his disappointment. Julian Redruth intends to step down from Parliament at the next election and so has a little under a year to make his mark. This goes some way to explain that jiggle in his left foot. He believes, I suspect, that in this anonymous complaint, in this investigator of his, he has found a wedge with which to—

'Aphra has considerable expertise not just in assessing material but in evaluating the origin of that material,' says Julian Redruth. 'What ulterior motives may be at work, what bias, what unseen pressures have nudged the operation in question one way or the other. You yourself may find a fresh perspective illuminating. Aphra's ability to understand sources will allow—'

Sir William has had enough.

'You have led us, Julian, in your solidly competent way, to a *diagnosis* of the problem,' he says.

Call that a micro-aggression, I'll show you a micro-aggression. Sir William's smile is fast and discreet, a marker that will allow him to retrieve and feast upon this moment once he's seen off the immediate threat.

'These words,' Sir William continues, 'these words we bandy around: "investigate", "source". For those of us who inhabit the secret world' – hands open expansively, regretfully – 'these terms have a different meaning. With the greatest will in the world, Aphra, what you are is a *researcher*, not an investigator. A researcher looks backwards. But an investigator looks all around, even into the future. One activity is passive, the other is active. An investigator considers risk, resource, mitigation, contagion. Live threats mutate and spread in a way that those from the Middle Ages cannot. Think of the difference between studying a dinosaur fossil and the monster itself as it rears before you. As for sources . . .'

Again, that regret. My vocation is my yoke, he seems to say.

'In our world, a source is a creature with complex and competing motives,' says Sir William, 'not a dusty tome summoned from the archives with one of your little pink slips.'

'They're not pink,' she says.

'I stand corrected.'

Gracious to the end, he is, for surely this is the——

'*Sola fide*,' she says.

'Excuse me?' says Sir William Rentoul.

'Luther's rallying cry,' she says, 'expressed in his ninety-five theses that may or may not have been nailed to a church door in Wittenberg. The church said that ordinary people couldn't understand the Bible. The church said that it was too complex for the uninitiated. They insisted upon a doctrine of sacerdotalism, according to which priests were required to act as intermediaries between God and humankind.'

She leans forward.

'A lot of people *investigate*, Sir William. A lot of people collect information discreetly and assess its reliability. To be honest with you, a lot of people run sources, although they might not call it that. There's really no need to pretend that you alone have that power.'

Sir William looks at her. To engage in debate with this quarrelsome woman would be to concede something he is not prepared to concede.

'Let me speak directly to God,' she says.

'But my dear,' says Sir William Rentoul. 'You already are.'

~

Sir William Rentoul stands ramrod straight in front of the floor-to-ceiling window that gives out over the Thames. His thoughts, like the water, are grey, unsettled. He recalls a visit to Tintagel Castle with his youngest grandson, and a conversation about the difference between a battlement, a bartizan and a drum tower. The ice cream van played an out-of-tune 'Greensleeves'. This is nothing compared to the Theodosian Walls of Constantinople, said Sir William, kneeling down and using twigs to illustrate his point, which was: moat, first wall, open ground, second wall, open ground, final wall measuring 12 metres high and 5 metres thick. He watched a ladybird climb the first twig while his grandson ate an ice cream.

Or something like that. There are the things I see and the things I hear, all of which you can take to the bank. Then there's the rest of it – thoughts, feelings. I've never understood it when people talk about pulling the wool over someone's eyes, because that's just what it's like, it's like looking through wool, and let me tell you, you can *see things* through wool. I'm not saying you can drive a car with wool over your eyes, but you can tell a story, you can do that. You can tell one hell of a story.

The unyielding stiffness of Sir William's posture suggests that his instinct is to say no to Julian Redruth. He has good reason to feel that way, even though he has agreed in principle that the Intelligence and Security Committee should be allowed to receive complaints directly from his officers. He never thought it would amount to anything. And of all the cases . . . Boy, have they picked a messy one. *The* messy one, let's be frank. It's one of those cases which are laudable if they go well but very, very, very hard to justify if they go badly. It's partly this whole thing of using an innocent person in an operation without their knowledge, bringing risk to their door that they have not accepted, that they cannot take steps to mitigate, since they are not even aware that it exists. It's also that it involves an assassin. It's also that lots of people have died. There's that too.

But would blocking the Committee have the unintended effect of drawing attention to the case? Probably, yes. And what's the worst that could happen if he *did* let them in? Their representative, Aphra McQueen, is unlikely to get very far: the organisation Sir William runs has decades upon decades of experience in frustrating outsiders intent on getting to the bottom of things. In fact, he thinks, in fact . . . Is there any way he might *benefit* from letting them in? He's long wanted to deliver a sharp warning rap to the knuckles of Julian Redruth and his Committee, and if he grants them access, an opportunity might present itself. He thinks of it as a piece of elastic. Maximum stretch equals maximum bounce. The further they are allowed to intrude, the further back they shall be thrown.

The file itself won't be a cause for concern, he thinks. No doubt the paperwork was drafted with precisely this sort of scenario in mind. The best documents are. Say what you like about lawyers, but their ubiquity in this building has made everyone a little more careful when it comes to the official record. In the nineteen sixties, would you believe it, there was so little need for legal advice that all three agencies shared the services of a single lawyer who was nonetheless so under-consulted that he spent most of his time guiding staff through property sales and divorce settlements.

Now they're everywhere, stuffed into the cracks of this building like insulation.

You can do this, Sir William. *We* can do this.

~

Things move quickly once the decision has been made.

'May I ask you to wear your visitor's pass around your neck rather than carry it in your hand, Miss McQueen?'

'Please,' she says, 'call me Aphra.'

'Aphra's an unusual name.'

'As a little girl I would have given anything to be called Susan.'

Susan is from the Service's team of building escorts, who accompany visitors at all times to ensure that they go directly to and from their meetings without straying into areas they are not cleared to enter.

'May I also confirm that any electronic devices in your possession have been stored in the lockers?' she says.

Aphra nods, smiles.

'I was surprised to find that noise-cancelling headphones are on the list of prohibited items,' she says.

'I suppose you do plug them in.'

'Hard to steal information through a pair of headphones, I would have thought,' says Aphra.

Susan stops, turns, leans in. She lowers her voice as though to share a secret at a cocktail party.

'The Chinese are *very* clever.'

She presses the lift button.

'I'm afraid all of the normal meeting rooms were booked,' she says.

'I'd be happy with a broom cupboard as long as it's quiet, Susan. I do like a bit of peace and quiet when I'm working.'

'Oh, we wouldn't dream of putting you in a broom cupboard. I've managed to find a desk in a corner of the registry. On the whole they're a quiet bunch. I'm afraid I've got to remain with the file at all times, so you'll have to put up with me sitting opposite you.'

'Are you sure it's quiet in there?'

~

Susan leads the way through the registry to an empty desk in the corner, stopping to say hello to a couple of women. Aphra McQueen removes her seal-black raincoat, sits, swivels one way and then the other, pulls a lever to glide upwards but overshoots, lets the chair back down with a series of bumps, each accompanied by a tiny pneumatic gulp of astonishment. A rubbish bin is threateningly close; she leaps up and places it by the window. She adjusts the blind to allow in more light. Back in the chair, she takes a wet wipe from her bag and polishes the surface of the desk until it glistens.

With a widening of those large hazel eyes that says she knows just how ridiculous she is, Aphra says: 'Susan? Hit me.'

'Excuse me?'

'The file. I'm ready for it.'

Susan places a file on the desk before her. Aphra centres it, then takes a notebook from her bag, opens it at a fresh page and writes something.

'If you write anything in your notebook,' says Susan, 'you'll have to leave it with us.'

'I've written the date.'

'Your notes may well be as sensitive as the file itself, you see. If you copy things out verbatim.'

16

'That makes sense.' Aphra McQueen screws up her face. 'I'd rather keep my notebook.'

'I'll bring you some paper,' says Susan. 'You can make your notes there and we'll keep them safe for you.'

Susan crosses to a printer, pulls open a drawer and removes a single sheet of paper. She hands it to Aphra, who says: 'Out of interest, when it comes to it, how shall I write my report?'

'We'll provide you with a computer.'

Aphra nods once, briskly. She opens the file and begins to read.

If every file tells a story then your standard police file is a procedural, each step made explicit and buttressed with evidence. It is a chain that relies upon the integrity of every single link. If a suspect – a character – passes the time of day with a shopkeeper then the reader will be provided with a written account of their conversation, however banal. We will be told what time the characters woke up, what they said to their partners, the models of car they drove to work. This could not be more different to an intelligence file, which is, by comparison, a work of modernist complexity. It is possible to read an entire intelligence file with no real idea what it is about, or what the problem was in the first place, or what the spies have done to make the situation better.

Fortunately for Aphra McQueen, this particular case is unusual. Most files that originate in this building are opened on the basis of a piece of intelligence. A source report that casts suspicion on an individual, say, or a piece of anomalous phone data. Intelligence files typically begin and end in uncertainty. But this particular file begins with a police report. It's a murder story before it's a spy story.

'Susan,' calls out one of the women in the room, 'did you or your guest want anything from the cafeteria?'

'We're fine, thank you, Mary.'

Aphra bends over the first document. The year is 2017, and an exiled Iranian journalist named Aresh Karimi is living in the Netherlands with his Dutch wife and their two young children. One Tuesday morning Karimi walks his children to school, kisses them goodbye, buys a carrot juice flavoured with ginger to help dislodge a lingering cold and takes the train into Haarlem, not far from Amsterdam, where he has arranged to meet someone. CCTV stills from the train confirm the timings of his journey, and a statement from the head waiter reports that Karimi seems in good spirits when he takes a seat at table 14, on the corner of Hoofmanstraat and Merkmanstraat.

A man approaches Karimi, according to two regulars at the café. It's cold; there's nothing odd in the fact that this second man wears a hat and a scarf. They shake hands. The day is fine and they set out together from the café, heads inclined in conversation that to the world around them seems friendly. Much analysis is devoted to the route they took. It appears random, particularly when marked in blue dots on a map, but its randomness must be by design because they end up at a very particular place.

Aphra looks up. There's a noise at the door as a woman comes in pushing a trolley laden with files.

'Oh hello, Susan,' she calls out. 'To what do we owe the pleasure?'

'Looking after a visitor.'

'Oh yes. Did you get any overtime at the weekend?'

'Had my grandkids in the end.'

'Oh lovely. I hope they didn't wear you out.'

Aphra continues reading. The two men turn into a cobbled mews. The second man emerges at the other end, on his own, exactly 196 seconds later. To walk the length of the mews without pausing would have taken anywhere between 46 and 59 seconds. Two-thirds of the way down the mews is a small two-storey house that has been rented via a website for a three-day period. No useful information can be retrieved from the property company about the individual who rented the house. Late the following day the body of Aresh Karimi is found in the downstairs living room following a search triggered by a missing persons report filed by his wife. The crime scene report suggests that the attack was so ferocious – his body was found without its left ear and left eye – that it would have caused significant blood splatter. When the second man appears at the end of the mews, he is no longer wearing his jacket.

One of the women seated by the door exhales noisily.

'Can anyone remember what the appraisal markings are?' she says.

'Lower achiever, higher achiever, top achiever. I think there's a fourth one but I can't remember what it is.'

'Isn't excellent achiever one of them?'

'It always reminds me of Starbucks. What is it? Tall, grande, venti? Nobody wants to buy a small coffee these days.'

Aphra takes the red scarf from her bag, wraps it under her jaw, over her ears, and secures it above her head with a large knot.

'Looks like you've got a toothache,' says Susan.

'What's that?' says Aphra, lifting the scarf from her ear.

'A toothache,' says Susan, pointing at the scarf. 'Looks like you've got a toothache.'

The knife and the jacket are never located.

There are assumptions made in the police report that Aphra would certainly question, if that was her job. But she's not here because of a murder. She's here because of what the spies did next.

~

Let's get it out the way, this question of who or what I am. I don't know how specific you want me to be, or how literal. It's not as though I'm entirely sure myself. If someone asked what you were, you might give your name, which is nothing more than a meaningless label. You might refer to the arbitrary construct that is nationality, or to your profession, which could change at any given moment. Even if you described yourself as a human, you'd probably be doing little more than applying a term you've heard but don't really understand. Hopefully you can understand my predicament. All I really have are questions. They might seem different, one from the other, but a strong family resemblance leads me to conclude that they all descend from the same ancient throb, which is, can a community have a soul? Can an organisation?

And if so, would it look, would it feel like . . . this?

A moment's thought and you'll realise that it makes perfect sense. When individuals come together, particularly under the umbrella of an organisation with a distinctive purpose and history, something new comes into being, something connected to those individuals, yes, something that draws on them, *yes*, but something that is larger than them. This might be called an organisation's spirit, or soul, or ethos, or character, or simply its identity. No doubt management consultants and motivational speakers have a snappy term for it. The question that follows is whether that collective identity is an entity in its own right. Personally, I think the quickest glance at recent history will confirm that it is. There's no other way to explain how an organisation is so much more than the sum of its parts; how it is capable of behaving in ways that are antithetical to the professed morals of its members. There's clearly a guiding force at work that operates according to a higher set of values. Now, I'm not interested in questions of whether that guiding force is organic or inorganic. I don't know whether there exists a laboratory machine that could detect its presence, and I have no intention of putting myself under the microscope. In fact, I'm not going to bring this up again. I only mention it because it's impossible to give a full account of events while ignoring the elephant in the room, as everyone always does, but I really don't mind whether you believe me or not. I suspect you'll dismiss it as a metaphor. I'd rather you didn't believe that I'm the spirit of spying, to be honest. That would suit me just fine.

~

Two men in their thirties walk towards each other along a busy corridor. As agent handlers, they're both pretty good (temperament plus training) at hiding their feelings, but it's evident there's some bottled-up tension here in the way one of them grabs the other by the elbow and steers him into an empty room, pulling the door shut behind them.

'I've just heard that Sir William is allowing some parliamentary researcher to look into our case,' he says.

'Not "is allowing",' says the other one. 'Has allowed. She's upstairs reading the file right now.'

'Jesus Christ. What the hell is he thinking? I've heard the rumours but I thought someone would step in if he did something really stupid. Do we know exactly what the complaint is?'

'It was submitted via a private email system that goes directly to the parliamentary committee. For security reasons the complainant isn't allowed to go into detail. From what I understand, it referred to the assassinations and our response to them, alleging gross negligence. I don't think it went into details.'

'An anonymous complaint seems a massively flimsy pretext for giving a parliamentary researcher access to a live intelligence operation.'

'Agreed. But let's be clear: we've got nothing to worry about. The case is complex, yes, but we're trying to stop a hostile foreign state from murdering innocent people on European soil. If that doesn't justify pushing boundaries a little, I don't know what does.'

'You're rehearsing your lines.'

'How did it sound?'

'"Pushing boundaries" is certainly one way of putting it. The problem is that it sounds like an admission of something.'

'Fair point.'

'I wouldn't say "European soil" either. We don't care about European soil these days. Who else is the researcher speaking to?'

'The ethics counsellor and the analyst. Possibly a lawyer too. And us, of course.'

'The analyst? You don't mean Peter, do you?'

'Yes.'

'Oh God,' he says.

'Don't worry, he's been briefed. Besides, he genuinely doesn't know anything.'

'What's her name, this researcher?'

'Aphra.'

'Aphra?'

'Aphra.'

~

'Aphra? Aphra?'

Aphra lifts the scarf from her ear.

'It's time for your first interview,' says Susan.

'What interview?'

'With the analyst.'

Aphra McQueen pulls the scarf away. 'What analyst?'

'His name's Peter,' says Susan. 'He works on this case.'

'I haven't finished reading the file yet,' says Aphra.

'He's off on holiday tomorrow, it's now or never.'

Aphra closes the file, stands, picks up the file.

'That'll have to stay here, I'm afraid,' says Susan. 'There's material in it that the analyst isn't cleared to see.'

Aphra follows Susan down a series of corridors. Susan moves at her own pace, sets down each step gingerly, wincingly, as though walking barefoot through icy water. At every turn, Aphra taps the sharp corner of the wall. She looks into open doorways, sees people, pages being printed, tea being made, clocks set to Islamabad, Washington, Moscow, Beijing, Tehran. Susan, whose purpose as a building escort is to make sure that visitors do not roam freely, feels uncomfortable about this, even though Aphra is technically doing nothing wrong. Susan approves of curiosity in theory – in her grandchildren, say, as they read a book about the construction of the pyramids or the way that flowers are pollenated – but believes that its gratuitous display elsewhere, particularly inside this building, is evidence of a highly questionable character.

Or something like that.

They reach their destination: a small, brightly lit meeting room with a single round table and three chairs.

'I thought there weren't any rooms available,' says Aphra.

Susan ignores her.

'Hello,' says the young man standing awkwardly on the other side of the table. Mid twenties, blue suit trousers worn to a shine, white shirt purchased when he was a size smaller. A thin beard covers acne scars. 'My name's Peter.'

'How lucky you are, Peter, to be off on holiday,' says Aphra. 'Where are you going?'

'Scotland,' he says quickly.

'Where autumn leaves lie thick and still,' she says, then adds, seeing his confusion: 'It's from "Flower of Scotland". My brother and I used to sing it on our way to school each morning. At least you'll be in the UK. We might have another opportunity to talk then, once I'm a little more familiar with the case.'

'From there to Norway.'

'Oh, I've made that journey,' says Aphra. 'It's a wonder to behold. Where are you going to in Norway?'

'I haven't booked my ticket yet,' he says. 'Bergen? Is that——'

'Shall we get started?' says Susan.

They all sit. Aphra turns over the single sheet of paper she has been given and prepares to write. 'Out of interest, Peter,' she says, 'how do you identify yourself?'

He thinks about the question. 'Male?'

'Oh, no, sorry,' says Aphra. 'I mean, within the organisation. Do you have a designation or a number?'

'Give her your staff number,' says Susan.

Peter holds up a plastic pass hanging from a lanyard around his neck, shows her the number, is visibly relieved to be starting with a question he can demonstrate he is answering truthfully.

'Your pass looks newer than some of the others I've seen about the place,' says Aphra. 'Does that mean you've only joined recently?'

'I don't see how that's relevant,' says Susan. 'Peter might be fairly new but you can be confident that we wouldn't put someone in front of you who was unfamiliar with the material.'

'As a matter of fact, Susan,' says Aphra, 'I find myself leaning towards the theory that the most helpful witnesses will be those who have spent the *least* time working here.' She winks at Susan. 'Now, Peter, where do you think we should start?'

He considers her question.

'Before Iran was an empire,' he says, 'it was home to some of the first settled civilisations on earth. Cyrus the Great ruled over three continents from Persepolis. The Parthians, the Safavids, the Seljuks, the Timurids.' He looks at Aphra, looks down the barrel of history, decides to change tack. 'There are limits to this approach,' he says, 'but I sometimes think of countries as characters. Like every former empire, Iran is having difficulties adjusting to its demotion on the world stage – in this case a demotion that has been particularly sudden and humiliating. Think of a proud man who's been told that he's ruined the family name, or a devout man who can't convince anyone that he's right, or a boy who's bullied every time he sets foot in the playground. Iran is angry, and to release some of that anger it's decided to kill Iranians abroad who criticise the regime.' Peter looks intently at Aphra. 'Aren't you—'

'When did it start?' says Aphra. 'The killing, I mean.'

'How far have you got in the file?'

'The murder of Aresh Karimi in the Netherlands in 2017.'

'That was the first one,' he says. 'Then there were two murders in Belgium in 2018, then one in Spain in 2019, one in Slovenia in 2020, two in Germany in 2021 – but one of those was the victim's neighbour who disturbed the killer during the attack and was also murdered. Twenty twenty-two was a bumper year: two in Germany and one in France.'

'Were the victims all critics of the regime?' she asks.

'To some extent. I think this is why it went unnoticed for so long. One of them ran a Twitter account that posted Iranian jokes, but very little of it was political material. Another one was notorious for complaining about the clerics but mainly to neighbours and friends. Some of the other victims were more obviously in the anti-regime camp.'

'Was any forensic connection made between the murders?' asks Aphra.

'No. Which was odd, considering the level of violence used. Things were . . . cut off or cut open, skin was slashed, two of them were burned with acid before being killed.'

'How did the police connect the murders, if there was no forensic evidence?' asks Aphra.

'The police weren't the first to spot that something was happening. A German-Iranian journalist linked the murders in a 2021 newspaper article that got a lot of attention. That forced the authorities to look into it.'

'So we have ten murders across Europe in six years,' she says.

'Yes.'

'But none in the UK.'

'Correct.'

'All the victims were, to a greater or lesser degree, critics of the Iranian regime.'

'Except for the unlucky neighbour,' he says.

'And the killer?'

'Our European counterparts studied travel data, flight records and the like, and identified an individual who appears to have travelled from Iran around the same time as the ten murders, using a number of different aliases. He's been allocated the codename CASPIAN.'

'What's his real name?'

'I don't have it to hand. He's a professor of chemistry at Tehran University. He flew to Portugal a week before the Spain murder, Germany three days before the Belgium murder, the Czech Republic two days before one of the German murders. He probably went through Turkey by coach ten days before the murder in France, so we think he was travelling across Europe to France on yet another alias passport. GCHQ has done extensive analysis of his phones. There's plenty of evidence to suggest links between the IRGC – the Iranian Revolutionary Guards, who would be in charge of things like this – and Tehran University, but it's hard to go much deeper than that. Are you familiar with Stuxnet?'

'The cyber-attack?'

'The cyber-attack on Iran's nuclear programme. Carried out by—'

'Are we wandering off track?' asks Susan.

'Sorry,' says Peter. 'My point is, as a result of Stuxnet, Iran upgraded its technical capabilities. Things that were easy to see pre-Stuxnet went dark.'

'Let's stick to this case,' says Susan.

'I'm trying to explain why our technical tools proved unable to give us much clarity around CASPIAN, and why we ultimately looked elsewhere for the answers,' says Peter.

'Elsewhere?' says Aphra.

'HUMINT,' says Peter. 'We recruited an agent.'

'What can you tell me about the agent?'

'You'll have an opportunity to speak to the agent handlers directly,' says Susan. She glances at her watch. 'Peter has to go soon.'

'What's your analysis, Peter?' says Aphra.

'Of what?'

Aphra appears taken aback by the question.

'Why, of the case,' she says.

'What aspect of it?'

'Take your pick.'

Peter's eyes widen, he looks to Susan for help.

'Has the agent been a success?' asks Aphra.

'A colossal success,' he says. 'He was recruited to provide intelligence on the murders, which he has done, but it turns out he also has the potential to reach deeper into the Iranian regime. It's been a game changer for the UK.'

'Has his reporting been accurate and reliable?'

'Consistently.'

'So your analysis is that you've all done a bloody good job,' says Aphra. 'I wonder why someone made a complaint.'

'There's always someone with a complaint,' says Susan. 'The real question is why you lot took it at face value.'

'It must be frustrating that in your world success by definition is something no one ever finds out about,' says Aphra. 'Perhaps that gives us a clue about who made the complaint. Someone wanting recognition, perhaps? Their moment in the spotlight?'

'No one works here for the spotlight,' says Susan.

'You strike me as someone who craves notoriety,' says Aphra.

'I beg your pardon.'

'I'm pulling your leg, Susan. Seriously, though, it is a little hard to imagine that a serial killer just stopped killing.'

'What serial killer?' asks Peter.

'CASPIAN. He killed ten people, at least one a year between 2017 and 2022. Then he stopped.'

'He's an assassin. Not a serial killer.'

'Couldn't he be both?'

'One is following orders, the other is acting out . . . impulses,' says Peter. 'Dark impulses.'

'Didn't he cut off the genitals of his victims in Belgium and Slovenia?'

'The police think he was trying to make them look like crimes of passion.'

'I thought you only read as far as the Haarlem case,' says Susan.

'Were you at St Andrews?' asks Peter.

Aphra looks at him. 'I was,' she says.

'History?'

'Did I teach you?'

'You taught a friend of mine. It's a really good department.'

'Is there anything else to do with this case that I should know?' she says.

'Didn't you leave . . . abruptly?' asks Peter.

'I suppose it might have seemed that way to your friend,' says

Aphra, putting the cap back on her pen. 'As far as I'm concerned, I left at precisely the right time.'

Susan can't take her eyes off Aphra.

'Thank you, Peter,' says Aphra. 'Have a wonderful time in Norway.'

His blush runs deep as a fjord.

~

These days you simply can't compare something to the Stasi in a positive way, but what fills me with pride about this organisation is the discipline and vigilance that characterise its officers, whatever their level or grade. You definitely have the sense that everyone's pulling in the same direction. For a while I was worried that it was a generational thing, that you'd find less commitment to the cause the further you travelled through time from the great wars, but the truth is that the vast majority of younger officers are gratifyingly loyal when it comes down to it. Of course these things have to be allowed to look a little different in this day and age. No one likes to think of themselves as obedient to the state. But if you whisper something like 'this person here is a threat', 'this person is not one of us', 'this person does not share our values', staff generally fall in line without a murmur of dissent.

Sometimes even a whisper isn't required. Take Susan here. You won't believe me but the truth is that I've said nothing to her. This is all her own work. She is obstructing Aphra's progress out of an entirely home-brewed hostility towards an outsider charged with investigating a complaint.

It's not that Susan can't imagine a world in which the complaint is justified. She knows better than most that things are imperfect around here. Despite once having her sights set on travelling the world as an agent handler, Susan has only ever worked in support roles (HR, Goods In, IT, Change Management and now Building Services), only ever earned in the lower quartile of staff pay (topping out at £26,495), only ever achieved mediocre appraisals from her managers ('Susan is careful to pace herself'). She's even submitted official complaints on three occasions (canteen prices, bullying, pension reform).

This is the thing, though. The organisation she works for likes to describe itself as a bubble, in reference to its airtight, sealed quality, and the thing about a bubble is that it is either wholly intact or it is no longer a bubble. Susan sees Aphra as one vast jagged edge. You can't compromise with that. All you can do is blunt it with a heavy object.

As a building escort, Susan understands that she is limited to a walk-on role. A walk-on and sit-there role. But she is coming to the conclusion that she is capable of far more than that.

~

The story that Aphra reads in the file goes like this.

Embarrassed into action by media revelations that the Iranians had been killing people across Europe for several years, the intelligence services directly involved – Dutch, German, Belgian, Spanish, Slovenian – set up a working group in 2021 under the codename HAARLEM, chosen for the scene of the first murder. Although no act of violence had taken place on British soil, the UK was invited to attend out of courtesy, an invitation that was accepted not out of any interest in the murders but because the working group was seen as an opportunity to deepen European relationships at a time when they were under strain.

The HAARLEM working group met on five occasions between early 2021 and late 2022, producing seventy-two pages of minutes and action points. In December 2022 the body of a young Iranian pop singer was discovered in a tributary of the Seine. As a result, French intelligence was invited to join the working group, prompting fresh hope of a breakthrough, but there was no useful forensic evidence. It was, however, discovered that the individual assigned the codename CASPIAN had once again travelled to Europe shortly before the murder, this time via Scandinavia, using yet another alias identity, further strengthening the assessment that he was responsible for the murders.

Early 2023 saw the turn of British intelligence to host the HAARLEM group. Cooperation between the UK and their European counterparts had fallen to an all-time low, and the meeting was seen in London as an opportunity to reset key relationships. This would be achieved, Aphra read, by hosting a dinner for all participants in a private dining room in the Palace of Westminster, arranging an after-hours tour of the Tower of London and establishing a UK cross-agency intelligence cell for a period of one week prior to the arrival of the HAARLEM delegates.

The UK cell convened early one Monday morning, charged with making an investigative breakthrough that would demonstrate UK prowess. They began with a review of relevant material held in their databases. It was without exaggeration the first time anyone had even looked. Within the first twenty minutes an analyst found a 2016 CIA report on the Iranian diaspora community in which it was stated that a forty-one-year-old mature student completing an MBA at the prestigious École des hautes études commerciales in Paris had a maternal uncle with the same first name as CASPIAN who taught chemistry at Tehran University.

The analyst took the report to her boss. They agreed that the nephew would make a good source, as he could potentially provide intelligence on his uncle's career, finances, friends, character and travel plans. They wrote to the CIA, asking for permission to share the report with the HAARLEM group so that the UK and France could make a joint recruitment approach to the nephew, but the CIA refused, citing sensitivities around the access that had generated the intelligence.

This created a quandary for the British. They could try to recruit the nephew in Paris on an undeclared basis, keeping the French in the dark, but, seeing as the entire point of UK involvement in the case was to rebuild relationships, it was felt that it would be counterproductive to attempt something that would enrage the French if it came to light. The only other option was to lure the nephew to the UK and pitch him there, something that wouldn't require French permission. If the pitch went well and the British agent handlers recruited the nephew then they could share disguised intelligence with the HAARLEM group, protecting the identity of the nephew. If the pitch went badly, it was very unlikely that he would return to Paris and tell the French authorities about it. Everyone agreed this was the best way to proceed.

But how to lure the nephew to the UK?

~

Susan leaves Aphra on her own and hurries downstairs to get them both lunch. She has something to do first, and walks as quickly as she has in a long while. She wears a grimace from the strain, though, and her face reddens. She manages a breathy hello to the first person she encounters, a former mentee of hers in his thirties who now runs a twelve-strong team of analysts tracking the remnants of Islamic State across the globe. The room numbers don't quite pass in a blur but she couldn't tell you exactly what they are, the speed she is moving. A polite nod to a young woman whose mother works in Information Management, she can't remember what the daughter does, it's either the Irish or the Far Right. The carpets have been replaced here, they can find money for that. The lift is crowded with people and notices: a cake sale, auditions for the panto, a history lecture, a warning that film crews will be shooting exteriors for a TV drama outside the building next Tuesday. The doors ping. She's out, turns left, up the stairs, through the doors and sits at the first available computer terminal, underneath a sign that reads Internet.

Badge number: B1D13.

Password: Susan1959. She knows you're not supposed to but how's anyone meant to remember a different password for everything.

A reminder about the risks of browsing: Accept.

A reminder about the need to close the session at the end: OK.

Aphra McQueen, she types.

St Andrews University.

Why did she leave.

~

What happens next is definitely what you would call a red flag moment.

Once Susan has left the registry, Aphra stands and stretches, touching her toes and flinging her thin arms violently across her body. She surveys the room, coming to a conclusion about its two remaining occupants, before walking with purpose towards the door.

She's going to ask one of the women for permission to leave the room. Either that or for one of them to accompany her to the toilet. Technically speaking, Susan shouldn't have left Aphra unsupervised, as she's the escort, but I'm sure one of these two will implicitly understand that Aphra shouldn't be going anywhere, although I'm not sure whether Susan informed them of that fact. They will probably tell her to wait for Susan. Aphra knows full well that she is not allowed to leave the room on her own. In case any doubt existed, the pass she wears around her neck has the words ACCOMPANIED VISITOR written across the bottom in red, so she's definitely not going to leave the room on her own.

She leaves the room on her own and walks at a steady pace down the corridor. The two women working at their desks don't even look up. Aphra turns left at the far end. She leans in to study a set of fire instructions stuck to the back of a door; it comes with a floor plan displaying room numbers, stairwells and lift shafts. Those hazel eyes close on the image like a shutter.

As she walks off, she reverses the pass hanging around her neck so that ACCOMPANIED VISITOR is not visible to anyone she comes across. Oh, this is bad. This is very bad. She picks up her pace, turns left and then right, pushing through a set of heavy wooden doors to the stairwell at the very edge of the building, which happens to be rarely used. Does she *know* that? It's one floor up to Russia, two floors up to China, three floors up to a lot of very, very senior people. There's no telling the damage she could do.

The doors swing shut behind her. She walks to the window, rests her forehead against the cold glass. Her shoulders shake once but by the time I move in she's got herself back under control.

∽

Susan's smile dances like the lid on a boiling pot. She is brimming with a sense of self-satisfaction that cannot be explained by the contents of the tray she carries: lentil soup with croutons, a slice of white bread, a bruised banana. For herself, Susan has bought a cheese and ham sandwich and a packet of crisps.

'May I read the file while I eat?' asks Aphra.

'If you had anything but the soup,' says Susan with a face. 'Keep me company.'

You don't spend forty-two years working in an organisation like this without absorbing something of the art of espionage. Susan has to decide what kind of encounter this is going to be. An interrogation? She's always fancied doing one of those. But does she have sufficient authority to compel Aphra to disclose the reason she left St Andrews? Or will she have to go undercover, slide out facts like wooden blocks? The fun, she imagines, lies in watching the tower wobble, that moment like the dawning of consciousness, as though it is weakness that brings the tower to life, but then it has to just *be*, aware of the possibility of its impending collapse but unable to see how or where it was weakened, or by whom.

Or something like that.

'I'm afraid they don't do haggis in the canteen,' says Susan.

It looks like she's opted for undercover.

With her spoon, Aphra pushes the croutons towards the edge of the bowl. She would have preferred them on a side plate. No doubt once cubes, they now exist in a place beyond shape or form.

'I expect you ate a lot of haggis in St Andrews,' says Susan. She selects a crisp and inserts it into her sandwich. She takes a bite, ruminates, gives Aphra space in which to respond if she chooses, which she doesn't. Susan selects another crisp. 'When you weren't busy at the university, that is.'

There's something about the bread–crisp–bread combination that thrills Susan. She could take or leave the cheese and ham filling, to be honest with you, but you can't buy a crisp sandwich.

She decides to introduce a direct question.

'Would you recommend St Andrews for a holiday?'

'If you like golf,' says Aphra.

This undercover lark isn't as fun or as productive as Susan expected. Presumably even interrogations can sometimes start with a bit of chit-chat, before they get going in earnest. No reason she can't switch, now that she's put Aphra at ease.

'Funny that Peter should have come across you before,' she says. 'It's a small world, as they say. History, was it, that you were teaching up there?'

'Medieval history.'

'Quite a jump to what you're doing now.'

'It might look that way.'

'Sounds as though you left quite abruptly, from what he said. Middle of the term, lots of angry students preparing for exams, wondering why you'd left them in the lurch.'

I'm not totally sure that Susan's striking the right note here.

'I imagine social media must have been agog with rumours.'

Or disguising the fact that she's just done a Google.

'Was it something in particular that made you leave?'

Susan makes it multiple choice in the hope that'll smooth Aphra's way to an answer.

'Another job offer? A death in the family?'

Nothing to lose now, may as well go for the theory with the most traction online. Hard to tell if there's anything to it, students being what they are. Sometimes there's smoke because there's fire, sometimes it's a piece of bread stuck in a toaster.

'A love affair with the wrong person?' asks Susan.

Okay, this obviously won't produce the result that Susan is hoping for, but there's value here, there's value in keeping Aphra uncomfortable and off balance and squarely under Susan's thumb, in making sure she knows that this is a hostile environment, that the people she encounters in this building are arrayed against her like a battery of cannon.

Aphra raises a spoonful of soup and looks at Susan.

'I bet you've fucked a colleague or two in your time,' she says.

~

The story that Aphra reads goes like this.

The UK intelligence cell had identified a potential source in the Paris-based nephew of CASPIAN, the chief suspect, but concluded that making a recruitment approach in France without the permission of the French was too high a risk. GCHQ phone analysis revealed that the nephew had a single UK-based contact, a forty-three-year-old British-Syrian dentist who lived and worked in the Smethwick area of Birmingham. Could the dentist somehow be used to lure the nephew to UK soil?

A character assessment was required. The cell dispatched an undercover officer to register with the surgery as a new patient who claimed to have been living in France for the past dozen years. It was hoped that this might lead to a conversation about life in France, prompting the dentist to mention that he knew someone living there, which might shed light on the nature of their relationship.

The officer reported back that the clinic was sandwiched between a discount firework outlet and a fabric store, that the front window was cracked, the electronic check-in system broken and the newest magazine on the coffee table fourteen months old. The dentist himself was pleasant enough, and mildly apologetic about the state of the clinic, but his own dishevelment ('uncombed hair, red-eyed, grimy white coat') undermined his apologies, leading the officer to conclude that the problems here were endemic.

A recording was made of their encounter; a transcript is included within the file. Much of it is taken up with medical comments made by the dentist to the dental nurse, but there were several brief opportunities for general conversation.

Dentist: Are you new to the area?
Officer: Yes, I moved back from France about a month ago.
Dentist: Whereabouts in France were you living?
Officer: Paris.
Dentist: Paris to Smethwick. We don't get many of those.
Officer: What about you? Are you a local?
Dentist: Upper left eight missing. I've been here for three
    years. Open wide, please.

And then a little later:

Officer: What's there to do in the area?
Dentist: It's a bit of a dump, to be honest.
Officer: Are you thinking of moving somewhere else?
Dentist: We'll see.
Officer: I'd recommend Paris if you want to work abroad.
Dentist: [Grunt]
Officer: It helps to have someone who can show you around.
    It's that sort of place, you need to know where the good
    things are.
Dentist: You've got a touch of gingivitis, nothing too serious.

The intelligence cell judged that the deployment had met its minimum objectives, which were to facilitate an assessment of the dentist's character ('down to earth, taciturn, bordering on glum') and ascertain how readily he could be persuaded to talk about his Paris-based contact ('the patient–dentist context is too restrictive. A different setting is required'). The cell set about looking for another opportunity to engage with him. An analysis of his weekly routine based on phone location data indicated that he spent two hours every Tuesday evening in a Pentecostal church not far from the Hagley Road. The church's website didn't list any events on a Tuesday night, but the address was given elsewhere as the location for a weekly Narcotics Anonymous meeting.

A second undercover officer was dispatched.

~

'The ethics counsellor is ready to see you.'

'Oh Susan, dear Susan,' says Aphra. 'It's all go–stop–go–stop here. Can I really not finish reading the file first?'

'She's just one floor down, we can walk.'

It's purely by chance that the quickest route to the ethics counsellor's office takes them down the same stairwell that Aphra fled to earlier. She does a good job of looking as though this is the first time, though. The only giveaway – and you'd have to know what you were looking for – is that she touches the window in the same cold spot where she rested her forehead just an hour or so before.

'We've got off on the wrong foot, Susan,' says Aphra.

It doesn't look as though Susan has a right foot, the way she walks. She never signed up for this much to and fro. An average day in the life of a building escort might require several hours of sitting in the general proximity of an electrician or a builder called in to repair something. Even them, she resents. Even sitting down, a book of crosswords on one knee, a cup of hot milky tea between her feet, Susan doesn't have to swing low to find more than enough resentment for someone simply doing their job. That one looks Russian, she thinks, or what's he *really* doing with those wires? This us-and-them thing is powerful. This *identity* thing. You arrive on day one – in Susan's case, Tuesday, 16 March 1982 – your head expanded with ideas of what you will do, what you will become, and when none of that happens, you realise that you need somewhere to put all those thwarted hopes. In Susan's case, she has taken what were once aspirations for a career in global covert action and reshaped them into something that makes a plumber unblocking a toilet feel mildly uncomfortable.

'Let's be friends, shall we?' Susan says to Aphra. 'I do think that name is so, so . . . pretty.'

There used to be a training exercise a long time ago in which the student had to empty a shop of customers. Shout fire, act crazy, pretend you're the manager – whatever it took. That exercise was all about asking the student to find the edges of their character. Most people are a blob. In this job, you want people who are a shape. You want a shelf full of shapes, one for every occasion. Susan is a shape.

'I looked it up,' says Susan. 'It means dust. Your name is dust.'

How can this be my first meaningful encounter with Susan? I think . . . I think I might be in *love* with her.

~

'It depends entirely on your mood,' says the ethics counsellor. 'If you're feeling zesty, I'd recommend either Liquorice & Spearmint or Spiced Ginger. At the other end of the scale, if it's calmness you're after, there's the Budding Meadow Camomile.'

She stands before an extensive selection of herbal teas, considering them with fingers outstretched, as though about to play a springtime melody.

'What are you going to have?' asks Aphra.

'Beetroot.'

'Beetroot tea?'

'Why don't you try it? It's very good for the digestion,' says the ethics counsellor. 'Where have you got to in the file?'

Aphra receives an outstretched mug emblazoned with some sort of Mum of the Year thing, places it on the low wooden table. 'An undercover officer is about to attend a Narcotics Anonymous meeting.'

'Aha. Good timing.'

'How so?' says Aphra.

'That's the point at which I was first consulted.'

'How often are you consulted on operations, out of interest?'

'My diary is full.'

'You're part-time.'

'Oh my, you've got sharp eyes,' says the ethics counsellor, her own eyes flicking to a weekly timetable stuck to a cork board, its Wednesdays and Fridays blocked out in green. 'You're quite right. I suppose it's a question of perspective. From my vantage point, people want to talk to me about the ethics of espionage constantly, but if I had to guess I'd say it probably constitutes a lowish percentage of all the operations run out of this building.'

If I had to guess, probably, lowish. That's one way to put it. You wouldn't believe how carefully the numbers are monitored and evaluated, along with the precise nature of the complaint, currently divided into seven categories, but I'd expect those to subdivide into at least twelve before the end of the year.

'Why do you think the number is lowish?' says Aphra.

'Because most of the work we do is pretty uncontroversial. You might be surprised to hear that. An agent handler recruits a source to provide intelligence on a terrorist network; a technical operations officer installs an eavesdropping device in the car of a Russian spy; a surveillance team follows a Chinese diplomat – as remarkable as such things may sound to an outsider, within this building they are entirely run-of-the-mill. They are all conducted legally and with

41

the aim of keeping the UK safe. Although they involve things most people would frown upon in real life, such as lying or intruding or betraying trust, such behaviours are unfortunately baked into the profession.'

'If you have a problem with deception, you're in the wrong job.'

'I'm afraid that's true.'

The official justification for creating the role of ethics counsellor (no more than colourful wrapping, let's rip through it) is that it provides an opportunity for staff to explore ethical concerns with an experienced blah blah blah. In private they say it reduces the chances of a British Snowden. It's no accident that the role was created in the same year that Ed boarded a flight to Hong Kong. *Whistleblowers welcome*, reads the caption beneath a newspaper cartoon stuck to the cork board. You'd have to be an idiot to believe that this is where you come to blow the whistle on anything, but I suppose there are stages along the way to becoming a whistleblower, and this is somewhere you might visit early in that process, when your concerns are still small enough – or imperfectly understood, which is the same thing – that you're willing to be persuaded that they could be dissolved in a Mum of the Year mug of organic rosehip tea. How bad can it be, how bad can *we* be, the ethics counsellor seems to say, smiling through the steam that rises from a spring meadow as the sun climbs into a perfect—

'You're typically consulted when an officer feels that something is close to the line,' says Aphra.

'Yes.'

'Where is that line?'

'It depends entirely on the person.' The ethics counsellor picks up her beetroot tea, hunches, smiles, blows little ripples across its surface. 'I can't discuss any specific examples, but there are some themes that won't surprise you.'

She takes her first sip. It might be single malt, the way she rolls the beetroot around her mouth.

'Drone strikes, for example,' she says. 'If your operation produces intelligence about a target in Syria or Iraq, is it ethical to share that intelligence with the military, knowing that it may lead to a targeted strike?' She takes a second sip. 'Another thing that comes up frequently is working alongside the intelligence agencies of certain countries. Does cooperating with country X mean that we are complicit in any human rights abuse they carry out?'

'Why were you consulted on this case?'

'Collateral intrusion,' says the ethics counsellor. 'People divulge very sensitive, very personal information at a Narcotics Anonymous meeting. Is it necessary and proportionate for us to send an undercover officer into that environment? How can we make sure that we only collect and retain information essential to our mission? Are we confident that we won't impact anyone's recovery?'

I don't know if it's intentional, but this habit of framing every-thing as a question is very effective. Every doubt can be expressed as a question, after all. The trick lies in preserving it at that stage, before it rots into a conviction that can't be ignored.

'I'm a bit behind the curve,' says Aphra. 'Can you tell me what happened?'

'An undercover officer joined the Narcotics Anonymous group. After the second or third meeting, he sought out the dentist, claimed to identify with elements of his story and asked for support on his own journey towards recovery.'

'He asked the dentist to be his sponsor.'

'Effectively, yes. They went out for meals, walks at the weekend, even watched films together. At an appropriate moment, the officer said that he was considering doing an MBA somewhere in Europe. The dentist replied that he had an acquaintance who had studied in

Paris and offered to put the officer in touch with him for advice. It was as straightforward as that.'

'So the dentist put your officer in contact with the nephew of the Iranian assassin.'

'Yes,' says the ethics counsellor.

'What is his name, by the way?'

'Whose name?'

'The Iranian assassin.'

'We use the codename CASPIAN.'

'Ah, yes. The idea was that your officer could establish some sort of relationship with CASPIAN's nephew as a step along the way to recruiting him as a source.'

'You'll have to speak with the agent handlers about what happened next,' says the ethics counsellor. 'But that's basically it, yes.'

'And the dentist?'

'Shortly after being put in contact with the nephew, the officer told the dentist that he was moving away from the area. He stopped attending the NA meetings and eventually broke off contact with the dentist. That's where my involvement in the case ended.'

'You'll be aware that the complaint we received doesn't go into details, so part of what I'm doing is working out what aspect of the case might have triggered it,' says Aphra. 'Allow me to play devil's advocate. What would you say to the charge that the intrusion into the dentist's privacy was neither necessary nor proportionate? Presumably he's vulnerable, otherwise he wouldn't attend NA meetings. You introduced someone into his life and then abruptly withdrew that person.'

'We took extensive advice from our operational psychologists. The officer played the part of someone *receiving* support rather than providing it, which will have mitigated the impact of his withdrawal. Remember, too, that according to the principle of proportionality the level of intrusion is pegged to the size of the threat. The greater the threat, the greater the level of justifiable intrusion. In this case, the purpose was to prevent the murder of Iranian dissidents in Europe. I'm sure you'd agree that's a very serious objective.'

'That wasn't the objective of the operation.'

'Excuse me?'

'The objective of the operation was to curry favour with European partners,' says Aphra. 'We didn't really care about the murders. The file is very clear on that point.'

'That may be a secondary objective, but the fact remains that people were being murdered.'

'If the objective was solely to curry favour with European partners, would you have put your foot down?'

'Put my foot down?'

'Would you have said no to the plan?' says Aphra.

'It's not my place to say no to anything. I'm a sounding board, an opportunity for officers to work their own way towards an ethical solution. We recruit people with a strong moral compass. They usually find their way to the right answer.'

'"Usually" being the operative word, I suppose.'

'What do you mean?' says the ethics counsellor.

'Well, there has been a complaint.'

'Look, the dentist didn't know what was happening around him. He wasn't aware of our involvement at any stage. As far as he was concerned, he was able to be a good friend to a fellow addict in his hour of need. I'd like to think that we left him in a better place than we found him.'

Beetroot was a bad choice. The ethics counsellor's digestion must be really messed up for her to have judged that *beetroot* is the right tea for today of all days. Today is a day for something light and insubstantial. But beetroot? Beetroot is subterranean, dusty, bloodsoaked, beetroot is—

'What if he *was* aware of what was happening around him?' says Aphra, leaning forward. 'What if the dentist saw through your operation?'

'But he didn't.' The ethics counsellor smiles, confident on this point. She blows murderous ripples across the surface of her tea. 'There is no way he had any idea what was going on.'

⌐⌐

He is aware that it would look odd if anyone peered through the window and saw him. There are chairs on the market that do something similar, he knows this, but his budget would only cover a deckchair or sunlounger, both of which he mistrusts because of his size, or a second-hand La-Z-Boy, but he's always found they require so much force to jolt them into movement that you're flung backwards and then basically have to execute a stomach-crunch–leg-curl manoeuvre back up to optimum recline. He can't imagine a worse way to relax. Besides which he'd have to somehow get it up the narrow stairs to his flat.

Or something like that.

There's also the adjustable spotlight. The glow it casts on his open book is forensic and warm. *Fitzroy Martial ran a hand through his mop of unruly hair*, he reads. *He surveyed the vast bank of MI6 hard drives in front of him, their lights twinkling like stars in the night sky.* He's not sure this book will add much to his growing list of insights, despite the claim on the cover that it was written by a 'former intelligence officer', that it contains 'revelations that will make your jaw drop'. Anyone who chooses writing spy novels over spying itself can't have been much good in the first place, he thinks. *Although a field man of the old-school variety, Martial understood that technology was transforming espionage in ways no one had ever anticipated. He sat in front of the screen, his fingers instinctively seeking out their familiar resting places on the keyboard like pigeons returning to their coop.* He shifts position, his back causing him some pain. He never uses the tiny tap and sink next to the chair but appreciates having them to hand. He won't admit it's because he likes the smell of mouthwash residue. He tried switching to an alcohol-free brand but it's less effective and he can't justify imposing it on his patients because of his own character flaw. *Far above him, Martial heard the familiar sound of the Wildcat CTS800 landing on the MI6 helipad. It was time. He reached for his Glock 19——*

He throws the book at the wall. It hits a framed poster entitled 'Anatomy of the Tooth', cracks the glass and falls to the floor.

~

The story that Aphra reads goes like this.

One day, the undercover officer was discussing with the dentist ways in which he might get his life back on track. Their conversation ranged from the importance of relationships to the ingredients of a healthy lifestyle to the various ways the officer might tear himself free from a career in tech start-ups that had driven his stress levels through the roof and contributed to his addiction. Money was not a problem. The officer was keen to start his own business – something small, something focussed on well-being – but lacked a sense of how to begin.

Aphra reads:

Officer: I've thought about an MBA but don't know where to
   look.
Dentist: Lot of good places in London, I would have thought.
Officer: I know too many people there. I need a fresh start.
Dentist: Pick a city, then.

Officer: In the UK? Outside of London, there's nowhere that's prestigious enough.

Dentist: What a thing to say out loud.

Officer: No, I mean, these things are all about reputation and networking, the educational content of the course isn't what counts.

Dentist: That doesn't make what you're saying any better.

Officer: I'm thinking European capitals. Somewhere liveable, you know? Good food, nice to look at, close enough to London for family visits.

Dentist: We should go and get some food. It's getting late.

Officer: Brussels? Amsterdam? Berlin? You know, I've always had a thing for Paris.

Dentist: How about a kebab from the Turkish lads on the high street?

Officer: Do you know anyone who lives there?

Dentist: On the high street?

Officer: Paris, you idiot.

Dentist: I know an Iranian guy who studied there, can't remember what it was. Let's go, get your arse off the sofa.

Officer: Do you think he'd be a good person for me to speak to?

Dentist: Who?

Officer: Your Iranian friend. Just, you know, what's it like to live there, best neighbourhoods, that kind of stuff.

Dentist: I thought you said you'd been there loads.

Officer: It's different altogether, living there.

Dentist: Come on, I'll give you his email, just get moving, you lazy bastard.

Within a week the officer was in contact with the nephew in Paris, first by email, then text, then phone call and finally

FaceTime. The nephew was able to provide a wealth of information about the MBA programme at the Hautes études commerciales, which he broadly recommended, albeit with some minor misgivings. Although he had already graduated, he offered to arrange for the officer to attend a lecture in order to make up his own mind.

This required an awkward manoeuvre on the part of the intelligence cell. They couldn't send the officer to Paris because of the risk that the French would realise what was happening and accuse the British of operating on their territory without permission, but they wanted to close out this final phase of the recruitment. The officer was instructed to tell the nephew that he'd changed his mind and now planned to study in New York. However, to thank the nephew for all his help, he wanted to invite him to Manchester for the weekend to attend a football match. According to the officer, he'd been given the tickets by a relative and couldn't find anyone else who wanted to go.

The nephew said yes.

It was a 2–2 draw.

Before he returned to Paris, the nephew was pitched by two British agent handlers.

~

Aphra follows Susan down the corridor. Susan's got this thing about Aphra peering through open doorways so tries to keep her busy with chat about the prospects for rain that weekend.

'The grandkids don't mind it but I'm not so keen,' she says over her shoulder.

'I'm with you,' says Aphra. 'I saw enough rain in St Andrews to last me a lifetime.'

They take a left, walk straight, take a right. It's oddly busy, as though staff are returning en masse from an event of some sort.

'They'll even go swimming in the rain, given the chance,' says Susan.

'Have you got a local lido?' says Aphra.

'We go up to London Fields,' says Susan.

They turn into the lift area, congested with people waiting, giving up waiting, not even bothering to wait in the first place, just threading their way through bodies to get back to their desks.

'Oh my,' says Susan.

Even when the lift doors ping it doesn't seem to make much of a difference since as many people exit as enter.

'Excuse me,' says Susan imperiously. Her slow pace works in her favour here; the crowds part grudgingly but just fast enough to allow her to make steady progress to the other side. 'What were we talking about?' she says to Aphra. The lift area narrows into another corridor. There's a few stragglers here but nothing to slow them down. 'Oh yes. Do you know London Fields at all?'

She doesn't get an answer. She turns to repeat her question, thinking it worthwhile to keep the conversation going after the earlier hostility between them, not that she regrets that, but she's starting to understand that a bit of warmth makes the knife slide in more smoothly.

Aphra's not there.

She stops, stares back down the corridor the way she's come. There's no sign of her. Susan starts walking back towards the lifts. She doesn't waste time thinking that Aphra's stopped to tie a shoe-lace, or she's got confused, or I'll spot her any second now.

There's a wall-mounted phone by the lifts that connects her to the security office. It's the first time in forty-two years that she's used it.

'I've had a visitor go missing,' she says. 'Aphra McQueen. Second floor, by the lifts.' She wants to say something equal to the occasion, like approach with extreme caution or shoot to kill, but the guards don't have guns, and they're generally a polite bunch. 'I think it may be deliberate,' she says.

A guard arrives quickly, a walkie-talkie in one hand.

'We've pulled a photo from the pass she was issued with,' he says. 'There's a few of us looking. Don't worry, she can't have gone far.' He listens to a crackle. 'Why do you think it might be deliberate?' he says.

Susan leans in, lowers her voice. She doesn't want to be overheard.

'She's rotten, this one. She's got evil in here.' Susan taps her breastbone. 'There's a dark cloud that descends whenever she's around.'

The guard raises his eyebrows.

'I feel . . . I feel under unspeakable pressure,' she says.

The guard's radio beeps. He puts it to his ear and listens intently.

'They've found her,' he says. 'Apparently she got separated from you in the melee, thought she saw you getting into the lift so followed you in. As soon as she realised her mistake, she came down to the main security office in the lobby to let us know.'

'Her mistake,' repeats Susan.

'There was a Town Hall meeting downstairs, that's why it was so busy. They're changing the pensions again.'

Susan forces a smile. 'Making them worse?'

'Do they ever make them better?'

~

It wasn't always like this, but the dentist has come to understand that what he values most about his job is that people make appointments, then they come to see him. Isn't it brilliant? He doesn't even have to be involved in the bit when they phone up. The genius lies in the way the process circumvents the question of whether or not he is motivated. It simply doesn't matter how he feels. Someone turns up, they open their mouth, he fixes it. The alternative is unimaginable. Managing a team? Developing strategy? Identifying opportunities for growth? Where would he start? *Would* he start? There's no way he could do a job that left him to his own devices. He doesn't trust his own devices, knowing what he does about them.

But the past is the past. You should see him now. Something has happened. Fortunately there's no need for speculation. You can literally see where the idea started, how it grew, where it now sits, where it might go next. If only everyone depicted the contents of their mind on the wall in such a clear pictorial fashion, it would make my life a lot easier.

I would guess that he's done it this way because he's seen it in the films. It's what brooding detectives do, in the hours after midnight, nursing a whisky, their shirtsleeves rolled up. It's also what spies do, and *what spies do* is a topic that is clearly on his mind. It explains the stack of books on the table, borrowed from the library, he's not made of money. The authorised histories of MI5, MI6 and GCHQ, a memoir or two (they're thin on the ground), spy novels praised for their 'authenticity', journalistic exposés.

He stands in the middle of his small living room. Stuck with Sellotape to the wall in front of him is a piece of paper. It appears to be the record of a patient who came to see him six months ago. Underneath, on a separate piece of paper, he has written, in bullet points:

- *Moved from Paris*
- *Telephone number: no response*
- *No social media*
- *Not at address – abrupt departure*

He's taped a strand of what looks like dental floss from that record to another piece of paper, stuck higher and to the left. On this piece, under the heading Narcotics Anonymous, he's written:

- *Interested in Paris*
- *Telephone number: no response*
- *No social media*
- *Abrupt departure*
- *MBA coincidence*

A strand of floss connects to a third piece of paper, this one a printed selfie of a man at what looks like a Manchester City game. Underneath he's simply written *???*

The way he's positioned the three items on his chart, leaving most of the wall empty, indicates that he expects his investigation to yield plenty more evidence. I can't fault his optimism, seeing as how he's made such a solid start. Laid out like that, it certainly does look as though we have been clumsy. On its own, the Paris coincidence was minor, and abrupt departures do happen in real life. I can't imagine his patients are all long-term regulars. But that MBA thing, that was deeply unfortunate. If the dentist had known all along his friend had done an MBA, the coincidence wouldn't have registered so violently. But to hear that his *new* acquaintance wanted to do an MBA in Paris and *then* discover that his *old* acquaintance had *also* done an MBA in Paris? And *then* to see that *old* acquaintance attending a football match in Manchester with his *new* acquaintance?

It's a tower built too high and too fast. No wonder it landed with a clatter.

The dentist takes a new piece of paper. Under the heading Conclusions, he writes:

- *It was a spy operation*
- *They picked me to play a role*

He inserts the word 'pivotal' before the word 'role'.

He stands back and considers his work. An expression crosses his face. This is worrying. I'm accustomed to suspicion. Anger I can deal with. Ridicule, indifference, vengefulness, resentment – I've seen it all. But this is something different. Unless I'm mistaken, he feels . . . pride.

As though he's one of us.

But of course he's not.

~

'You really don't have to apologise,' says the first of the two agent handlers. 'We've passed the time grappling with the eternal question of which ice cream flavour is best. I'm a staunch defender of traditional vanilla, but Ned here has pulled the kilim out from under my feet by proposing Turkish ice cream, which apparently has a delicious mouthfeel – is that the right word? – which they make by adding—'

'Mastic and salep, which comes from orchid root,' says Ned.

'Does that qualify as a flavour? Isn't mastic a thickening agent?' says Aphra.

'Aha,' says the first agent handler, 'she has a point.'

'You can certainly get flavours like Gaziantep pistachio or sour cherry,' says Ned, 'but it's also sold as *sade dondurma*, which translates as plain ice cream. I would argue that mastic and salep *is* the flavour.'

'This is the sort of profound global insight one brings back from a posting in Istanbul,' says the first agent handler. 'Speaking of sour cherries, who was that woman who brought you here?'

'Her name is Susan.'

'Why does she look like that?'

'We got separated. The corridor was crowded. She suspects I had some sort of ulterior motive.'

'In giving her the slip?'

Aphra shrugs.

'What did you do with your freedom?' says the first agent handler. 'Poison the water supply? Garrotte a dinner lady?'

'Which brings us to the subject of our meeting,' says Aphra.

The first agent handler sprawls like an off-duty marionette. A string is pulled: his limbs snap together, he sits up, he sits forward.

'Death,' he says. 'Death and destruction.' He wears a Stone Roses T-shirt under a blue linen blazer. 'Anything you want to know, just ask. We're normally very tight-lipped indeed about agents, but the word has come down from on high that there's been a complaint, so we want you to consider yourself granted an access-all-areas pass.'

He mimes the act of handing Aphra a pass, which briefly confuses her.

'We're also keen to hear how your thoughts are evolving,' says Ned, wearing desert boots, beige chinos, a blue Oxford shirt and a moustache. 'People who work here are as prone to group think, unconscious bias and herd instinct as anyone else. There's material you'll have seen in the file, material that may have caused you concern but that we're blind to. I'm totally open to the possibility that we've screwed up along the way.'

'Me too, I'm totally open to the possibility that Ned's screwed up along the way,' says the Stone Roses T-shirt. 'Seriously, though, if there's lessons to learn or mistakes to put right, we want to know.' He puts his fists up. 'And we'll be in your corner if you get any push-back from management.'

Just as you want a locksmith who doesn't leave what they call 'hesitation scratches' behind, so you want an agent handler with unshakeable faith in their abilities, someone who approaches new people with the confident forward thrust of a well-oiled skeleton key.

'Can we start with the nephew's recruitment?' says Aphra.

'We pitched him just before he boarded the Eurostar on his way back to Paris,' says Ned. 'As you know, he'd been to Manchester to attend a football match with an undercover officer who he believed was a friend of the dentist. A recruitment pitch is always unpredictable, so you want to minimise the likelihood that the person being pitched will create a fuss. We had a support officer keeping an eye on us in case. But he couldn't have been nicer.'

'The nephew, he means,' says the Stone Roses T-shirt. 'The support officer was and remains an arsehole.'

'I'd love to claim that he was hostile and argumentative,' says Ned, 'that we had to draw on our voodoo skills to calm him down and talk him round, but the truth is that he was urbane, intelligent, calm, reflective and very open to coming back to London a week later to sit down with us.'

'Still the nephew,' says the Stone Roses T-shirt. 'The support—'

'Did you tell him it was about his uncle?' says Aphra.

'Not at that stage,' says Ned. 'Even at the next meeting, we took it slowly, talking in very general terms about the situation in Tehran, his views on the regime, that sort of thing. I think he brought up his uncle, I want to say in the third or fourth meeting we had with him, but only in the context of a discussion about family rifts. He hadn't seen or spoken to his uncle in years, and described him as an old-school, pro-government type. He was supportive of the crackdown on unveiled women, for example, which the nephew abhorred.'

The Stone Roses T-shirt watches Ned as he speaks, nodding in agreement. 'It was both good and bad for us, this rift,' he says. 'Good because, well, if there's no love lost between them, he might be willing to report back to us about his uncle. But bad because they simply didn't see each other.'

'Once we felt confident in the strength of our relationship with the nephew, we shared our suspicions about the murders,' says Ned. 'He was horrified, utterly horrified.'

'He cried in front of us. He told us his mother – it's her brother we're talking about – would die if she found out.'

'Once he'd calmed down, we told him that when he next returned to Iran on holiday, we wanted him to begin the process of rebuilding the relationship with his uncle so that he could collect intelligence about him and pass it to us.'

They've either worked together for a while, these two, or they've rehearsed this.

'Did you talk about the risks involved in acting as your agent?' says Aphra.

'More than any other topic,' says Ned. 'But there was no stopping him. He hated what his uncle was doing, he hated what the regime was doing, he hated that his family was being shamed by his uncle's conduct.'

'But motivation alone isn't enough for us,' says the Stone Roses T-shirt. 'If he's going to be safe then he also has to be good – very good.' A brief pause. 'The trainers told us they hadn't seen an agent with his raw ability for a long, long time.'

'He went back to Tehran and returned with so much intelligence that it took us a long weekend to debrief him, staying up past midnight most days,' says Ned. 'He had talked his uncle into taking him on a hunting trip, a kind of let's build bridges exercise, so the two of them had lots of quality face time. He didn't admit to the murders, that was never on the cards, but we got phone numbers and email addresses and social media usernames, we got a rundown of the uncle's personal life, we got his views on the regime, the names of his friends, dates and details of his military career. He even admitted that he had travelled to Europe, which was huge for us, because we know for a fact that he hasn't travelled under his own name, so it was confirmation that he's used an alias and therefore is probably the assassin.'

'We've shared some of this with the HAARLEM group, but disguised it so that it seems to come from a number of different sources, including technical sources, rather than just one person. We don't want them to know we've got an agent in play,' says the Stone Roses T-shirt.

'Because they're leaky?' says Aphra.

'It's always a risk with the Europeans,' says Ned.

'A key part of what we've been able to do is identify a Facebook account that the uncle uses to send messages to his masters when he travels into Europe,' says the Stone Roses T-shirt. 'If we see that account being used again, it'll tell us that the uncle is on the move. We'll share that data with our European counterparts so that they can intercept him.'

They all listen to Susan pass the time of day with someone in the corridor outside.

'There's huge additional potential with the agent that we've barely tapped,' says the Stone Roses T-shirt. 'He went to school with half a dozen or more people who now work for the Iranian government, all of whom he's in regular contact with. But let's turn the tables.' He mimes spinning the table around, groaning as though it's really heavy. 'What do you think? What have we done—'

'Are there any areas of the case where you feel doubt?' says Aphra. 'Where things could have been done better?'

'To be completely honest, I feel that way about *every* aspect of the case,' says Ned. 'Did the nephew really feel able to say no to us? Did he think he'd be in trouble if he walked away? Was he seduced by the glamour of spying? We did everything we could to make sure he gave us an honest answer, including insisting that he consider our proposal for a few days to let the idea sink in.'

'And still he said yes,' says Aphra.

'This is unfortunately one of those operations where there's risk everywhere you look. A risk that we'd upset the French. A risk that we'd harm the dentist by using him as a stepping stone to the nephew. A risk that the nephew would say no, that he would side with his uncle, that he would go to the press, that he would go to the Iranian embassy to complain of harassment. If he'd done that, the Iranians would have spotted the connection to his uncle in a heartbeat and realised that we knew he was the assassin. We would have lost any chance of catching him.'

The Stone Roses T-shirt sits forward. He's very excited about something.

'I've got a great idea,' he says. 'Why don't you come to our next meeting with the nephew? It'll give you a sense of the rapport and trust we've built up with him over time.'

It's perfectly safe to suggest this, there's no way that management will green-light it.

'We're due to see him next week,' he says. 'What do you think?'

I think I might swallow this, if I didn't know what I know. It's hard to tell what Aphra thinks.

'We'll tell him you're a colleague evaluating the case,' says Ned, joining in. 'You can ask him anything you want.'

Everyone's heard of the good cop, bad cop routine, but it still works, because it generates a threat (the bad cop) and a safe haven from that threat (the good cop). Of course, the price of admission into the safe haven is a confession. But these two are not interested in making Aphra confess to anything. They're interested in *hiding* something from her. What they're deploying, I would argue, is the lesser-known good criminal, good criminal routine. Stay with me, I'm thinking on my feet here. Imagine you're trying to hide something from the cops. Imagine the cops are on their way to your home with a search warrant. You could put the thing you're hiding in a room and lock the door, but it's just a matter of time before the cops get to that door and think, it's behind this door. They're not idiots. But according to the good criminal, good criminal routine, you muzzle the dog, switch off the alarm, throw open the front door, hand round mugs of sweet tea and give them a guided tour yourself.

Ned and the Stone Roses T-shirt both say 'Well?' at the same moment, and turn to each other with warm, affectionate smiles.

The Stone Roses T-shirt places a hand on Ned's shoulder, massages it. He looks at Aphra.

'What do you say?'

~

Much later Susan says 'Follow me', which leads to some confusion because she wants to walk behind Aphra. After what happened earlier, she wants to have her eyes fixed on Aphra every step of the way. There couldn't be a more embarrassing time to lose her than this, given where they're going, given that the corridors are bone empty at this late hour. They're both carrying coats and bags. It's dark outside. The file has been stored away in a safe, the combination lock has been spun first one way and then the other, the *tick tick tick* of the dial always sounding to Susan like time itself, you think it'll spin forever, but the heavy mechanism slows down surprisingly fast.

Or something like that.

'Okey-dokey,' says Susan. 'Here we are. Do you want to leave your bag and coat with me?'

~

'I hope you don't mind being diverted here on your way out, Aphra. A little bird told me that you had finished for the day.'

Sir William Rentoul stands before a wooden cabinet now open to reveal a selection of bottles, all the same size and colour, like organ pipes, each with no brand label except for a small handwritten tag identifying the contents. He didn't start the tradition, it's always been done this way.

'Nobody knows,' he says in response to a question nobody asks, 'but the story goes that one of my predecessors was due to host his Russian counterpart and worried that his preference for one brand of gin over another would give away aspects of his character that could be exploited.'

A less welcome inheritance has been the large metal safe in the corner of Sir William's office, first used by the original holder of his post over a hundred years ago. Despite a number of increasingly tense sessions with the locksmith, Sir William hasn't mastered the art of opening it. He can close it fine, that has never been a problem. After one of those sessions he suggested replacing it with a modern cabinet – you can open those touch keypads in seconds – but it has never materialised, so he keeps a lot of the day-to-day material in his desk drawer, contrary to regulations.

'Nothing like a glass of sherry to signal that the day's work is done,' says Sir William.

When important visitors are due, he summons the locksmith from his basement workshop to open the safe and leave it slightly ajar, allowing Sir William to spin the dial with brio before his audience.

'What can I offer you?' he says.

Julian Redruth is also present. He's spent most of the day in Parliament but his mind has been down here among the spies. He holds his sherry glass just below the knot of his tie. A table by the window is laid for two. Fresh linen, folded napkins, polished silver. There'll be a fish course, by the looks of it.

'Thoughts?' says Sir William.

'Excuse me?' says Aphra.

'Fino, amontillado or cream?'

'I don't mind.'

'I'll give you a cream, it was my late wife's favourite.'

Sir William selects a bottle, uncorks it, pours a small measure.

'I hope you are finding Susan helpful,' he says. 'Did you know we joined on exactly the same day? The 16th of March 1982. In those days there wasn't much mixing between the officer class and the rank and file, other than at the Christmas party once a few sherries had been drunk. I remember twirling Susan a bit too energetically to something from Bucks Fizz. She was an avid butterfly collector in those days. Might still be. You'll have to let me know. Had a pokey room in Bow somewhere, a glass-fronted box on the wall filled with the bloody things, I remember thinking how creepy it looked.'

He lifts his glass.

'To a successful investigation.' He takes a sip. 'I've set up a few more interviews for you. Timothy, head of Legal, will talk you through the relevant legislation at 10 a.m. tomorrow. You'll be able to see the signed warrants that apply to this case, as well as the RIPA legislation that authorises our use of the agent. Then, after lunch, I've asked a few of our security advisors to present you with a case study and discuss the tradecraft we've used to make sure that all involved remain safe and well.'

'I speak on behalf of the entire Committee,' says Julian Redruth, 'when I say how much we appreciate you leaning into this, Sir William.'

'Safe, legal, ethical and successful – those are the targets we aim for,' says Sir William. 'Now . . .'

The pause is long enough to make it apparent that Sir William has forgotten her name.

'Aphra,' says Julian.

'Put us out of our misery, Aphra,' says Sir William. 'How have you got on today?'

'It's too early to say.'

'I think we understand that it will take time to reach a nuanced judgement,' says Sir William. 'I suppose what we are asking, to put it crudely, is whether you have found a smoking gun on your first day.'

There is an awkward silence. Aphra doesn't appear to understand that she's being asked a question.

'I agreed to your . . . investigation, shall we call it, on the basis that a complaint had been made,' says Sir William. He's being very patient. 'Now, if that complaint was prompted by a serious error on our part, I shall wish to take urgent steps to correct it.' He waits, then has one final attempt, speaking slowly this time. 'In other words, if this matter is serious enough to warrant an investigation, it is also serious enough to warrant an update.'

Aphra looks at him. I suppose, technically speaking, he hasn't asked a question, but that's beside the point.

'Julian, perhaps you can better explain our position,' says Sir William.

Julian Redruth clears his throat.

'Can you please tell us, Aphra, if you have uncovered anything of concern during the first day of your enquiries?' he says.

'No,' she says.

'No, you can't tell us? Or no, you haven't found anything of concern?'

'I haven't found anything of concern,' she says. 'But—'

'Wonderful,' says Sir William, clapping his hands once. 'Dinner's ready, Julian. Thank you so much for stopping by, Aphra. Susan is waiting outside. She'll show you out of the building.'

~

The dentist has tried it both ways, typed and handwritten, but both have their issues. Spy shows often use that typewriter font, the letters B E R L I N or M O S C O W hammered out one by one across the bottom of the screen, but when you write a whole letter like that it looks like a ransom note, which is not the effect he wants.

In its favour, a handwritten letter looks personal. After all, someone has taken the effort to write it. If he was sending a letter to a close friend – let's assume he had one – he would most definitely write it by hand. Furthermore, having concluded from his research that the person charged with opening the mail will have been trained to a high level in the art of graphology, he has taken steps to adjust his handwriting to reflect honesty, integrity and all-round good moral character. This will mitigate, he believes, the fact that the majority of those who send handwritten letters to intelligence agencies are likely to be certified lunatics, or possibly children wanting to be spies when they grow up. He's seen lots of that on their social media. He doesn't want to be confused with them either.

Or something like that.

The best course of action, he decides, is to write the letter by hand but on paper headed with the name of his dental surgery alongside the NHS logo. People trust the NHS, even spies, presumably, insofar as they trust anyone. It runs the risk that the letter opener will think it's been delivered to the wrong address, but he plans to reassure them with a strong and clear opening.

Dear Sir/Madam, he starts. He crosses it out.

To whom it may concern.

Hello. Hi. Hi there.

I hope you're well. I hope you are well. I hope this finds you and your staff well. Please do not be confused by the heading. This letter does not concern dentistry.

It's more difficult than he expected. He doesn't waste time asking the internet. Even the internet will be incapable of telling him what register to adopt when writing to the spies, he's sure of that. Where else might he find inspiration? He looks around for a letter he received last week, recalls something about its tone that was authoritative, personal and straightforward.

I am writing in reference to a number of recent outpatient appointments that you have missed. I am very sorry if this has been caused by a recurrence of the personal difficulties that we discussed, but I would encourage you to attend your scheduled session this Thursday at 2.30 p.m. so that we can explore your current situation together and, if necessary, amend your course of treatment by increasing the dosage of—

Okay, he's ready to give it another go.

I am writing in reference to the intelligence operation your officers carried out in the Smethwick district of Birmingham in March this year. I am very sorry if the contents of this letter come as a surprise, but I have a number of important matters I wish to discuss.

He's learned a lot from the library books. Spies are actually called 'officers'. They either 'carry out' or 'conduct' 'operations', never 'missions', and members of the public who work for them are 'agents'.

As you will be able to verify from your records, approximately six months ago I was approached by an undercover officer purporting to be a patient at my dental surgery. Shortly afterwards, I was approached by a second undercover officer attending a Narcotics Anonymous meeting held in a Pentecostal church near the Hagley Road. The purpose of the operation appears to have been connected to an Iranian acquaintance of mine who lives in Paris. I wish to make it clear that I bear you, your organisation and your officers no ill will. I do not need to know the reason for your operation. I understand and respect the principle of NTK that governs your work.

He originally wrote 'need to know' in full but the acronym will make it clear that they're not dealing with an idiot.

You will be aware from my attendance at the NA meeting, as well as from my medical records, that I have experienced some personal difficulties over the past few years. It is because of this that I am so gratified to have been of service to you. You have seen a value in me, whether in the form of an aptitude or a strength of character, that at times I have struggled to see myself. I would very much like the opportunity to discuss this with you, and to explore ways in which I might continue to work as an agent for your company.

Your organisation.

Your service.

Your Service.

Your estimable Service.

I look forward to hearing from you.

It's been such a stressful experience, writing the letter, that he opens a bottle of mouthwash and pours himself a small measure.

~

Aphra takes her coat and bag from Susan and follows her down the corridor. Susan is like a kettle stuck on boil. She's walking fast, she's turning to check on Aphra every few paces, she's stroking Aphra's upper arm, she's giggling at nothing at all.

At the security booth, a guard retrieves Aphra's headphones from a locker and hands them to her. He reaches for her bag, places it on a table to conduct a brief search, takes out a scarf, a purse, a paper-back, tissues, a notebook, mints, a file marked top secret.

He speaks to her, a frown on his face, but she doesn't hear him. She just turns to look at Susan, several feet away, who is so over-come with the stress of her first ever covert operation that she starts to cry.

~

It's easy to jump to conclusions in a situation like this, and that obvi-ously applies to me too, but on reflection there's no *actual* evidence that Susan planted the file in Aphra's bag.

Look at it this way. Since the moment of the discovery, Aphra hasn't spoken a single word in her defence. She has refused to provide any explanation whatsoever for what has happened. At the very least, such uncooperativeness is not the behaviour of a person who deserves to hold the highest level of government security clearance. There's also the matter of her two unauthorised, unaccompanied forays into the office for goodness knows what purpose, as well as the fact that Susan's forty-two-year disciplinary record is entirely blemish-free.

And see how she shivers. It's true that she is naked except for her underwear while two female security guards search each item of her clothing, but there's shivering caused by cold (it's not cold) and shivering caused by fear (the guards are being perfectly polite) and shivering caused by guilt.

But, as I said, it's best not to jump to conclusions.

~

Aphra sits, fully dressed, on a chair in the corner of the security office. Her bag has been searched, X-rayed and placed by her feet. Sir William Rentoul and Julian Redruth stand before her. That Sir William still wears his napkin is a reminder to all present that he has been interrupted, that he intends to return to his sea bass at the earliest opportunity.

'I do appreciate you being so understanding,' says Julian Redruth.

'I'm not doing it for your bloody appreciation,' says Sir William. 'If we called in the police, they would have to arrest her. This file would become part of the evidential chain. We cannot allow secret intelligence to enter the courts for every Tom, Dick and Harry to paw over.'

'Call the police,' says Aphra. 'I didn't take the file.'

Julian Redruth twists the neck of his napkin. He knows what's coming, wishes there was some way to put the future out of its misery.

'I suppose she didn't remove the file from the building,' he says, 'so you could argue that technically speaking no crime has been committed.'

'We're a lawyer now, are we?' says Sir William.

Susan watches them from a distance. She has been told that she can go home but prefers to stand in her duffel coat beside the vast ornamental crest that dominates the lobby.

'Poor Susan,' says Sir William. 'This has been most upsetting for her. Now we know why Aphra was behaving so oddly upstairs. When she put the file in her bag, the last thing she expected was to be brought to my office.'

'Do you really think I would try to walk out the front door with a classified file in my bag?' says Aphra.

'It is puzzling, Sir William,' says Julian Redruth. 'She's been with us for two years, has an exemplary record.'

'So you say. Would you know, though, if she'd been up to all manner of things?' says Sir William. 'The parliamentary estate is so large, so much happens up there, that I'm not convinced you would notice. I'm told that she gave Susan the slip today, was roaming unaccompanied around the building for fifteen minutes. She's clearly got some wiles about her.'

Sir William thinks. He had no clue this was going to happen, I am sure of that, but he is astute enough to recognise an opportunity when it comes into view. 'If we are not going to involve the police, Julian, we shall still have to find a way to recognise formally what has happened tonight,' he says. 'Something that compensates us, as it were, for the fact that she will go unpunished.'

Here it comes, thinks Julian Redruth.

'This has been an experiment,' says Sir William. 'Allowing you and your Committee to receive and investigate complaints from my officers has been an experiment. We deserve full credit for attempting it, you and I, for assembling our beakers and burners, but sadly it has blown up in our faces. You clearly don't have the right sort of people to carry out a complex and sensitive investigation of this sort. We shall of course continue to respect your remit as an oversight body, but I am afraid to say that the closer cooperation, the greater access for which you have been arguing, will no longer be possible. It is time for you and your Committee to take a step backwards.'

This, then, will be his legacy. A reduced, a restrained Intelligence and Security Committee. Julian Redruth once had a fierce ambition to bring the spies down a peg or two. They've learned how to speak to politicians, how not to write things down, how to use a grey puff of history like a second-rate magician to hide their tired sleight of hand. Those bottles, those bloody bottles. He's heard Sir William explain those fucking bottles three times. He was surprised Sir William didn't tell Aphra how the safe in the corner had been recovered from the rubble of the old HQ during the Blitz, its locking mechanism still in good working order. She's probably not important enough for that story.

Or something like that.

'You'll terminate her contract, I assume,' says Sir William.

'I resign,' says Aphra.

'At least she was able to confirm that there was nothing wrong with our operation. Unless you disagree violently, Julian, I think we can mark complaint number one as resolved.' Sir William smiles. He's got everything he could have wished for out of this. 'One for one,' he says. 'A hundred per cent record.'

'Oh do shut up,' says Julian Redruth.

Sir William goes to adjust his tie, is surprised to find the napkin still there.

'Come, come, old friend,' he says. 'Let's finish off that sea bass before it dries out completely.'

∽

They call it crown shyness, the way the uppermost canopies of two trees will grow towards each other and then stop, leaving a slender winding margin that allows daylight to pour through to the forest floor. I've often wondered whether the night sky has a similar arrangement in place. After all, there's so much colour, so much light up there, that it's not clear to me where all this darkness pours from, if not from crooked fissures of coal-black between those milk-flecked blues, dusted with peach, those greys like a winter's breath.

She walks with her head bowed, her black raincoat wrapped tightly around her. One end of her red scarf blows free.

I expect that Aphra McQueen will return to academia. She's only been away for two years, and her experience working for a parliamentary committee will enhance her academic profile and lead to new opportunities. St Andrews won't have her back, not after her abrupt departure, but it rains so much up there, and she's always wanted to teach in southern Europe. With the benefit of time and perspective, she will look back on this period with gratitude. Some people are just not cut out for the secret world. I ascribe no malice to her, despite what happened. I put it down to an excess of curiosity, even to a desire to do the best job possible, which to her mind required the opportunity to study the file at her leisure, in the privacy of her own home, without Susan staring at her.

One end of her red scarf blows free like a severed noose. A new lease of life, that's what she's been given. A reprieve.

Peter the analyst turns the page of his Russian-language text-book. He's surprised at how bad he was at lying, how uncomfortable it felt. But thrilling, too. It's not really lying, is it, when the government tells you to do it. By the end of the year he will apply to move into operational work as an agent handler. His application will be rejected, but he will be given feedback, which he will spend the rest of his career addressing.

The ethics counsellor sits on the edge of her youngest child's bed. He's got a fever, calls out in his sleep. She presses a lavender-scented flannel to his forehead.

One of the security guards finds Aphra's paperback. He's just come on shift, doesn't know it's hers, put to one side during all the commotion over the file. He frowns at the title but opens it to the first page and begins to read.

Ned is at the BFI, watching the latest in their Kubrick season. He prefers the early films, if he's honest. The Stone Roses T-shirt is on a second date with a cardiologist he met on a dating app.

Susan was too upset to go home. The security guards made up a camp bed for her in the corner of the museum, and she's fast asleep next to a radio transmitter concealed inside a shoe, still wearing her duffel coat.

Aphra is walking. She must have covered six miles already, shows no sign of letting up. It's fortunate that she didn't get to the bottom of the case, but I am hopeful that the attention she has brought to bear will help resolve some of the underlying issues. That would be in everyone's interest. It's tempting to look at this sort of thing in terms of individual lives, in terms of how people *feel*, but those simply aren't useful yardsticks when thinking about national security.

Julian Redruth walks alongside the Thames in the direction of Parliament. His sea bass was undercooked.

He is a man of science, Julian Redruth, a man of medicine. If one were to strip out the emotion and – let's speak plainly – ambition, and look at this story through a scientific lens, one would see the following arc: a body is attacked by hostile bacteria; a natural antibody is produced; the bacteria is repelled; the body is strengthened. It's a story we can all get behind.

Sir William Rentoul phones down to the garage and asks them to ready his car. He writes a note to himself. He writes a lot of notes to himself these days, since his memory started to play tricks on him. He's not too worried about Aphra, has half a suspicion that it was Susan who put the file there. What else was all that blubbering about? He's much more worried about the anonymous complaint. Julian Redruth might have been seen off, but there remains the fact that an officer of his saw fit to complain directly to the Intelligence and Security Committee. He places the note in his desk drawer, to be actioned in the morning.

Aphra McQueen unlocks a door and climbs forty-three steps to a small flat on the third floor. She must have covered fifteen miles tonight. Her long walk has exhausted her, but it's also given her time to reflect. Her edges are softening; dawn is replacing the lunacy of darkest night. She knows, I think, or is on her way to knowing, that she made a mistake, that she has nobody to blame for any of this but herself.

Or something like that.

I wish her well. We all do.

She switches on her computer, types *dentist*, types *Birmingham*, types *Smethwick*.

She clicks on a tab marked Make an Appointment.

Oh bloody hell.

PART TWO

The dentist wakes at 3 a.m. and spends some time looking at his wall chart. The string of dental floss that connected the evidence – *Paris, abrupt departure, no social media* – to the assessment – *they selected me to play a pivotal role* – lies crisply twisted on the floor. It's been six months since he last encountered an undercover officer, four days since he posted his letter to the spies. He hasn't received a response. It's early days, he tells himself, but still. He thinks he's right, that he was briefly caught up in a clandestine operation, but out of nowhere a new idea lands, one that he knows he won't be able to shake off.

They didn't pick me because I'm brilliant.

They picked me because I'm not.

He knows this about himself, that disappointment lands heavily. In his universe, disappointment has a mass that is out of proportion to its size. Grey skies, a difficult conversation with his mother, even the loss of a sock – they have all, at various times, hit the ground with a thump that knocked him off balance for weeks. There's no logic to it. Smethwick doesn't depress him, for example. Being overdrawn or overweight isn't a problem. He felt light-hearted upon signing his divorce papers, even though he had sought reconciliation at every step, and miserable on the day he graduated from Imperial College with a first in bioengineering. The ups and downs

77

are one thing; it's the inability to see them coming that he finds most difficult. It's like moving through life and constantly misjudging the temperature as you go, bursting into rooms wearing too many layers or stepping outside with nothing to protect you from the cold. That was until prescription medicine levelled him out. Then it didn't, and he had to deal with that as well. And now this, the thought that the spies don't want him after all, that they haven't seen something special in him, that there'll be no life of travel, camaraderie, excitement, glamour, service—

There's a twenty-four-hour shop down the road. His dressing gown wrapped tightly around him, he shuffles along the pavement, considering his options.

~

Aphra waits open-mouthed for him to finish. He's got the armamentarium of a professional: dental assistant, chair, waiting room, leaflets about oral health, last year's magazines. He says those things that dentists say, like 'UL5 MOD Composite' and 'gingival pockets all within normal limits'. But beneath all of that he's a wreck. His eyes are bloodshot. He's sweating. His sickle probe rattles against her teeth as though he's sending a farewell message from behind enemy lines. Even through his mask, the alcohol fumes make her eyes water.

'Your teeth are fine,' he says, standing back. 'I really don't understand why you said this was urgent.'

She came in here with a strategy. Or rather, given how quickly this is all unfolding, she came in here thinking that a strategy would surely present itself to her at some point. Failing that, she would be blunt. This is who I am, this is who you are. We have both been used and tossed aside.

'I'm sorry to have wasted your time,' she says. 'I just had a funny feeling . . .'

She pulls herself to the edge of the chair, prepares to leave. She steals one last glance at him. It's the last thing she expected. She thought he was in recovery. There's no way that she can involve him in what she is planning to do, given its complexity, its ambition, its sheer—

'Pick a city,' he says.

'Excuse me?'

'Any city. Any *capital* city. What are there, 200, 201?'

'I'm not—'

'Don't think about it. Just pick one, the first one that—'

'Paris,' she says.

He stares at her. Obviously the odds aren't 200 or 201 to 1, because of its proximity. Paris doesn't have the same value as Gaborone, say, or even Helsinki. But even if the true odds are more like 50 to 1, or even 20 to 1, her answer strikes him as significant.

'Is this . . .'

'Yes?'

'If you're not here about your teeth,' he says, 'are you here about my letter?'

'Tell me about your letter,' she says.

~

Sir William Rentoul sits at his desk, going through his schedule with his chief of staff. He's got the Secretary of State for Defence at ten, the US ambassador at eleven, lunch with the editors of the *Spectator* and the *Telegraph* at one, a board meeting at two thirty and at seven he's dining with the Service's alumni network at a private members' club in Piccadilly.

'Set up a cell,' he says. 'Six officers, until we know what we're dealing with. Two data analysts, two investigators, one admin support and a team leader. Prepare for the possibility that we'll need more.'

'Yes, sir. Any operational staff?'

'Not at this stage. The cell will report directly to me.'

'Understood, sir.'

As usual, Sir William's alarm woke him at 5.45 this morning. He had been dreaming about the first ever operation he ran, as a freshly minted young officer, against an IRA quartermaster who tried to buy weapons from a group of Colombian rebels, except that in Sir William's dream the rebels who emerged from the jungle included his driver, the woman who cleans his office, half the members of the board, even the chief of staff who stands before him now.

'Two administrative questions, sir.'

'Yes?'

'Operation name?'

Sir William thinks. 'BOGOTA,' he says.

'Target?'

He considers it betrayal, nothing less. If he could have called it Operation TRAITOR or Operation MOLEHUNT he would have done so.

'The target is whichever officer sent that fucking complaint to Julian Redruth and his committee of MPs.'

∼

'Wait,' says the dentist. 'Is this about the letter or not?'

It's like one of those books she read as a little girl, the ones where you're given a choice at the end of each page. There's always an easy question near the beginning to warm you up. *Do you climb through the window of the abandoned house or go home to bed? Do you overcome your fears and follow the smugglers into their cave?* The lesson being that an excess of caution is the surest way to bring your story to an end.

'Yes,' says Aphra. 'This is about the letter.'

'Huma,' he says to his assistant, 'can you give us a minute?'

She leaves the room.

'Well?' says the dentist. 'I'm listening.'

This is what Aphra thinks. What just happened must be related in some way to the intelligence operation. Why else would anyone suspect that a dental appointment was a pretext for something else? It was her mention of Paris that seemed to tip him over the edge. The two undercover officers had both talked about Paris in an attempt to get him to open up about his friend there. Does he know they were undercover officers? Has he written to one of them? Is that the letter he means? As the first officer was pretending to be just a patient, it's unlikely the dentist would write to him, but the second might have left a forwarding address. But why would a letter to the second officer trigger a visit from a woman pretending to need urgent dental care?

In short, she doesn't know what to think.

'No,' she says, '*I'm* listening. It was your letter, after all.'

Because he's excited, she can see that. He's not scared or anxious. He's happy that she's there. Which means that she has a certain amount of power over him. She doesn't know why or how far she can push it, but she knows that he isn't going to ask her to leave just yet.

'Sorry,' he says. 'I didn't mean to sound abrupt. Can I ask, though, why did you let me check your teeth? If you came to talk about the letter?'

'I didn't know whether Huma would be in today.'

In that sentence Aphra McQueen reveals just how dangerous she is. I wouldn't expect you to understand. But that 'Huma', that 'today' . . .

The dentist nods. 'She's been off sick a lot recently,' he says. He's helping Aphra with her answers. He wants to be persuaded. 'Shall I just repeat what I said in the letter?' he says.

'Say it as it comes,' she says. 'It'll feel different, saying it aloud to a person.'

There's one final thing on his mind.

'Do you have a badge or something?' he says.

'A badge?'

'To identify you as— you know, as a spy,' he says. 'I mean, as an intelligence officer.'

Until this moment Aphra McQueen hasn't known what role she is supposed to be playing. Now she knows. Now she is wondering how to present as a spy. She's met more of them in the last twenty-four hours than most people meet in a lifetime, but the truth is that none of them has quite met her expectations. Sir William Rentoul's patrician stiffness, the Stone Roses T-shirt's tiresome bonhomie, the ethics counsellor splashing around in hibiscus shallows – their styles would be inappropriate for the situation facing her. Susan was too bitchy, Peter was too nervous. Ned came the closest, perhaps. Certainly no one has provided her with an act she can easily imitate. Is that the point, she wonders, is that the spies' slippery genius, that any attempt to grasp hold of their essence leaves you empty-handed?

She nods at him as though she's heard the question many times before.

'I understand why you're asking. But the purpose of an intelligence officer is to operate below the radar,' Aphra says, realising in that moment that it's impossible to talk about spying without sounding like the back of a cheap paperback. 'We aren't issued with badges.'

He nods. He suspected as much, from his research.

'Can you tell me something you wouldn't otherwise know?' he says.

What her answer lacks in substance it makes up for in speed. 'You've lived in Smethwick for three years. Now,' she says, looking at her watch, 'shall we talk about your letter?'

'I want to help,' he says. 'I want to volunteer.'

'Let's go back to the beginning.'

'A new patient came to me a little over six months ago,' he says. 'Like you, I suppose. He said that he'd moved here from Paris. In hindsight, the way he talked about things seemed a little deliberate. I don't know how else to describe it.'

She makes a gesture. Hand aloft, thumb and index finger pinched together, she draws a shallow concave arc, or a smile, or a rope bridge over a ravine. In isolation it would make no sense, this gesture, but she knows that his cart has tipped over the top of the hill, that he's already rolling downwards, that any gesture will do. What's more, at this stage, given what she's pretending to be, a little mystery is no bad thing.

Or something like that. It's also possible the gesture has a precise meaning that neither of us understands.

'It was as though,' he says, looking for the right words, 'it was as though he was driving from A to B, but instead of using the roads he drove over pavements, he drove through gardens.'

Her nod says: I know. I already know.

'Then there was the man at my Narcotics Anonymous meeting. He wanted to do an MBA in Paris. I introduced him to someone I know who lives there, and it turned out – I didn't know this – that he *also* did an MBA in Paris. I don't mean to insult your colleague. I'm sure he's a good officer. It's just a lot of coincidences. I tried to track down the first one, the patient, but he's not at the address he used to register, his phone number doesn't work, he's nowhere on social media. Same pretty much for the NA guy, and it's an NA rule, sort of, that you reply when people reach out to you. But he doesn't.'

She's got him under her control, but it's not clear to me whether that's down to her abilities, which appear to be considerable, or a weakness in his character, or some unholy marriage of the two.

'There's also . . .'

'Yes?'

'There's a smell that real addicts give off. I don't mean this,' he says, waving a hand in front of his face. 'I don't mean the smell of alcohol. I mean the smell of . . .'

He looks for the word, finds only a shrug.

'Only' is the wrong word. A shrug is a lift and drop manoeuvre. With him, there's sufficient height and weight involved for the lift to be significant, for the drop to reverberate.

'Why do you want to volunteer for an organisation that you believe is incompetent?' says Aphra.

The dirty white coat is a few sizes too small for his big shoulders.

'I didn't use that word. Maybe I have a talent for seeing through deception. I thought I could put it to good use.' In case that sounds too utilitarian an answer, he adds, 'In the service of my . . .' but quickly feels foolish and drops his eyes.

'Your country?'

He thinks she's mocking him. 'Alright, alright,' he says quietly.

'Motivation is important to us,' she says. 'It's rare to hear anyone talk about acting in the service of their country, particularly—'

'Particularly someone who's not properly British,' he says.

'I was going to say, particularly in this day and age. I don't care one bit that you've got two passports. I'm assuming that anyone whose primary loyalty is to the Syrian state after the last decade or so is not capable of holding a rational conversation like this.'

'Rational?' he says. 'You're the one who faked a dental emergency to have a conversation that we could have had over the phone, or in the car park outside. It's a weapon, that word. Like the way that men tell women they're being irrational, like the way—'

'I'm always grateful when men point these things out to me,' she says.

'Anyway, since when is loyalty to a country *rational*? It's emotional all the way down. I think if you'd put a gun to his head, no pun intended, my dad would have picked Syria over England, despite the fact that he spent three years in a prison outside Damascus.'

'Your talent for seeing through deception,' she says, bringing him back to the point.

'Your name's definitely not Susan for a start,' he says. 'I don't care what you've written on the paperwork. You don't look like a Susan.'

'What else?'

'Huma says she's happy here but secretly she's applying for other jobs. My therapist pretends to be compassionate but I feel her judgement like I'm a schoolboy again. My ex-wife was angry with her father but it always came out directed at me. I don't know if deception is the right word. Everyone around me is pretending, that's what it feels like. Everything has something hidden behind it, even if that something is nothing, is emptiness. I remember watching cowboy shows when I was a boy – *Zorro*, *Bonanza*, *Champion the Wonder Horse*. It surprised me that no one else could see the sets wobbling. Little Joe Cartwright isn't going to get shot by a cattle rustler, I used to tell my mother, he's going to get squashed by the hotel.'

He feels stupid, drops his eyes.

'At least that's what I thought,' he says.

'All the world's a stage,' says Aphra.

'Look around,' he says. 'Wouldn't you want this to be a film set? Wouldn't you want to step out of Smethwick into the Californian sunshine?'

She smiles at him. As a medical man and a patient, he's familiar with professional smiles: what they mean, what they hide. He hasn't yet learned to read hers so hurries to make up lost ground.

'I'm not showing myself in the best light,' he says. 'I'm actually lots of fun.' He smiles back at her. 'What is your real name? If you don't mind me asking.'

'Do you realise,' she says, 'that volunteering to work with us will involve telling me things about your friend in Paris, including—'

'Yes,' he says.

'Don't interrupt. It will involve you telling me things that feel deeply personal and private. It will involve us travelling together to Paris. It will involve you meeting with your friend and afterwards reporting exactly what happens.'

'I understand.'

'You will have to follow my instructions to the letter.'

'I will.'

'It'll feel like betrayal.'

'I'm prepared for that.'

'No one is. You will need to stop drinking.'

'Tick.'

'Excuse me?'

'I mean, yes.'

'Are you drunk now?'

'A little bit.'

'If you have a drink or take a drug while working for me—'

'I won't, I promise. When are we going?'

'Now.'

'Now? As in—'

'You'll need to cancel your appointments and close the surgery with immediate effect.'

'Huma can arrange all that.'

'What shall I call you?' says Aphra.

He's taken aback. 'You don't know my name?'

She smiles as though she's been here many times before. 'I like to redo introductions when things are on a new footing,' she says.

He looks at her, doing the maths, checking it all adds up.

'My name's Aphra,' she says, helping him with the sums.

The dentist takes off his white coat, steps forward, extends a hand. 'Nice to meet you, Aphra. I'm Zak.'

~

Sir William Rentoul is counting down the seconds. The clock on the far wall, recently hung by his staff to ensure that he maintains strict time discipline after the emergence of a tendency to lose focus in meetings, is wholly unnecessary this morning. He can't wait for this to be over. He desperately wants to be elsewhere. Sitting opposite him is the second US ambassador he has met during his four years as Head of the Service. US ambassadors are political appointees, often with no international or diplomatic experience, which explains why the CIA London bureau chief has unexpectedly also turned up at the meeting.

'We'll have to get you over to Little Rock, Sir William,' says the ambassador, 'have you fitted out with your own pair.'

Although in the diplomatic hierarchy a CIA bureau chief is junior to an ambassador, this particular CIA man clearly considers it a logical impossibility that anyone sporting cowboy boots could be his superior.

'You must get the English version while you're here,' says Sir William. 'We refer to them as "wellies". You'll need a pair if you want to blend in.'

'What do you think, Charlie?' says the ambassador to the CIA man with a chuckle. 'We should buy some of these "wellies" for your undercover officers so they blend in with the locals.'

The CIA man chuckles back. 'We wouldn't dream of doing undercover work in the UK,' he says.

'I've got a good man on Jermyn Street, ambassador,' says Sir William. 'In fact, leave your size with us and we'll have a pair sent to your residence.'

Which allows Sir William to press a button, summon his chief of staff to make a note of the task and hasten his visitors' departure.

This is what confuses him, that in the same meeting he can pull off a nimble move like that and yet address the ambassador by the wrong name. *Twice.* His annual pension statement landed on his desk yesterday. He has six months left to retirement. Until recently, he had all sorts of plans lined up: non-executive director of something connected to oil, a charitable role for balance, plenty of punditry. Everyone's doing podcasts these days, but, if he's honest, he doesn't really understand what one is, or rather, how it's different from the radio.

But the last few months have made Sir William re-evaluate his plans. It's not just his wife's unexpected death following complications arising from a fall. It's also that he is aware of a new difficulty remembering things. He is deeply averse to attaching a name to this condition, even in his most private moments. He doesn't even like the word 'condition'. The odd thing is that he can feel his mind going through the usual motions, reaching for names or numbers which are simply no longer there. He is trying to take some comfort from this. *He* hasn't changed. His mind is doing the same thing it always did, his mind is working fine. It's the facts that have backed away.

Or something like that.

'Lucille is here to run through the figures before this afternoon's board meeting, sir,' says his chief of staff.

'Cancel it,' says Sir William.

He doesn't even acknowledge Lucille as he hurries through his outer office and into the corridor, pursued by his chief of staff. He's got half a mind to cancel the board meeting itself.

'Where's the cell?' Sir William says over his shoulder.

'Where's the what?'

'The cell, you idiot. Operation BOGOTA. They're supposed to be tracking down the officer who complained to the Intelligence and Security Committee.'

'Room 5.8, sir. But—'

Sir William always knew that the prospect of retirement would trigger some emotion but nothing has prepared him for the grief and terror that now grip his heart. The CIA man and the ambassador will already be laughing about it. A note will no doubt be drafted to Washington. *Sir William appears distracted and forgetful. Wherever possible, we should postpone substantive discussions until his successor is in post.* He quickens his pace. Is it possible, he wonders, that his sanity depends in some unseen way upon his job, that his mind is a flower drawing nourishment from the soil of his career, that retirement will be at best a slow decline offset by sudokus and fish oil, at worst a sudden plummet into—

'Sir, I need to explain—'

Sir William waves a dismissive hand. The defiant spirit of an old spy reasserts itself. He has been in tight corners before. Let's assume the worst, he thinks. Let's assume I'm in decline and retirement will only make matters worse. I have six months left in post. Enough time for one final operation, for one last bracing plunge into the icy depths of the secret world. He's read about fasting, the way it can recharge dying cells, so he knows that such reversals are possible.

He pushes open the door to room 5.8.

That fucking officer will wish they had never been born, he thinks.

The room is empty. He turns to his chief of staff.

'They've concluded the investigation, sir. I was trying to explain. Their report is already on your desk.'

'What do you mean?' says Sir William. 'They only started two hours ago.'

'They've gone through everything. It's clear beyond a shadow of a doubt.'

'What is? The traitor? Who is it?'

'What traitor?'

'The complainant, damn it. The officer who made the complaint.'

'There is no complainant, sir.'

'What?' says Sir William. 'No complainant? How can that be?'

'There is no complainant because there was no complaint.'

~

Susan spent the night in the museum. She wakes up with the strangest of convictions, wanders the corridors for a good twenty minutes.

'Is this like a confessional?' she says, settling into the chair.

'In what sense?'

'Confidential.'

'Oh, I see. Yes. Totally confidential.'

Susan is still wearing her duffel coat. There's a flask of something on the table. It must be hot, she thinks, the build-up of steam inside escaping in soft bursts, like the whistle of a freight train, like a trapped canary.

'It's taken me by surprise,' she says.

'What has?'

'Being here. Coming here.'

'Take your time, Susan.'

'I'm only here by accident, really. I was just walking past.' Susan yawns. 'I slept really badly.'

'That's often a sign of something.'

'Is it?'

'Has something recently happened that might be causing you anxiety?'

'I can see what you're doing,' says Susan. 'You're not going to talk me into anything.'

'I wouldn't dream of it.'

'I planted a file on someone leaving the building,' says Susan. 'That's all it is. I planted a file and then they got caught.'

'Tell me more,' says the ethics counsellor.

~

Things are moving very fast now. Aphra McQueen called a taxi to drive them to St Pancras, and their Eurostar train is already approaching the English coast.

'Here's what we're going to do,' she says, putting her elbows on the table that separates her from the dentist. 'How do you refer to him, your friend in Paris?'

'Just Ali.'

'Alright. You're going to send Ali an email, saying that you're on your way to Paris and would like to catch up with him.'

'I've got a better idea.' He types for a minute or so. 'There. Done.'

'While you're on your phone,' she says, 'will you please go into settings and share your location with me?'

He follows her instruction.

'How long do you think it'll take him to reply?' she says.

'Let's see. He's on Instagram most days.' He glances at her. 'You're in a hurry, I can see that.'

'We are.'

'You tried that thing with the patient, then you waited a few weeks, then you tried again with the NA guy. That was months and months ago. You seemed happy to move slowly. But all of a sudden you're in a hurry.'

'The context has changed,' says Aphra. 'We were a little worried then, now we're a lot worried.'

'About Ali?'

'Yes.'

'What's he doing that's got you so riled?'

'How well do you know him?'

'Obviously not as well as I thought.'

'Have a guess,' she says. 'Harness your prodigious talent for seeing through other people's lies.'

He laughs at her gentle dig, his face tilting towards an imaginary sun, his eyes flooding with gratitude, his body heaving. It takes him a minute or so to collect himself.

'Well,' he says finally. 'He comes from money, and I imagine any Iranian family with that kind of wealth is going to have government connections. What could that mean? Is he procuring material for their nuclear programme? Laundering money for Iranian elites?' When she doesn't answer, he says, 'Am I warm?'

'If I don't tell you everything, Zak, it's not because I don't trust you. It's just not helpful to fill your head with things you can't say in front of Ali.'

'Maybe he's walking round Paris trying to stick a veil on every woman he sees.'

'Because he's religious?' she says.

'No, it was just a joke, you know, because of the regime.'

She's amazed to see it play out like this before her eyes, the way that a joke that falls flat is enough to dent his mood. It's a reminder to her to keep things on an even keel.

'Tell me how you met him,' she says.

'I used to spend summers with my father in Aleppo. Ali's father ran an import–export company in Tehran. My father once inter-viewed him for a trade magazine and they became friends. Anyway,

Ali's father would leave him with us for weeks at a time while he went off to do the rounds of his Syrian and Lebanese customers.'

'Did you like him?'

'Ali? Not really. We were both odd boys, I suppose. Not very good at making friends. I was getting into weightlifting around then and wanted to spend all my time at the gym with Walkman headphones clamped over my ears.'

'But you stayed in touch.'

'There's a connection there, a historical connection. I guess time counts for something. He came to my wedding. He came to my dad's funeral. But we're not close.'

'Do you know his family?'

'He's not married.'

'What about his parents, his uncles and aunts?'

'I get an email card from his father at Iranian New Year. I think his uncle is a professor of something.'

A trolley comes down the aisle. Although they both say no, his eyes flicker towards the beer, the wine, and then he feels self-conscious, knows that she's seen it too, slumps back in his seat, looks out the window. Mid forties, I'd put him at. You might eventually arrive at Syrian but chances are you'd stop at Greek or Italian on the way. Dark beard, little round tortoiseshell glasses, at least six two and big with it. Not all muscle by any means, but his shoulders look strong. One of those hands could easily span a basketball. His ears are long and narrow and protrude like wing mirrors on a truck.

His phone makes a noise.

'See?' he says, holding it up, excited again. 'I told you he'd reply.'

~

Sir William glares at the leader of the investigative cell.

'Speak plainly, for God's sake,' he says.

'Imagine an electronic pipeline that runs from this building to the Intelligence and Security Committee up the road in Parliament. We created a system that allows an officer in this building to send a message down that pipeline. Now, every time a message is sent, it is accompanied by a kind of covert electronic signature, a little like an IP address, that will tell you which terminal it was sent from and at what time. If you remember, you insisted on this, so that we would be able to find out who was making—'

'Get on with it.'

'We have been able to gain remote access to the computer belonging to the Committee. The complaint is there, logged entirely as you would expect.'

'Yes?'

'But there is no covert electronic signature attached to it.'

'Meaning?'

'It was not sent from this building.'

'Meaning?'

'It was not sent at all.'

'Meaning?'

'The original complaint was written on the Committee computer.'

Sir William looks at his chief of staff.

'We've found a way to access pass data from the parliamentary estate, sir. On the day the complaint was written, Julian Redruth was in his Lancashire constituency.'

'The other Committee members?'

'The complaint was written late at night. No Committee members were on the parliamentary estate at that time. The only person who was there—'

'The researcher.'

'Yes, sir. Aphra McQueen. I'm afraid it looks as though she

turned up here to investigate a complaint that she had written herself.'

'Well, well,' says Sir William. 'This is even better than I expected.'

~

Sir William Rentoul stands in front of a small team, hastily recalled to their desks. Two data analysts, two investigators, one administrative support officer and the team leader, although the team leader is also acting as an investigator since Sir William has very much taken charge.

'Surveillance?' he says.

'They've taken up positions on her street, sir. No sign of her at the window. A covert search team is on standby to deploy when we know the property is empty.'

'Get one of the team to knock on her door and confirm that she's there. Make up some sort of cover. Survey for the council, a prisoner selling tea towels, that sort of thing.'

Sir William has cancelled his lunch with the editors of the *Spectator* and the *Telegraph*. He tried to cancel this afternoon's board meeting too but was told there are workforce planning decisions that can't be delayed. If necessary he will authorise one of his deputies to chair the meeting and make the decisions. There's no way he's leaving this room, there's no way he's delegating the investigation into Aphra McQueen to someone else.

'What's the update on her phone?' he asks.

'The emergency warrant has been signed, sir. As of a few seconds ago the intercept is live. We'll get any calls she makes.'

'Do we know where her phone is located?'

'No, it's still switched off.'

Widening his stance, Sir William indulges a private thought that running an intelligence cell in the middle of a live operation is like racing a chariot, with life charging at you from all directions while you struggle to guide a pack of surging, muscular, sweaty—

'Surveillance has rung her doorbell, sir. No answer.'

He'd rather they didn't call him 'sir' all the time, it reminds him of his seniority, it reminds him that they all find it profoundly odd that the Head of the Service is running a small intelligence cell rather than lunching with the prime minister or flying to Washington or even—

'Ideas, people,' he says, tapping the table to get their attention. 'Aphra McQueen is not in her flat and her phone's not telling us where she's located. What do we do?'

'Internet browsing history?' says an analyst. 'In case she's bought a ticket, made plans with a friend, gone to the—'

'Get on with it.'

'Yes, sir.'

'No need for the "sir",' he says. 'It's good to be back on the factory floor where I started my career. "William" is just fine.'

'Late last night she made an online appointment to see a dentist,' says the analyst. 'The appointment was . . . this morning. Eleven a.m.'

Sir William looks at the clock on the wall.

'She should be done by now. Get the address of the dentist, send it to the surveillance teams, have them send a car there.'

'It's in Birmingham.'

'What is?'

'The dentist's surgery. An area called Smethwick.'

'She went from *London* to *Birmingham* to have her teeth checked?' says Sir William.

'There's something on our system about the dentist,' says one of the investigators, peering at his screen. 'He's got a file reference next to his name.'

'Meaning what?'

'He's connected to an agent operation in some way. I haven't got authorisation to access the file. It's something to do with Iran.'

'Shit,' says Sir William. 'I know the case. Can you see where the dentist's mobile phone is located?'

'The data is all jumbled, I'm not getting a clear picture. It looks like . . .'

'Yes?'

'It's saying he's in the middle of the Channel but that's probably an error, it does sometimes happen that—'

'Check his passport. Check hers too while you're at it.'

'Both passports were swiped by the Border Force at St Pancras just over an hour ago,' says the other investigator. 'His first, hers a few seconds later. They're definitely travelling together.'

'Assemble an operational team,' says Sir William. 'Call Ned, call that one he always works with. We'll need to deploy in pursuit.'

'Do we tell the French,' says the team leader, 'request that they stop the two of them in Calais?'

'God, no,' says Sir William. He rolls down his sleeves, puts on his jacket. 'My phone number's on the whiteboard. Send updates the moment they come through.'

'Where are you going, William?' asks the team leader.

He bristles at the informality, speaks with more severity than he intends.

'Into the field.'

~

They don't make an attractive pair, these two, particularly given the competition on display in this Parisian park, located in the fashionable neighbourhood of Neuilly-sur-Seine. The autumn sunlight is thin and pale, barely hoisted up the flagpole, but sufficient to tempt students, office workers and a few local residents outside. There is a force that emanates from Aphra. It's definitely not coming from him. If anything, he's absorbing energy rather than emitting it, his hangover and fatigue and anxiety so on display that he catches the attention of passing dog walkers, whose eyes flit from the large bearded man to the slim woman on the bench next to him, single-handedly keeping his world under control.

'Ali might be out,' he says. 'He said he had a few things on today.'

'Let's see, shall we? No harm in ringing his bell.'

'He might invite me to stay with him.'

'Tell him you've already paid for a hotel room,' says Aphra.

'He might insist.'

'Tell him you'll stay with him next time. If you stay with him tonight it's going to be difficult for you and me to talk, which I think is going to be important.'

It's not easy to work out what Aphra's doing here. She knows that the nephew, Ali, is a recruited agent of British intelligence. Anything out of the ordinary and he will tell his handlers, which means that the dentist has to be extraordinarily skilful, something that at the moment looks unlikely.

'Are you feeling okay, Zak?' she says.

'A bit nervous. I didn't think I would be but . . .'

'How do you normally deal with nerves?'

'Beta blockers,' he says.

'Do you want to take one now?'

'We left in such a rush that I didn't bring them.'

'Is there anything else you left?' she says. 'Any other medication you usually take?'

'A few things for anxiety and depression.'

'Did you take them this morning before work?'

He nods. 'The alcohol is interfering with them.'

If Aphra feels at all guilty for what she's doing, she doesn't show it. She just nods, as though the dentist's sorry state is unavoidable rather than something she has deliberately and unnecessarily willed into existence.

'The best way to handle feelings like this,' she says, 'is to make them part of your cover story. Don't try to pretend they don't exist. If Ali says to you that you seem stressed, or something like that, just admit it. And when he asks why, tell him that you've been working really hard, which is why you decided last minute to close the surgery and come away for a break.'

The dentist is wearing a thin grey woollen overcoat with a curiously feminine collar. He pulls it around himself, scratches his beard.

'Why won't you tell me where all this is going?' he says.

'Do you remember what you said to me about that first officer who came to you, the one pretending to be a patient? You said he was in such a hurry to get from A to B that instead of using the roads he drove over pavements and gardens.'

He nods.

'I don't want you to do that,' she says. 'Think of me like a satnav. I'm going to show you the stretch of road that's right in front of you, and maybe the next turning. That's all you need.'

We're all in the same crowded boat here: the dentist, Sir William, the entire Service, me. We're all blindly following Aphra McQueen to God knows where.

'I guess I can always walk out if he's being a dick,' he says.

'Is that likely?'

'When I started going to the gym,' he says, 'this is when we were teenagers in Aleppo, the only way I could get extra protein was eggs. It was long before you could buy creatine and whey and other powders in whatever flavour you wanted. My father's housekeeper cooked meat for us, of course, but lots of Syrian food is vegetarian, and I was trying to consume as much protein as I possibly could, like lots of other idiot teenage boys. Ali hated all of that stuff. I took him to the gym with me a few times but the trainer said he couldn't come back, he sulked so much. Then one day Ali said out of nowhere at the breakfast table that he had an egg allergy. My father declared the kitchen an egg-free zone, so from then on I had to cook my eggs on a camping stove in the garden.'

'You think he made it up?'

'I know he did. A few days later I came home and found that someone had thrown all my eggs against the garden wall.'

'Ali?' she says.

'You're a professional, I can tell.'

'My first suspect was actually the housekeeper.'

'What would her motive have been?' he says.

'She didn't like having a rival cook in the house.'

'Eliminating the competition. I never considered that.'

'Then there's your father,' she says.

He smiles, he's enjoying this. 'Go on.'

'He's a good host. He takes the whole cooking eggs in the garden thing as an affront to Syrian hospitality.'

'The story doesn't end there,' he says. 'When Ali came back the next summer, I was keeping a dozen or so chickens in the backyard.'

'For the eggs.'

'For the eggs, right. One of the neighbours had a dog that was always trying to get in, so I built a coop out of wood and chicken wire to house them. Except that one day, this was probably a week or so after Ali arrived, I went out early morning and all the chickens were dead. Blood and feathers and bones everywhere. Someone had peeled the wire back to let the neighbour's dog in.'

'How high was the wall between your yard and your neighbour's?' she says.

'Chest high.'

'Could the dog jump over by itself?'

'No,' he says.

'So Ali would have had to lift it over.'

'Unless . . .'

'The neighbour did it,' she says.

'He's got to be a candidate,' says Zak. 'Along with Ali, the house-keeper and my father.'

'There's enough plausible suspects to reopen the investigation,' she says. 'I think they call this a "cold case". By the way, I'm assuming you're definitely innocent.'

He laughs, closing his eyes and turning his face towards the lemony sun, pale as a boiled sweet in a tin of powdered sugar.

'Tell you what,' she says, 'let's make a game out of your visit to Ali. To take the pressure off. Forget about me, forget about national security. Your new objective is to find out what happened to your chickens all those years ago in Aleppo. Maybe enough years have passed for Ali to feel he can finally tell you the truth.'

He smiles at her. 'I didn't use to be like this. I used to be able to do things.'

She smiles back at him. 'I think you're going to do just fine.'

~

'From left to right, there's Buttermint, Camomile, Cherry & Cinnamon, Earl Grey, Mango & Strawberry, Rooibos & Honey, Rosehip—'

'Wait,' says Susan. 'Have you . . . Is that alphabetical order?'

'You know, I'm not sure I ever noticed that before,' says the ethics counsellor.

'You missed out Builder's.'

'It's under Y for Yorkshire. Is that what you'd like?'

'I'm not staying,' says Susan.

'What are your plans?'

'I've got work to do. I asked for the day off, after last night, but they said we've got too much on.'

'It must have been stressful, what happened with the file. Tell me about it.'

'That woman . . . That woman is *dangerous*. Someone had to do something.' Susan accepts a mug of tea, takes a sip. 'What is rooibos anyway?'

'It's from South Africa,' says the ethics counsellor. 'Lowers blood pressure.'

'They didn't call the police so there'll be no real consequences for her,' says Susan, 'other than losing her job, and she's only been doing that for a couple of years.' She slurps from her mug. 'She'll be able to go back to her old life without too much difficulty, I should expect.'

'Did someone ask you to plant the file on her?' says the ethics counsellor.

'No.'

'Did you know she'd be caught?'

'Yes. You see, she'd wandered off on her own around the building, earlier on, when she was supposed to be sticking with me. The guards would definitely search someone who did that.'

'That was naughty of her,' says the ethics counsellor.

Communities are defined by what they're *not* more than by what they *are*. If I spend too long wallowing in the warm bath of mainstream opinion, I run the risk of forgetting what makes this particular community distinctive. I forget that there's an *us* and a *them*. That's what's so valuable about spending time in this room. Nothing gives me the warm glow of home like watching someone realise they don't belong here.

'I know we're whiter than white these days,' says Susan. 'But I see things, as a building escort. No one notices little old me. I hear people saying: don't write *that* down, or make sure *that's* not in the paperwork, or let's cover our arses, *chaps*.'

She drains her tea, stands up to go.

'History's where the bad stuff happens. History's a *mess*. Thank goodness we're not like that any more. It used to rain a lot; now it's sunny every day. Do you buy that? I don't. We get our hands grubby all the bloody time. It's just that this was my first go at it. That's why I feel a bit wobbly. No more than that.'

'Can I do anything for you, Susan, before you leave?' says the ethics counsellor.

'I still don't feel quite right, if I'm honest.' Susan sits down again. 'Maybe a mug of that rooibos tea will help after all. What do you think?'

~

It's only once he gets down to the exit pods that Sir William Rentoul realises he hasn't left this building alone and on foot for close to five years. These days, given how often his picture is in the papers, even short journeys are undertaken by car. His predecessor selected an ordinary-looking Volvo as her official vehicle, with the necessary upgrades made to horsepower, acceleration, tyres, things like that, but Sir William's first decision in post was to replace it with a Jaguar, having learned over the course of a long operational career that first impressions can rarely be dislodged. Without his Jaguar's tinted windows to hide behind, though, is there a chance he'll be recognised? Might a lurking Russian surveil him, an angry teenager pull out a knife? He considers rummaging through the lost-and-found cupboard for a cap or an umbrella, but the key is in the security booth, and if those goons know he's planning to leave on foot, they'll insist on accompanying him. Screw it, he thinks. The sting of salty language emboldens him. He holds his pass to the card reader, watches the pod door slide open. To his astonishment, he feels something similar happen inside him. A door long sealed slides open and in gusts fresh air, danger, mystery, new life, new life, new life. It's all Sir William can do not to break into a run.

~

Susan is still wearing her duffel coat. She holds the mug of rooibos tea clasped in her hands while she studies the walls of the ethics counsellor's office, taking in the children's drawings, a framed oil painting of the building, a calendar with a daily quotation. *Real integrity is doing the right thing, knowing that nobody's going to know whether you did it or not.*

She shakes her head.

'You don't agree?' says the ethics counsellor.

'It was odd, sleeping in the museum. I woke up at two, went for a wee, walked around a bit, had a good look at the exhibits. It's all that Special Operations Executive stuff that gets me. The things they did behind enemy lines. I was trying to imagine what it felt like. They didn't have a rule book, they didn't get to check with an ethics counsellor before they did something. It was sink or swim, it was dog eat dog. If some Nazi accuses you of being a spy and you've got the drop on him, what else are you supposed to do? Quote, I don't know, quote . . .'

She leans forward, peers again at the quotation on the wall.

'Oprah Winfrey.'

She says the name slowly, as though it's someone in Accounts she's meeting for the first time.

'It's a balancing act, that's how I would characterise it,' says the ethics counsellor. 'We need to be tough and resolute but in a way that is consistent with our values.'

'You should have your office in a little room off the museum,' says

Susan. 'Anyone having a wobble, send them out on a tour of the real world. Send them to look at the bomb that killed Mountbatten, or, I don't know, the perfume bottle the Russians used to carry novichok. They've even got one of the black flags those monsters hung up in the background while doing unspeakable things.'

'We are given more flexibility in these matters than almost any other part of the state apparatus,' says the ethics counsellor. 'We are able to steal, to lie, to manipulate and to exploit, all in the interests of keeping this country safe. Those monsters, as you describe them, are now either behind bars or dead, so we must be doing something right.'

'It's the Hitler question.'

'How do you mean?'

'If you met Hitler before he became Hitler, knowing what you do now, what would you do? That's the choice I faced,' says Susan.

'You think this woman, the one you planted the file on, you think she's like Hitler?'

'Not literally, of course not. That's not what I'm saying. I'm just saying, someone needed to stop her in her tracks.' Susan takes a sip of tea, pulls a face. 'It tastes like . . . cigarettes. Are you sure it's good for you?'

'Things that are good for you don't always taste nice,' says the ethics counsellor.

Susan smiles. 'I like that. Clever. You should put that up on your wall.'

'I'm glad we had this conversation, Susan. Sometimes we need to vocalise things to realise how we really feel.'

Susan nods, but absent-mindedly, as though her thoughts are elsewhere. When she speaks, it is in a faraway voice.

'I want to come clean,' she says. 'I want to make things right with Aphra McQueen.'

~

Sir William survives the solo walk, arrives at his destination in a matter of minutes. No one stops him, no one gives him a second glance. He enters the parliamentary estate using his pass. Julian Redruth is not in his office, not in the tea rooms, not in the Intelligence and Security Committee chamber. Sir William sits in the visitors' gallery for long enough to study the benches below and confirm he isn't involved in a debate. He has to ask someone where the smoking area is. On the way he passes the library. He draws the line at checking the toilets. The only reason he pops into the Strangers' Bar is to see whether they'll sell him a sandwich.

'Old friend,' says Sir William.

'Hello,' says Julian Redruth. He sits in the corner with a pint of mild watching the river outside as it coils, uncoils, recoils.

'I was here on other business, spotted you lurking in the corner.'

'Care to join me?'

Julian's vowels have a cautious, slippery sound, like footsteps on ice, that suggest he's been here a while. He expects a polite refusal, is taken aback when Sir William accepts the invitation with a nod.

The barmaid's polishing glasses. Waiting until she's poured half a pint, he says, 'Looks a bit cloudy. First one of the day?'

'It's had a bit of use already,' she says.

'Oh, really?' Sir William glances at Julian, puts his elbow on the bar, lowers his voice. 'He's giving a speech later to a group of visiting schoolchildren. Do I need to slow him down?'

'It's really not my place to say.'

'Understood.'

'My kids prefer me when I've had a couple,' she says.

He chuckles. 'Is that where we're at, a couple?'

'Give or take.'

Sir William nods, picks up the glasses, crosses the room to join Julian Redruth. Drinking with someone can be a very effective way of eliciting useful intelligence, but turning up once they're already drunk is a different thing entirely. Solitary drinking is rarely undertaken in a spirit of joy. The stew darkens, thickens, burns, turns bitter and inedible.

Julian is still staring at the river.

'Where's your nearest water up north?' asks Sir William, placing the two glasses on the table. 'The Calder? The Ribble?'

Julian ignores him, takes a big gulp of his mild.

'Don't be too hard on yourself, Julian,' says Sir William. 'We've all made mistakes over the years.'

Julian Redruth sighs, blows a rag of foam onto the table, takes another gulp.

'These things happen – it's the nature of the game,' says Sir William.

'I'm going to miss her,' says Julian.

It isn't what Sir William expects to hear. He frowns. 'There isn't . . . There wasn't anything, how shall I put this delicately, there wasn't—'

'We're all going to miss her,' says Julian. 'She made our lives easier in so many ways. Did you know that she single-handedly arranged for our records to be transferred to an electronic database? Sat with each Committee member to explain the new system. For hours, for *days* sometimes.' He takes another drink. 'Her drafting skills were second to none. Succinct, thorough, witty when appropriate, surprisingly barbed when she felt the Committee was being disrespected by your lot.'

'I'm sorry it's come to this,' says Sir William. 'If there was any other way.'

'Never took a sick day, never complained. She brightened the place up no end.'

'I once had a secretary who would buy flowers for my wife. Even picked up my dry cleaning. You can't ask someone to do that for you these days.'

'Aphra would do it.'

'You old fool,' says Sir William, carefully measuring out nine-tenths affection, one-tenth chiding.

'She was a terrier; at least, that's what we all liked to think. Wouldn't let anything go. We loved it. In her first month she went to war against Housekeeping when they said they only had the resources to hoover our rooms once every two weeks. Then there was the time someone started putting their drinks on our bar tab. It was just a few pounds here and there, but Aphra threw herself into it, finally discovered a pad of our chits in the coat pocket of the Lib Dem chief whip. He denied it up and down but eventually paid us back to avoid a scandal. We started calling her Columbo, Mother Brown, Poirot of Parliament. Last Christmas we did a secret Santa. Someone gave her a brass plaque to put on her desk. Investigator, it said. Supposed to be a ten-pound cap on gifts. At the time I thought *that* was the rule that was being bent. Now I've a hunch she gave the bloody thing to herself. Now I've a hunch she put the missing chits in the whip's pocket.'

'You mean—'

'She was positioning herself, William. She was hired as a researcher, nothing more, but by the time the complaint came through from your office, we all referred to her as an investigator. She was the natural candidate to have a first look.'

'Can you remember how that played out?'

'She said, they'll be wary of letting you have a look at their files. They'll be wary of a politician they can't bully. Let me have a first look. That way when you get involved, you'll already have a good sense of what they're hiding and where you should dig.'

Julian drains his glass, waves angrily at the barmaid's back.

'Whatever it is she's up to,' says Sir William, 'it's not opportunistic. That's what you're telling me.'

'If I'm right about secret Santa and the Lib Dem whip, she's been planning this for a while. What I don't understand is how she allowed herself to be caught with a file on her first day. It was such a careless mistake.'

Sir William nods. It does seem inconceivable that Aphra would make such a mistake. He remembers his theory that Susan planted the file on Aphra, concludes he was right, except that he can't remember Susan's name, experiences a flare of panic, he can see her face, he can see her pokey room, he can even see the Chequered Skipper and Meadow Brown and Purple Hairstreak all pinned in their glass case, so why can't he remember her bloody name?

Julian waves again at the barmaid.

'Remind me how Aphra came to you,' says Sir William.

'From St Andrews university. She left at short notice. I remember there was a stink around that. But she told us a relationship had soured and she wanted a change of scene. The truth is, she was head and shoulders above every other applicant.'

'Personal life?'

'Single, lived alone. Her parents are dead. Every holiday she would spend hiking in the Alps.'

'Any strong connections abroad, other than the hiking?'

'No.'

'And not an activist of any sort?'

Julian shakes his head, looks again for the barmaid.

'She didn't mention characters like Snowden or Assange.'

'Come to think of it,' says Julian.

'Yes?'

'She'd visit the Ecuadorian embassy every Tuesday afternoon like clockwork.'

'Julian, please.'

'Stop asking stupid questions, then. If that's the best you can do, you're sunk. You're *sunk*. She's cleverer than the lot of you.'

Experiencing a soft, steady vibration in his chest area, Sir William worries that on top of everything else his heart's aflutter, but he quickly realises it's his mobile phone. There's a message from the head of the intelligence cell.

Your Eurostar leaves in one hour.

Susan, he thinks. She's called Susan.

Sir William stands, pushes his untouched pint towards Julian, walks out.

~

Someone's inside the apartment, the conversation is perfectly audible, but Ali's not answering the door. Zak is in two minds whether to give it one more go. He's already knocked twice. He can feel his heart racing and knows he'll sound out of breath when he speaks. The stairs were going to be his excuse for that, but the longer he stands here the less plausible an excuse that will be, the more it will seem that he's hyperventilating, that he's having some sort of inexplicable panic attack. Ordinary social encounters have become more difficult for him, so doing this, approaching an old acquaintance on behalf of British intelligence, with a whole secret agenda he's not allowed to disclose, it terrifies him. The only thing pinning him there is the prospect of disappointing Aphra, so he lifts a hand to—

The door opens. Ali is holding a mobile phone to his ear. He points to a doorbell set so expensively into the mahogany door frame that Zak didn't even notice it. He takes Zak by the upper arm, pulls him into his apartment, waves towards the room as though to say make yourself at home.

Zak heads to the window, breathing heavily. He strains to catch a reassuring glimpse of red scarf on the street below.

Actually, no: Ali's wave doesn't say make yourself at home. I take that back. Ali waves towards the room as though backhanding a piece of waste paper towards a bin on the far side. That's what it looks like to Zak, who already seems defeated by the encounter.

No one likes to hear 'I told you so', but Zak's clearly not cut out for this kind of work. There's a reason the operational team used him unwittingly, or at least tried to.

'What the hell happened to you?'

Zak turns from the window, sees Ali still with the mobile to his ear but with one hand over the mouthpiece while he addresses Zak.

'What do you mean? Am I late?'

'You look terrible.'

'I've been working really hard,' says Zak, 'so I decided to close the surgery and come here on a short break.'

It's practically verbatim what Aphra told him to say. Zak is clearly prone to what we call 'legend vomit', the habit of blurting out your cover story in one unrealistic chunk rather than teasing it out more naturalistically. It's fortunate that Ali's not listening. He speaks in Farsi into the phone and hangs up.

'Sit down,' he says. 'You're making me nervous. What can I get you?'

Although Zak wants a glass of water, he suspects he'd gulp it down in one go, so chooses something that will give them a little more time together.

'A coffee would be great,' he says, sitting. He looks around for the first time. The top-floor apartment is double height, its walls hung with vast paintings in what Zak thinks of as an impressionistic style. The poured concrete floor is covered by a patchwork of silk Persian rugs. 'It's good to see you doing so well, Ali.'

'I expect you want coffee the old way.'

'Which way's that?'

'The way your father's housekeeper in Aleppo made it. What was her name again?'

'Umm Saida,' says Zak. 'She died last year.'

'I swear your dad was screwing her on the side. I came back one day and she had this flushed look on her face, she was adjusting her veil, and there was the smell of—'

'If you mean with cardamom, yes please.'

Ali opens one cupboard, tries another. They close with the slow heavy click of an expensive car door. 'I don't know why I offered, I'm not even sure I have any.' He has to stand on tiptoe to peer at the top shelves. 'Did she die of heartbreak?' he says over an array of vinegars, oils and low-calorie sprays. 'One year after your father, it certainly suggests there's something to my theory.'

'Cancer of the oesophagus,' says Zak.

Ali is small, dark and neat, his beard as precisely edged as an ornamental garden. He wears a deep blue shawl-collared cashmere cardigan with large buttons and an expensive watch.

'Have you ever tried a macchiato?' he says, giving up the search for cardamom. 'That's how coffee should be drunk.'

'I'm happy with anything.'

'You look like you drink those giant, what are they called, "Mocha Frappuccinos", is that right? The ones with whipped cream on top.'

Ali stands before his coffee machine. At one end he unlocks the portafilter, drums out the used grounds; at the other he turns a knob to release a plume of steam.

'Was that the last time you went back? For her funeral?'

'Umm Saida's?' says Zak. 'No, I'm not allowed to go back to Syria.'

'You're not? What about your father's house?'

'I don't own it any more.'

'It was bombed? Or you sold it?'

'One of the conditions of being released from prison was signing over any assets on Syrian soil to the government,' says Zak.

'Oh yeah, I heard about this,' says Ali, looking up from the machine. There is amusement in his glittering eyes. 'How long did they hold you for?'

Zak struggles to talk about this with his therapist; he's not sure why he opened this particular door for Ali of all people.

'Not that long. Tell me your news,' he says. 'This apartment is incredible. Where are you working these days?'

'I've bowed to the inevitable and gone into business with my father,' says Ali. 'I'm handling the European and North American markets, which allows him to focus on the Middle East. Less travel for him, which makes my mother happy. That was her on the phone.'

'Say hello to her next time you speak.'

'She won't have any clue who you are. Even my father barely knows who you are.'

'The business is doing well, I take it.'

'It's doing better now that I'm involved,' says Ali. 'I went to China a few times last year. There's a good chance we'll move the manu- facturing side of things over there.'

'Because of sanctions?'

'What?' Ali looks at him over the top of the coffee machine. 'Why would you say that?'

'Nothing.'

Ali stops what he's doing.

'Why do you think sanctions are a problem for us?' he says.

Zak didn't particularly say it because he thought the subject would interest Aphra. He doesn't know why he said it, or what to say now. If Aphra didn't exist, if he wasn't so nervous, he would probably double down, tease Ali about trying to bypass sanctions, but obvi- ously that's the last thing he can say under the circumstances.

'What's the matter with you?' says Ali.

'I know you do a lot of technology.'

'How do you know that we do technology? In fact, what *do* you know about my business?'

'Your father gave me my first ever radio,' says Zak. 'Do you remember? It came from one of his consignments. For some reason he had a crate of them in the back of his car. I still remember the tingle of excitement I felt, extending the aerial, turning the dial—'

'I know how a radio works, Zaki.'

He's turned his attention back to the coffee machine, the moment seems to have passed.

'I'm indulging in nostalgia, I admit it,' says Zak, relieved to have got away with it. 'It's a happy memory. I can't imagine exactly what that radio represented to me, but it must have been adventure, mystery, the promise of far-off lands.' He shakes his head. 'They're so intense, the things we feel in childhood.'

'You sound like a therapist. Have you been seeing a therapist? I wouldn't hold it against you, after what happened. I can't imagine a Syrian prison is much fun. What was it like? I bet you walk out of those places with a bunch of disorders.' He slides a coffee cup across the counter. 'Not that you were ever hyperfunctional, Zaki.'

Zak reaches for the coffee. 'Thank you.'

'Is that where you got the eating problem?'

'I don't have an eating problem. It's just that it's hard to find time to exercise. Work is really busy. Setting up and running my own surgery has been very demanding. It's one thing working for someone else but another thing entirely—'

'I heard you got divorced too,' says Ali. 'What's . . . What's—'

'Molly.'

'Molly, that's right. What's Molly up to these days?'

'You answer my question, I'll answer yours.'

'What was your question?' says Ali.

'Well,' says Zak, thinking it's time he took control of this conversation, 'I was going to ask you, do you not have any happy memories of the time you spent with us in Aleppo?'

'What I remember is how much I used to complain about getting dumped with you while my father went whoring around Beirut with his clients.'

'My father said it was so you would learn Arabic,' says Zak.

'Is that what he said?' Ali laughs. 'My father told me it was to learn humility and gratitude. You know, gratitude that I didn't live in a three-bedroom house that smelled of eggs, gratitude that we had a car with air conditioning and electric windows, that we had more than one servant—'

'We didn't really think of Umm Saida as a servant.'

'Your father certainly didn't, we've established that.'

'Do you remember the time you pretended to have an egg allergy just to annoy me?' says Zak.

'I do have an egg allergy.'

'Come on. I just saw a box of eggs in your cupboard.'

'My housekeeper buys them,' says Ali, wiping coffee grounds from the kitchen surface.

'Why?'

Ali looks up. 'Why does my housekeeper buy eggs? That's what you're asking me?'

'I'm just saying, it doesn't make sense.'

'You've come to Paris because your life is so stressful and the first thing you do when you get off the train is come here and ask me, like, three times why do I have a carton of eggs in my cupboard. Actually, no, before that you ask me if I'm moving my business to China to evade sanctions.'

None of this is working. None of this is going right. Zak can't keep that thought off his burning face. But it also seems to him that the damage has been done, the eggs are smashed, he may as well keep going.

'Even if they're for someone else,' he says, 'I just thought it would bother you to have eggs in your kitchen. Unless, that is, it's not really an allergy. You just don't like them.'

Ali stares at him across the expanse of marble countertop.

'You're even weirder than you were as a teenager,' he says.

His mobile starts to ring. He picks it up.

Zak picks up the coffee, turns the heat of his face away from Ali, crosses to the window. He searches for sight of Aphra in the city below him. She promised she would be close by. He wants to tell her that it's all gone wrong, that not only has he failed to get to the truth of the egg story but he's said something that has clearly alarmed Ali. Why did he think he'd be good at this? There was a moment, he still thinks about this, there was a moment when life simply emptied of promise, it's as simple as that. He's tried more than once to pin it down to a specific day, so he can examine each hour, each minute, as though with one of those screwdrivers that lights up when it encounters a current, to isolate the moment the power went out. Something like that is happening again. He thought he could do this, it turns out he can't. He really can't. The coffee smells flavoured, as if Ali found some other spice to replace the cardamom, something sweet like cinnamon. Aphra will call the whole thing off, he's in no doubt about that. He'll be back in Smethwick before nightfall. But then he drinks his coffee down in one, and the liqueur that Ali has added hits his empty stomach with a jolt, and suddenly everything is on its way to being alright again.

~

Aphra has found a table by the second-floor window of a bookshop café that allows her a direct view of Ali's apartment. Once or twice she's stared in that direction more intently, as though she can make out a figure at the window. I can't imagine what she thinks she can see or do from here. There's no operational value in sitting this far away. What would she do if something went wrong? I can only assume, and I am being generous here, that she feels anxious about

Zak and his deployment, and having line of sight provides an outlet for her anxiety, or if not an outlet then a place to put it.

He's been gone an hour now. She's long since finished her cup of tea. There's a stack of books on the table in front of her. It's to her credit that the titles, for the most part, suggest she's aware of her responsibilities: a practical guide for the families of addicts, a best-seller about the after-effects of trauma, an A to Z of Paris and a poet's memoir of a Syrian childhood. Apart from rotating between the books, she's only really moved once. Her eyes first, following a car on the street below, and then her head, drawn by something she'd seen. I wouldn't have registered it as anything special if I hadn't seen her eyes widen in surprise at the sight of the driver, who appears to have swapped his Stone Roses T-shirt for a black polo neck.

~

'It's been another good month,' he says. 'The numbers are pretty stable, so we can be confident that staff continue to view the role of ethics counsellor as relevant, as helpful, as the proper place to take a concern. That's down to you and your hard work, so well done.'

The sign on the door reads Director of Establishments, which is one of those job titles best passed over quickly. I wonder how the incumbent would explain it. He – Philip – is distracted by the curious sight through his window of a tourist boat shaped like a duck. It's stalled in dirty water, slowly spinning as though being tugged towards a plughole.

'Philip?' says the ethics counsellor, otherwise known as Elizabeth.

'Same time next month?' he says.

'There's one more,' she says. 'She only came to see me this morn-ing, so technically she'll be counted in next month's figures.'

Philip is already looking at his computer screen, scrolling through the emails that have accumulated in the half-hour since their meeting began. They have titles like *Shortfall in Recruitment Budget* and *Well-being Week launch event* and *Still on for squash?* and *URGENT: former officer detained in Dushanbe*. He deletes the last one, plants a red flag alongside a couple of others.

'It's an unusual case,' says Elizabeth.

'What is?'

Elizabeth feels more than ever that she's done her time in ethics. Her two young children are approaching school age. She wants to take them overseas, preferably to a European capital, preferably Scandinavian, where the office will cover school fees and the tempo of work will be manageable. The Swedish services take an entire month off every summer, she's heard. Ethics was sold to her as a role that would demonstrate the more corporate skills required to progress upwards, and she feels that she's close to amassing enough evidence to fill a promotion application.

'Her name's Susan,' she says. 'She's a building escort.'

'A building escort? Aren't they . . .'

He still hasn't looked at her. *Honours List for approval*, *You can't keep avoiding me Philip*, *Staff Satisfaction Survey Results—*

'They're the ones who sit with tradesmen while they fix the electrics or paint a wall,' says Elizabeth.

'I wouldn't have thought a building escort would be asked to do anything that might cause ethical concerns.'

'She was looking after a lady from the Intelligence and Security Committee up at Westminster. Not one of the MPs – a researcher. Anyway, Susan got it into her head that the researcher posed some sort of threat and so planted a classified file in this woman's bag.'

Philip stops typing and looks squarely at Elizabeth.

'She did *what*?' he says.

'I know. The guards found the file and this researcher got sacked.'

'Susan's not complaining about something that someone else did. She's *confessing* to something that *she* did herself, is that right?'

'Correct.'

'What do we think about this?'

'I've got a friend who works further down the corridor,' says Elizabeth. 'According to her, it's a very sensitive case. The Committee has been trying to "bring us into line", that was the phrase she used. So an admission of this sort from Susan would not be helpful.'

Philip leans back in his chair, looks out the window for the spinning duck boat.

'From one perspective,' he says, 'it sounds as though Susan was thinking on her feet. If she'd done something similar out there in the real world against, say, a Russian spy or a terrorist, we'd be applauding her. It's just unfortunate that in this case she did it to a representative of the body that oversees our work. I wonder whether . . . I don't know what you think, Elizabeth.'

'Go on.'

'Perhaps we should encourage Susan to be a little less hard on herself. It is Well-being Week, after all.' He looks for an email he just saw, in the process sees *IT infrastructure meeting*, *Pension Update*—

'Philip?'

'The important thing is that she understands it was the wrong thing to do. If she does, we can draw a line under it. I suspect it would be best for everyone involved—'

'Except for the—'

'Except for the researcher, that's true, but we have no responsibility to her,' says Philip. 'Let's do that, shall we? Praise Susan for her candour, embark on a period of discreet, supervised reflection, absorb this unfortunate incident and emerge stronger at the other end.'

Having solved the problem, Philip turns back to his email inbox, which continues to grow. *Draft schedule for CIA visit*, *B7739 disciplinary update*, *exterior refurb quote no. 34*—

'She doesn't want to do any of that.'

Staff canteen menus, manuscript approval letter for signature—

'Susan wants to apologise to the researcher,' says Elizabeth. 'She's very clear on that.'

'But that would—'

'I know, that's why I'm bringing it up. It would have significant consequences for us. Reputationally, I mean. Susan would have to be fired and the Committee would use the incident to reassert control over us. The problem is that I'm not sure how easy it will be to talk her round.' She looks down at her hands, drums her fingers together. 'I was wondering if this is one of those cases where we might want to consider triggering Operation WATERSLIDE.'

Philip stands, crosses to the window to see if anyone is coming to rescue the stranded duck boat. He can see children on board. It's beginning to rain.

'I was hoping we'd get through this year without resorting to WATERSLIDE,' he says. 'It doesn't sit well with me.'

'Me too. I just thought . . .'

'Mmm?'

'If we do use it,' says Elizabeth, 'can I oversee it? I'm gathering material in support of a promotion application, and it would be very helpful to be able to point to something—'

'You could never put WATERSLIDE on a promotion application. It's far too sensitive.'

'I know that, but I could make a vague reference to resolving complex problems in a manner that benefits the organisation as a whole, or something like that.'

'Sir William is very keen that we phase out older, unofficial prac-tices like WATERSLIDE,' says Philip. 'It's becoming harder and harder to keep things like that off the books. It's also that the potential fallout is growing by the year. If WATERSLIDE had come to light a decade or two ago, we could have weathered it. But now? No chance.'

Elizabeth leaves him to it. She knows what he's like. He prefers to creep up on a decision, wearing the opposite point of view like a disguise before – aha! – whipping it off and taking everyone by surprise.

'Having said that, WATERSLIDE does exist for a reason,' he says. 'I'd have to get Sir William's authorisation. Why don't you have a further chat with Susan to see how she's feeling? With any luck, you'll be able to talk her down from the lofty position she's adopted. If not . . .'

He smiles.

'I can't see any reason why you shouldn't be the one to nudge her off her high horse.'

~

'It took a while to get into it properly, but eventually he said that an allergy is not exclusively a medical thing, the term "allergy" can encompass a strong preference *not* to eat something,' says Zak. 'He has a strong preference not to eat eggs, that's what he said. When we were boys and he told my father he was allergic to eggs, that's what he meant.'

I have to hand it to Aphra, I've never heard of someone debriefing their agent while receiving a foot massage, but it seems to be working surprisingly well. At this time of day there's no other clients, and they're in a back room far from the curious glances of passers-by. As long as they keep their voices low, there's little chance that the women oiling their feet will pay them much attention.

'That sounds like nonsense to me,' Aphra says.

'I told him that from a medical perspective his statement is untrue.'

'What did he say?'

'He said, what does a dentist know about a medical perspective?'

The women are making long scooping movements with the base of their thumbs up the soles, starting at the heel.

Zak winces.

'Are you alright?'

'I'm reconsidering my long-standing belief that ticklish and painful are at the opposite ends of the sensory spectrum,' he says.

The smell is sandalwood. Imagine a series of tropical photographs put through the most garish filter available and you'll have some idea of the decor. Water trickles through a small fountain cluttered with plastic turtles.

'Ali sounds like an idiot,' says Aphra. 'But, look, whether he says it in these terms or not, he's basically admitted something pretty significant. I was thinking about this earlier. The last thing a person with an allergy would do is handle eggs, let alone throw them against the wall, let alone release their appalling contents into the world. You see what I mean? If he had an allergy, I'd wager it wasn't him. But now we know that he doesn't, he's squarely back in the crosshairs of the investigation.'

'Mmm.'

'What?'

'You're straining a bit.'

'You're forgetting who's the pro in this room,' says Aphra. 'Mark my words, you've opened the door to a full confession. It's just a matter of time before he admits letting the neighbour's dog into the coop.'

'We don't need to pretend that I did well in there.'

'I'm not pretending anything,' says Aphra. 'You've got to allow me to set the objectives at each stage. The objective today was to make contact with Ali, confirm where he lives, exchange basic news, get comfortable in your role as agent and arrange to see him again. Did you achieve all of those things?'

'It just didn't feel as natural as I'd hoped it would.'

'That's because it's your first time.'

'Can you remember your first time?' he asks.

She doesn't even break stride.

'I had the advantage of my first twenty or thirty deployments taking place in a training environment,' says Aphra. 'It might look real but you know there's a safety net. When you're tied to a chair and some thug is threatening to gouge out your eyes with a screwdriver, you can say to yourself, take a breath, it's not real, he's probably called Nigel or Keith and most days peels vegetables in the kitchens. It was totally different for you. You swung out on the trapeze with no training whatsoever, Zak, and you've swung back in one piece.'

'There was one bit where I definitely messed up.'

'Tell me.'

'He was talking about his father's company and said he was planning to move some of the manufacturing to China.'

'That's interesting.'

'Except that I said something about the real reason being to evade sanctions. I don't know why I said it. It was just a stupid joke. But he didn't like that.'

'Listen,' says Aphra, 'I've worked with plenty of people in your position who never do anything to provoke the target. They smile, they're polite, they say nice things and as a result we never get anywhere. The reason that you're going to do well is that you and Ali provoke each other. Sparks are going to fly. It's always been that way. That's why he made up the allergy story in the first place, that's why he threw your eggs against the wall. But that's also why you're the perfect person to do this. If you feel like saying something that might rile him, if it's something you might say if I didn't exist, if we weren't doing this, then just say it. I trust your judgement. The only person I want you to be is you.'

He looks embarrassed by this, as though she's given him something and he doesn't have anywhere to keep it.

'That fountain,' he says.

She cocks an ear. 'What about it?'

'Doesn't it make you want to pee?'

'Now that you mention it,' she says.

'Did I tell you about the Botox?' he says.

'What?'

'I'm pretty sure Ali's had Botox.'

'How can you tell?'

'You know when you sniff something,' he says, 'you have these lines that appear next to your nose? They call it bunny nose or bunny face. He was looking for cardamom among his spices and—'

'No bunny nose?'

'No bunny nose.'

'How do you know about bunny nose?' she asks.

'I've been thinking of offering fillers at work to supplement my income.'

'Do lots of dentists do it?'

'I don't know. Anyone can do it. It's just a one-day course.'

'Does it change your assessment of him, that he's had Botox?'

Zak considers the question.

'It's very in keeping with his style. He's very controlled, very . . . surgical. He's grown into himself, but that's the wrong phrase to use because he seems even smaller than he used to, although that might be because his apartment is so huge.'

'Is it nice?'

'It's horrible. Like a really expensive hotel for people with no taste.'

'I hope you like the place I've booked for us,' says Aphra. 'There wasn't much available at such short notice.'

'I'm not much of a sleeper these days.'

'Do you take anything at night?'

'Yes.'

'Have you always found it hard?'

'Just the last few years,' he says.

'Do you know what started it?'

'That's a big subject, Aphra. Big and messy.'

'Understood. I'm not a great sleeper myself. Perhaps I'll see you at 3 a.m. for some mint tea.'

He puts his head back on the chair, folds a scented flannel and places it over his eyes. He's quiet for at least a full minute.

'I went back to Aleppo for my father's funeral,' he says. 'This is three or four years ago now. I hadn't been there since the war started, in 2011. Some of my father's friends warned me not to come, but what kind of son doesn't go to his father's funeral?'

'Were they worried about something in particular?'

'Conscription. I got an official deferment of military service more than twenty years ago because of academic study, and my father had to pay a bribe, which is totally normal in Syria. But with everything that's happened in the last decade or so there was a chance the government would change their minds. That's what his friends said anyway. I thought it was worth the risk.'

The two women move up to their bare calves.

'This is okay?' asks one of the women.

'You can go harder,' says Aphra. She puts her head back, closes her eyes.

'It wasn't all bad,' says Zak. 'I got to attend his funeral. They could have arrested me when I arrived instead of when I was leaving. Instead I was there when they buried my father, and I stayed in his house, where I spent every single summer from the age of three to eighteen. His housekeeper, Umm Saida, was there too. I would wake up with the sun each morning, drink coffee at his kitchen table and eat foul mudammas with warm bread, traipse around the house in his sandals, wander among the tangerine trees at the bottom of his garden. He put a swing on one of the branches when I was little. I used to sail up so high that I could reach out and pick the ones that were ripest, and I'd run indoors to share them with him.'

'What happened when you tried to leave?'

'They stopped me at the airport. I spent seven days in solitary in Sednaya prison, which is really no time at all. They didn't torture me. I could hear all sorts of other things going on in other cells, all the things you'd expect, like beatings, rape, electrocution. In the winter they turn the heating off, in the summer they turn it on, so the temperature was pretty unbearable. The water they gave me was dirty. It made me very sick. I didn't get questioned. I suppose it must have been because I have a British passport as well as a Syrian one, although I would have thought that would have made things worse for me.'

'I can understand why that would keep you up at night.'

'Maybe you can explain it to me, then. I don't understand why I've found it so hard to move past it. I was the luckiest person in that place. I was even luckier than the guards. Can you imagine doing what they do every day? Can you imagine what that does to them?'

'That's a very generous perspective,' says Aphra.

'If I drew a chalk line on the floor and told you to walk along it, you'd do it without any difficulty. But if that line was drawn on a wooden plank stretched between two buildings, hundreds of feet up in the sky, it would feel terrifying, even though it's basically the same thing. That's how it feels. I try to do the same things I used to do before this happened, but for some reason everything terrifies me now.'

A young woman in her thirties with several shopping bags enters, sits in a chair at the far end of the room. Aphra glances at her.

'I'm trying to tell myself it's a good thing,' says Zak. 'It's knowledge, right? How can knowledge be bad? How can sanity depend on ignorance? I have a better understanding of what the world is like now. I've learned that the floor beneath the line is an illusion and there's nothing really there. So all this – the insomnia, the depression, the addiction – this is just a moment of vertigo before I adjust to the new reality and find my balance. That's what I'm looking forward to. Waking up one day and finding that everything's fine again. It's going to happen. It has to.'

'Did you ever get a chance to talk to your father about his experience in prison?'

'What's strange is that as a young man he was in Sednaya too.'

'Why did he stay in Syria after he was released?'

'He tried to leave. He came to London, where he met my mother. They got married, they had me. But he missed Syria too much, they got divorced, so he went back.'

'Do you think you'll be able to go back one day?'

'I wish I knew how he did it. I wish I'd asked him for the secret. He was in prison for three years, and as far as I know they tortured him most days. He always had difficulty walking after that, and bad teeth, and when I was little he'd do this clicking thing with his fingers that would make me laugh, but I'm pretty sure it was caused by broken bones that never reset properly. I don't know how anyone comes out after three years of that and finds it in themself to be a loving father. There are days when I can't get out of bed. But he was never angry with me, he was never impatient. When I was in England with my mother, he would write long letters every week. At some point he must have made a conscious decision not to pass it on to me, whatever it was they did to him. It would have been so easy for him to take it out on his weird son. I wouldn't have blamed him. But he never did. He just put all that stuff somewhere I would never see it.'

The two women take fresh towels and wipe the oil from their feet and legs. Zak lifts the flannel from his eyes, sits up and smiles at them.

'You've got really tickly fingers,' he says.

~

Sir William Rentoul watches from a discreet vantage point across the road as Aphra and the dentist emerge from the spa. He's supposed to use operational codenames in place of their actual names, in case his team's communications have been intercepted by a third party, but he can't for the life of him remember what they are. He touches his left earpod, still getting used to the fact there's no wire, has to stop himself saying something like 'Hello?' or 'Can you hear me?' every time he speaks.

'Stand by, stand by,' he says. 'Both subjects have exited the address and turned right, repeat right, heading in a north-east direction. She is wearing a black full-length mackintosh and a red scarf. He's in a grey overcoat.'

He counts to twenty and begins to follow them, confident that if he remains at a safe distance he won't be recognised. He barely recognises himself, truth be told. Before donating his favourite grey flannel suit to a charity shop, Sir William hurried around an upmarket department store to collect the pieces of an outfit that now strikes him as coming straight from Nantucket Sound, or wherever it was the Kennedys had their compound: pleated cream chinos, pink button-down Oxford, an unstructured blue cotton blazer and deck shoes. The day is bright enough for a pair of vintage aviators. 'Camelot', is that what they called it? Why would anyone leave this? he wonders. Why would anyone choose a life of boardrooms and budgets over the excitement of following two enemies of the state down a Paris street, he thinks, before realising that's precisely what he did.

Or something like that.

'Received,' he hears through the earpods. It could be the one called Ned, it could be the other one.

He watches as the two figures ahead of him turn down a side street.

'Subjects are turning right, repeat right,' he says. He glances at the road sign as he approaches. 'Rue de Longchamp. No indication of surveillance awareness as yet.'

It took the intelligence cell in London longer than Sir William would have liked to pin Aphra and Zak down to the spa, something they blamed on an unexpected lag in communications data. The same lag was also responsible for the delay in reporting that Zak had earlier been co-located with his Iranian friend for almost two hours – an update that caused considerable alarm in London and Paris. What was he doing? More importantly, what was *she* doing? The last thing they could do was tell the Iranian – their agent – that something was going on, as the news would suggest that his security had been compromised. How does someone outside your organisation even know that I am your agent? he would rightly ask; and any answer that required an explanation of the delicate relationship between the Intelligence and Security Committee and the spy agencies was never going to work. Much better, they all agreed, to find out what Aphra was up to and remove her and the dentist from the scene.

'Please update.'

'Still on Longchamp,' says Sir William. 'They've just passed the turning onto Rue Frédéric Passy.'

'Roger. I'm approaching Longchamp from the east, will take the lead. Prepare to drop back.'

He watches as the one who isn't called Ned comes into sight and turns left onto Longchamp, a dozen or so metres behind Aphra and Zak. Sir William is impressed to see shorts and a football shirt, mud smeared on bare legs. He's even carrying a football under one arm. Desperate times et cetera. It's not just that a team this small is unheard of in professional circles, it's that Aphra has sat down with all three of them in the last twenty-four hours. The odds really are stacked against them.

'Left, repeat left off Longchamp onto Neufchâteau.'

Sir William allows them to turn, followed by the one who isn't

Ned, and continues straight along Longchamp. There's no harm in dropping out of sight for a bit, as long as he remains close by. All they need to do at this stage is house Aphra and the dentist to an address where they are staying. That way, if the team loses control of them at any point, they can stake out that address and pick them up later. The alternative would be to stake out their agent's apartment in case the dentist returns there, but that would double the risk as their agent might spot Ned and the other one, his two handlers, loitering inexplicably on the street.

'Continuing along Neufchâteau,' he hears.

There's also the very real risk posed by French intelligence. No one has asked them for permission to operate in their territory, and, as Ned and the other one have gently pointed out, it's possible that Sir William's passport triggered an alert in Calais. The French would never expect someone as senior as Sir William to be engaged in covert operational work of this sort, but they would want to know if he was holidaying in France so they could ensure the necessary protection was in place.

Sir William spots an alleyway that runs parallel to Neufchâteau, turns into it. 'Update,' he says.

His team in London – chief of staff, deputies, secretary – have all sent messages gently asking what he is doing and when he'll be back. They will have learned – they will be *aghast* to have learned – that he's on operational business. It's totally unheard of for someone in his position to deploy overseas on a clandestine operation of this sort. His job is to steer the ship, as his chief of staff told him, not scrape barnacles from the hull.

'Update,' he repeats. 'Please provide an update.'

'I've lost them.'

'What?'

'They were at the bottom of Neufchâteau but they've disappeared.'

Sir William breaks into a jog. He focusses on the strip of azure sky at the end of the alleyway, relishing the feeling of movement, of urgency, of peril. Discounting his weekly game of squash, he hasn't run in years. He emerges onto a wide boulevard, the river opposite, looks right and left. Nothing.

Except that he hears something. A laugh that to his ears doesn't quite sound French, and the noise of a door, one of those doors with a closing mechanism installed above it, the *whoosh whoosh* of a heavy wooden door swinging out, swinging in, out, in, before coming to a rest.

He glances left and sees stairs ascending from street level to a door filled with a dozen or more glass panels, distorted like the bottom of milk bottles, but transparent enough to see the colours black, red and grey on the other side.

'Number 64, Boulevard du Général Koenig,' he says, touching his ear. 'Modern apartment block, seven storeys. There are several key boxes attached to the wall outside, suggesting some of the units are used for rental purposes.'

'Great work, sir,' he hears Ned say. 'We'll take it from here. You'll want to get back to London.'

Sir William sees the other one, the one with the football, emerge from Neufchâteau with a panicked look on his face.

'Take this down,' says Sir William.

'Excuse me?' says Ned.

'Number one. Recce the surrounding area to identify a discreet OP from which we can watch the entrance. Our friend Zinedine Zidane here can do that, once he's washed off the mud and changed his clothes. Number two. Task the cell in London to interrogate booking and credit card data to establish which apartment the subjects are staying in.'

'Sir, we'll take these excellent suggestions forward,' says Ned. 'London has been in touch to request that you return on the next train to deal with pressing matters in HQ.'

'Number three,' says Sir William. 'Get on to the embassy. Go there in person, don't call, the French are probably monitoring phones. In fact, don't go there, they'll have cameras outside.' He thinks. 'Contact HQ, have them instruct Paris Station to activate a dead-letter box.'

'What for, sir?'

'To pass us the covert eavesdropping equipment that we'll need.'

'But we'd have to wait for a specialised tech-ops team to install equipment like that, sir.'

Sir William breathes deeply, adjusts his aviators, smiles at the pretty young woman walking past him.

'No need,' he says. 'We'll do it ourselves. Tonight.'

~

It's best to avoid the personality side of the business. I know everyone likes a stellar-performing employee or two, and I have no issue with that, but the truth is that superstars require particularly close monitoring, because of the ways in which they can destabilise the collective. What I value more than anything is an even keel, a we're all in this together, *esprit de corps*, just another brick in the wall type of mentality. Yes, that's it. It's the uniformity of a wall that makes it strong. No one ever leaned in, widened their eyes in admiration and said now *that's* what I call a brick.

What I'm saying, I suppose, is that Sir William is entitled to behave like this if he's sitting on top of the wall. He's a figurehead; there's an aspect to his role that is ceremonial, even decorative. Within certain boundaries, up there, he's allowed to be his own man. But the moment he drops down several rows and tries to squeeze in among the other bricks, he has to adopt a brick-like shape, and accept that there are bricks above and below him, that he's one of the bricks. This is a surprisingly fertile metaphor. I don't like to criticise Sir William, who's evidently a very talented spy with a long and distinguished career behind him, but there's nothing more destabilising to a wall than a figurehead squeezed in four rows up, seven rows across, trying to pretend he's not there.

~

'So it's a normal rented holiday apartment, is that right?'

'Yes,' says Aphra McQueen. 'I should warn you, it's a little small, but we wanted something in the area. And it was short notice.'

It's a mistake, her first real one. Much better to say the size is intentional and not mention the short notice at all. I see it land, his frown like ripples from a stone cast in error. They've just left the spa. As they walk, Zak glances across to gauge her reaction.

'I'm surprised to hear that things like "short notice" apply to you,' he says. 'Doesn't your organisation have a dozen or more safe houses that we can use? This is Paris, after all.'

There's something sensuous about the way they are both walking, as though the massage has taught them to take new delight in their feet.

'Not quite a dozen, but we do have a few,' she says.

They turn onto a street called Rue de Longchamp. Suited security personnel form a guard of honour outside boutiques and jewellers. To her credit, Aphra has spotted her mistake and hurries to rectify it.

'Let's say we used one of our safe houses and Ali asked where you were staying,' she says. 'How would you reply?'

'I don't know. With a friend?'

'Who's your friend?'

He thinks. 'Someone from dental school.' He thinks some more, realises what she's doing. 'He's called Timothy. Married a French woman and moved here two years ago. They've got a new baby girl and a sweet cockapoo called Lulu.'

Aphra smiles. 'You came here because you were tired and stressed and you're staying in the same apartment as a newborn baby?'

'She's a very quiet baby.'

'I need a new dentist. Can you give me Timothy's number?'

Zak smiles. 'He's left the profession.'

'What does he do now?'

'He's a stripper.'

'A stripper?' She laughs. 'Where?'

'It's a very upmarket place. More burlesque than *Magic Mike*. Somewhere in . . .' He looks around for a street sign. 'Rue Frédéric Passy.'

'Can we go and watch the show?'

'He's a bit shy—'

'A shy stripper?'

'When it comes to his friends, yes. He's only really doing it to get out of the house at night.'

'I thought Lulu was a quiet baby.'

'She's got colic at the moment.'

'Hang on,' says Aphra, 'isn't Lulu the dog?'

He laughs. 'They're both called Lulu.' He holds up his hands to signal surrender. They walk in silence for a while. The problem with ripples is there's no stopping them once they're off. Her answer was a robust one, he can't fault it, but the doubt is still there. 'It's an unusual name, Aphra,' he says. 'What was it like as a child, being called that?'

He says it lightly but I know what he's thinking. If it's not her real name, she won't *actually* know what it was like to be a seven-year-old called Aphra. She'll shrug off the question with something generic, something like *I'd get teased* or *I begged my parents to change it*. It won't mean anything in itself if she's not called Aphra, but it'll be a useful barometer of her truthfulness.

'I have loved my name since the moment I could say it,' she says.

'In fact, there have been times when it was my favourite thing about me. Everyone else in my school was called Mary or Elizabeth or Jane. It was like being, I don't know, a Manchester City fan in a crowd of United supporters, or a maple tree in a forest of pines. Do you like your name? Is Zak short for something?'

'Zaki.'

'It's barely worth abbreviating.'

He laughs. The problem with her answers, he thinks, is that although they're good, they're just words; it's like pulling at a weed but leaving the roots behind.

'Do you have an equally unusual middle name?' he says.

They turn left off Longchamp onto Neufchâteau.

'Are you testing me, Zaki?' she says.

'What?' As though *appalled* at the thought. 'No!'

'I wouldn't blame you if you were.'

'Why would I need to test you?' he says.

'I'll tell you what,' she says. 'Would it give you some reassurance to meet one of my colleagues?'

I can't imagine what she's thinking, unless this is the moment that she reveals she's actually working for a foreign state, which, come to think of it, is a very real possibility. It would explain why she's so good at this. Is Sergei or Hao or Farhad waiting for them at the rented apartment, ready with Earl Grey and impeccable English, ready with a handshake and warm words of appreciation for Zak's service to his country?

'Pick left or right,' she says.

'What?'

'Left or right?'

'Left.'

They turn left off Neufchâteau onto a narrow side street.

'Pick left or right,' she says.

'Right.'

On the corner is a patisserie with a red check awning. Aphra leads Zak inside. She greets the woman behind the counter and they stand at the window, looking at the cakes and pastries on display.

'What are we doing?' he whispers.

'Do you remember asking ten minutes or so ago what it was like to be called Aphra?'

'Like being a maple tree in a forest of pines, you said.'

'And?'

'A football fan in a crowd of hostile fans.'

'Do you remember which team I said?'

'Manchester?'

She points with her chin to the street. A young man comes into view, dressed as though he's just stepped off the pitch, with mud smeared on his legs and a football under one arm.

'I'm not very good at football,' Zak says. 'Is that a Manchester City shirt?'

'He's wearing it because I gave it to him this morning,' says Aphra. 'It's his birthday. His name's Lionel, he's thirty-two years old, he lives in Croydon and he's worked with me for the past five years, specialising in surveillance and close protection. I'm breaching protocol by doing this, but I wanted to pull back the curtain just a crack to show you that there's a lot of people rooting for you.'

He nods, blinks, smiles to show her that he's reassured.

'Choose a pastry,' she says.

～

I'm mindful of my wider responsibilities. As all-encompassing as this is, there's yet another disciplinary case involving sexual impropriety among the ranks of surveillance officers, the operations room is trying to stay on top of a dissident Irish plot *and* a lone-wolf Islamist threat, a former officer remains detained in Dushanbe for unknown reasons, a lowball Treasury pay offer is causing disquiet on the staff intranet, the prime minister is visiting the building this week to give a talk, the official Instagram account was briefly hacked last night by environmental protesters who posted that climate destruction was a graver threat to national security than the Russians or Chinese, a fault in the gas supply to the building has led to a team of engineers being admitted without undergoing the usual security checks, the annual feedback survey has recorded the lowest morale score ever, the Belgians may have caught two of our officers in the act of photographing classified documents inside an EU building, and the cleaners are going on strike.

All this and with Sir William in Paris, there's no one at the top of the organisation.

And yet isn't it funny how gravity has a habit of bending us towards its darkest mass? I paused to have a quick look at one of the gas engineers, only to find that Susan is looking after him.

'So you're an escort, is that right?' he says.

'I've heard all the jokes,' she says, positioning her folding chair so she's close enough to keep an eye on him but not so close that he'll want to chat.

'If I want to go to the toilet, will you take me?'

She's got her paper, she's got her pen, she's got a mug of sweet builder's tea from the cafeteria. It's much nicer than that dusty mouthful of South African tobacco water she was given by the ethics counsellor. What was it called? Rufus? Rebus? She expects it's all part of the process. The ethics counsellor smiles, she nods, she even *tilts* and nods, but beneath the surface warmth Susan detected an icy undercurrent. It's probably just another way of making sure people mean what they say, she thinks.

Or something like that.

'How old are you?' Susan says.

'Twenty-six,' says the gas engineer. 'Why?'

'Have you ever done something you regretted?'

'That third pint last night was questionable.'

'I mean it. Ever done something you just felt in your bones was wrong?'

He's puzzled by the question.

'Is this a test?' he says.

'Forget I asked.'

'I put the wrong valve on a boiler the other week.'

This one should sign up to be a spy, she thinks. There's a reason they bring them in young. That was her mistake, thinking she wasn't too old to pivot into operational work without throwing something out of kilter. She thinks about her grandkids for a while. You can't do anything with an old bit of plasticine. It's a million different colours and crusty as an old dog turd. These kids, though, they're the colour of neon, they're fresh out the pot. You can make them into anything you like.

'Any chance I could get a cup of tea too?' he asks.

I can't stay here forever. I just wanted to check that he was being monitored, given his lack of security clearance. He's alright. Turns out it's his escort, it's *Susan* I need to be worried about.

'One of my colleagues will be along in a bit,' she says. 'I'll see what we can do.' She looks up from her paper. 'Have you ever tried rooibos tea?'

It's possible to read too much into a turn of phrase, but I really don't want Susan to feel *in her bones* that what she did was wrong. I'd happily swap *in her bones* for *skin deep*, if that were on the cards. She needs to remember the basic truth that we all agree on the end goal. Some like to run towards it in a straight line, others take a more bendy route, but at the end of the day it's just a question of preference.

Please, let's not talk about bones. Let's not bring bones into it.

~

Sir William Rentoul enters the station via the main entrance. He can see the logic of collecting the technical equipment from a locker in the Gare du Nord. After all, as Ned has explained to him, it's the busiest station in Paris and there are hundreds upon hundreds of lockers. At least one officer under diplomatic cover at the embassy routinely commutes home via the Gare du Nord, meaning that dropping off the equipment won't require a detour that might be spotted by French intelligence.

The problem for Sir William, however, is that being the head of an organisation means your preferences are always on show. Your preferences are the reason you're there. You're a walking display case of preferences, which is why Sir William insisted on a long discussion about his own preference, which was to locate the dead-letter box in Père Lachaise cemetery.

'But there's cameras everywhere these days,' said Ned.

'Near the graves that are more likely to be desecrated, I understand that. I'm not suggesting we go near Edith Piaf or Oscar Wilde. But in the more obscure corners? Remember that Paris was my first overseas posting. I know the territory very well.'

'The equipment is bulky. They'd have to dig a sizeable hole to conceal it, which in a cemetery would not go unnoticed.'

'There's no need for a hole. They can conceal a bag in the undergrowth. It'll be there for a matter of minutes before I collect it.'

'We also think that I should be the one to retrieve the equipment,' said Ned. 'There's some concern, sir, about your profile.

After all, you're a prominent public figure whose picture is often in the papers.'

It ended in a draw, with Sir William collecting the equipment from Gare du Nord. He walks at a steady pace across the main concourse. To his credit, Sir William keeps evidence of his anxiety well out of sight, in his left pocket, where his fingers dampen a slip of paper containing the locker number and access code. He was told to memorise them but doesn't trust himself to get it right.

The self-storage area is downstairs. Sir William stands on the escalator, casts a casual glance around in search of hostile surveillance. Once at the bottom, he heads for the rows of yellow lockers. Number 349 is tucked away in a corner. He checks the slip of paper, enters the code, swallows the piece of paper. The bag inside is a black canvas holdall.

Gripping it tightly, Sir William heads for the exit.

~

He arrives at the safe house to find Ned and the other one in a state of considerable excitement.

'We've done it,' says Ned. 'It's over – the operation's a success.'

'What?' says Sir William.

'The uncle's on the move,' says Ned.

'What?' says Sir William, putting the bag down. 'Who?'

'The uncle. The assassin. CASPIAN. A while ago we instructed the nephew to send his uncle an email with an invisible attachment that allowed us to gain remote access to his computer in Tehran. From there we identified a Facebook account that the uncle uses to communicate with his IRGC handlers when he's deployed in Europe.'

It's a densely packed sentence, delivered at speed. Sir William nods, trying to replay it, trying to decode each chunk, or are these what they call bytes?

'In other words,' he says.

There's a brief silence.

'In other words,' says Ned, 'the Iranian assassin is on European soil for the first time this year. Zagreb, to be exact.'

'I understand that,' says Sir William curtly. 'What I mean is, he'll be on the move. Zagreb is just a stopping post. When was he there?'

'The Facebook account was accessed three hours ago.'

'Deploy a surveillance team,' says Sir William. 'As many bodies as we can spare. Have them plot up north of Zagreb, somewhere around Munich, so they can intercept him as he travels into western Europe.'

'It takes an hour for the Facebook log-in data to come through,' says the other one. He wasn't expecting this. He wasn't expecting to have to push back against Sir William. 'It's extremely unlikely that one of our team will be close enough to his location to intercept him in the act of logging in. We also don't know what vehicle he's in or what identity he's using or whether he's altered his appearance.'

'Facebook is not our only data point, though,' says Sir William. 'Presumably we've mapped out a list of possible targets: Iranian exiles, regime opponents, querulous journalists. Once we get a second Facebook log-in, we'll have a general idea of his direction of travel. We then position our team around the possible targets.'

Ned and the other one glance at each other.

'We've actually got a plan already,' says the other one.

Sir William glares at him. That *actually*, that *already*.

'Sir, we think the best course of action is to alert HAARLEM to this development,' says Ned.

Harlem, thinks Sir William. Harlem. He once ran a source with an FBI agent named Johnny Harlem. Or do they mean Haarlem? He has a dim recollection of some Dutch connection to this case but can't for the life of him remember what it is.

'HAARLEM?' says Sir William.

'The European working group.' Ned sees that he'll need to go further. He would also like to communicate that he feels empathy for Sir William's increasingly obvious difficulties, but he can't see how to do that without sounding patronising. 'It comprises the intelligence agencies of all the countries in which there's been a murder.'

'Including France?'

'Yes.'

'No.'

The two officers' confusion is palpable. This stuff about a British team intercepting the assassin is so strictly for the birds that they can't believe it's coming from the man in charge.

'Let's say our officers plot up around possible targets, sir, as you suggest,' says Ned, treading delicately. 'Say that they manage to do that in the next few hours. And say that our assessment is right, and the uncle heads towards one of the individuals we've identified. Our officers can't actually do anything to stop a murder. They're not armed. Any intervention will have to come from a European police force.'

The biggest risk in making statements of fact rather than judgement is that he sounds as though he's talking down to Sir William, which he knows is a mistake.

'May I set out another possible plan?' Ned says quickly. 'We inform HAARLEM that through some piece of technical brilliance we have obtained coverage of communications between the assassin and Tehran. We don't mention the existence of the nephew. We pass HAARLEM every piece of intelligence relating to the assassin's location as soon as we get it. We let the Europeans intercept him, we let the Europeans deal with any evidence they seize, we let the Europeans carry all the risk in the event that he gets away or kills someone. Whatever the outcome, our hands are clean and we get huge credit for making the first ever breakthrough in this case.'

'It's a win-win from the UK perspective,' says the other one.

'There remains the matter of Aphra McQueen and the dentist,' says Ned. 'Our proposal there comes in two parts. Firstly, you speak to McQueen, tell her she's in hot water and order her to return to the UK. Secondly, and as near to simultaneously as we can manage, I knock on the nephew's door, tell him that as a reward for all his hard work as an agent on behalf of UK plc we are going to take him to the south of France for a luxury holiday at an exclusive château vineyard. The car's waiting outside, engine idling, Robbie behind the wheel. McQueen and the dentist are left high and dry. When they return to the UK, tails between their legs, we instruct the police to arrest her for the attempted theft of a confidential file.'

It strikes Ned as so neat a plan that he can't help but continue, even though he knows that it would be sensible to stop.

'It's bulletproof, it's win-win, just as Robbie said. You see,' – not a good phrase to use at the best of times – 'if it came to light further down the road that we were aware the assassin was in Europe and hadn't told anyone, the political consequences would be huge. London is not going to allow—'

'London?' says Sir William, raising his voice. 'Who the hell do you think you're talking to? London is *here*!' He bangs the table. 'London is standing right before you!'

The ocean washes away the turrets and battlements of their perfect plan.

'Who the hell is this Robbie you keep talking about?' says Sir William.

The one who's not called Ned puts his hand up.

'Listen, you two,' says Sir William. 'Listen and take fucking note. Espionage is not about collaboration – it is about domination. We do not leave it to the fucking Belgians to deal with the assassin. We do it ourselves. We do not leave it to the police to deal with Aphra McQueen. *We do it ourselves.*'

He can't bear the thought of what his beloved Service will become in the hands of such callow youth.

'Instruct HQ to deploy surveillance resources north of Zagreb. Let's see how things play out. It's what my generation used to call "holding your nerve".'

He lifts the canvas holdall onto the table.

'To remove Aphra McQueen from the board,' he says, 'we first need to know what game she is playing.'

He unzips the holdall, starts to take out the equipment.

'You two are responsible for following McQueen and the dentist. I'll install these bugs in their apartment.'

He's immediately struck by the complexity of the equipment, by the number of items, many of which he doesn't recognise. This bit could be a battery pack, or it could be the motor for a drill, or it could be the thing he's supposed to hide in the apartment, although it seems much too big for that. There are enough cables to secure a big top through a storm.

Wordlessly they watch him peer at each piece of equipment as though examining evidence of alien life.

He looks up.

'What are you two waiting for?' he says.

This is disastrous.

~

'Don't.'

'What?'

'Don't do it.'

'Don't do what?'

'Jesus Christ. You're going to do it.'

'It's on the menu, I'm not bringing it up, it's written there. What's wrong with you, are you allergic to the word *œuf* as well?'

'I feel that we covered eggs earlier, Zaki. I don't want to talk about eggs any more.'

'We're not actually talking about eggs, though.'

'What,' says Ali, 'they're a metaphor for something else?'

'They're not a metaphor, no. They're . . . they're a portal through time and space.'

'Please stop talking. Look at the menu and let's order.'

Ali looks around for a waiter, no one sees him, he waves his arm anyway to release a charge of irritation. It's not what you expect in a restaurant like this. The chandelier hangs above them like a burst of raindrops. The cheese has its own assigned waiter, standing stiffly, a single white-gloved hand resting on the edge of the trolley. It's not proprietorial: the cheese outranks him. He's clearly the junior partner in this relationship, he's *definitely* the expendable one.

'It's like when you see a painting and your eye is immediately drawn to an object because of its shape or its colour or the way the artist has used light,' says Zak.

'Keep your voice down,' says Ali. 'It's not that sort of restaurant.'

Zak is too large, too loud, too awkward, too poorly dressed for a place like this. He's also too cheap. There are no prices next to each dish – a detail he has noted with some alarm. He's not deterred, though. There's a new energy about him. He finds something liberating about having been given a specific set of objectives by Aphra. It changes this from being a purely social encounter – he tends to flounder in those, with no sense of direction or purpose – to a task with desired outcomes. It's the difference between dancing at a party and that game he once saw in an arcade in Birmingham city centre, where you match your feet to flashing coloured squares on the floor.

Or something like that.

'For some reason,' Zak says, 'when I look back through time—'

'Through the egg portal.'

'The first thing I see is you and me as we were then, as awkward teenage boys, with my headphones and your spots, and then I see my father's house, I see the blue tiles on the kitchen floor that are so faded that they only look blue for an hour of the day, when the light falls in a certain way, and then the bright orange of the tangerine trees at the bottom of the garden. My father is standing at the back door, waving at me.'

'All that from the eggs.'

'They're packed full of life,' says Zak.

'They're packed full of protein, that's what you used to say.'

'You know, I came here to get away from work and all the stress around that, and out of nowhere the idea came to me on the train, why don't you look up Ali? But now I'm thinking that my subconscious was nudging me in your direction because you're one of the few connections I have left to my father. I really don't know anyone who also knew him.'

'You shouldn't have divorced Molly, then.'

'She met him, sure, but not in Syria, not in Aleppo, in the place he came from. But you stood in his house, you shook his hand, you ate his—'

'If I tell you what happened with the eggs, do you promise we can change the subject?' says Ali.

'I promise.'

'I threw them against the garden wall.'

'I *knew* it,' says Zak.

Not quite the right comment, considering the reflective tone he has adopted in this conversation. It smacks of triumphalism, of

Objective Number One: tick. On the whole, though, he's doing a lot better. It's weird, it's just plain weird that he should travel to Paris and want to spend so much time with Ali, with a person he clearly dislikes. Whether or not Ali knows he's unlikeable, he's clearly registered the fact that this is weird. Which is why it's clever that Zak is suggesting this is really about his father. I'm still not sure what it does to advance Aphra's plan, which remains thoroughly opaque, but it does at least make the whole thing plausible.

'Now can we order?' says Ali.

'Wait, is that it?'

'What else do you want to know?'

'I want to know why you did it.'

'Why do you think?' says Ali. 'I wanted to annoy you. I hated the fact that my father dumped me with you for the summer. Those were supposed to be the best months of the year. But I was dragged away from my friends, my home, and dropped in this shitty house where I didn't know *anyone* and there was *nothing* to do except go to the gym and watch you lift weights like, like an ox, like a truck, listening to the same three tapes over and over again, Whitney Houston, A-ha and, and, what was the other one?'

'I can't remember.'

'Yes, you can.'

'Huey Lewis and the News?' says Zak.

'Who even listens to Huey Lewis and the News?'

'Actually some of their—'

'I don't know why I didn't admit to smashing the eggs at the time,' says Ali, 'because part of the reason I did it was to make sure I didn't get invited back the next year. I also read your father's diary. I also stole money from Umm Saida's purse and used it to buy cigarettes. I also crept around at night and looked through the neighbours' windows.'

Zak breaks a bread roll. It looks tiny in his oversized hands.

'You're right,' he says. 'It's odd that you did those things in secret if your objective was to not get invited back. Why break the eggs and then deny it? Why let the neighbour's dog into our yard to kill all—'

The waiter appears. The menus are hardback and cloth-bound, lengthy enough to warrant a tasselled bookmark in case you lose your place. Ali is sufficiently fluent – and his manner sufficiently brusque – to disable the waiter's professional condescension. Zak does his best. His French is seaworthy but built for short hops, like one of those cable ferries propelled by grit and determination.

'*Lapin*, is that rabbit?' says Zak, once their order has been taken. 'Do you not find it chewy?'

'Obviously not.'

'My father took me hunting once in the hills outside Aleppo.'

'Your father was a hunter?'

'Why's that surprising?' says Zak.

'I never saw a rifle in his house. Why didn't he take us hunting when I was staying with you? It would have been more interesting than going to the gym with you.'

'You only came to the gym twice. Anyway, I hit a rabbit with my first shot.'

'Pure luck.'

'I don't think you'd be a good shot,' says Zak. 'Anyway—'

'I'm a very good shot.'

'You're too short.'

'The last time I hunted,' says Ali, 'I hit six or seven birds. Easily.'

'I'm talking about real hunting, not what they do here, not when they stuff pheasants or ducks with so much food that they can barely get off the ground.'

'This wasn't in France, it was in Iran.'

I see what Zak is doing here. This is interesting. This is clever.

'You went hunting in Iran?' says Zak.

'With my uncle. He hit a wolf.'

148

'Is this the uncle who's a university professor?'

'What, does that mean he can't shoot?' says Ali.

'So your uncle, what's his—'

'He also clipped a gazelle but she got away.'

'What's his name, your—'

'He was very impressed by my aim.'

'What's—'

'This actually really annoys me,' says Ali. 'The thought that your father had a rifle in the house and never mentioned it. Why did he never suggest we go hunting? Why didn't you?'

I detect Aphra's hand in this. Zak has done nothing to suggest he'd be capable of coming up with a tactic like this on his own. That said, he delivered it very naturally. He's absorbed her advice, that he should be himself, that he should fit her requirements to the shape of his character, in the same way a hand fits into a glove, rather than the other way around. He also let it go just in time. You can't ask the same question three times.

'Well?' says Ali.

He's angry. It's hard to see how missing out on a hunting trip twenty-five years ago might trigger this response, but you never know, you never *really* know with a person which floorboard is going to creak, whether a cracked pipe will drip this way or that, where the rats have nested.

'He probably didn't trust you around guns,' says Zak.

He's making a joke, trying to lighten the mood, but I wouldn't have advised him to say that, speaking personally.

Ali looks at him for a while, even while the food is being served. It makes Zak uncomfortable. With a spoon he rummages among the contents of his bouillabaisse.

'I suppose that to know for certain what your father thought about anything you'd have to read his diary,' says Ali. 'Do you have it?'

Zak shakes his head. 'I didn't know he kept a diary.'

'You said that you came to see me to connect with the memory of your father. I think that's a really profound insight, Zaki. I applaud you for it. And I know that you'll want to connect with the truth, not just an idealised version, not just some warm words about kitchen tiles and tangerine trees.'

Zak is still looking into his bouillabaisse. He sees a mussel, he sees a piece of onion.

'Look at me, Zaki.'

'I don't want to talk to you about my father.'

'You know already, don't you. Your father was human like anyone else. He had mixed feelings about you, he had complicated feelings. You were his only son, yes. But you came out of a marriage that made him unhappy, you were from a country he didn't like. There were days when he would look at you and think, I don't recognise that boy. It's better that he spends ten months of the year with his mother. Did it ever seem odd to you that he invited me to spend summers with you – the only time he had with you? Did you ever think that maybe he wanted someone to distract you so that he wouldn't have to spend so much time with you himself?'

Zak prods a piece of orange peel, sets it rocking. A solitary prawn bobs, curiously human, curled and flayed.

'He always wrote in Arabic,' Zak says, still looking down. 'If he wrote a diary, it would have been in Arabic.'

'So?'

'I've heard you speak Arabic. It's not good enough to read a hand-written diary.'

'Really? With a dictionary, with hours to kill?' says Ali.

'You said he was sleeping with Umm Saida. I know that's not true. You'd know that wasn't true if you'd read his diary.'

'You don't *know* it's not true. How could you?' Ali lifts his cutlery for the first time, tears into the rabbit. Holding aloft a forkful of red meat, he continues. 'Why are you here, Zaki? Why are you *really* here? I'm sure you have plenty of other friends you could look up. What about that guy who wanted to do an MBA in Paris?'

He watches, chewing, as Zak blushes.

'I wouldn't say he's a friend,' says Zak. 'I haven't seen him for ages.'

It's like staring at a colour chart, it's like trying to pick the right shade of red for a feature wall.

'How did you meet him?' says Ali.

'I can't remember. He might have been a patient.'

'A patient? He told me you met at a Narcotics Anonymous meeting.'

So this is spying, thinks Zak. He feels curiously resigned. He is being outplayed, he can see that, and Ali has just given him a glimpse of the range and breadth of what's coming down the line. Take the revelation that Ali knows Zak attends NA. That he knew Zak had a problem with addiction and yet put a shot in his coffee is a useful reminder of his ruthlessness. But they both know that Zak didn't complain about the shot at the time, or even mention it, so now Ali also knows that Zak is either drinking again or vulnerable in that respect.

'Well?' says Ali.

Zak thinks about saying something to bring this to an end. If he were to admit exactly what he's doing, if he were to lay out the story of the patient who'd moved from Paris, and the undercover agent at the NA meeting, and Aphra's appearance at his surgery just that morning, then he wouldn't have to do this any more. It would all just stop. As much as he is disillusioned with spying, though, he feels affection for Aphra, he feels that she has treated him fairly, which he appreciates. He would like to withdraw from this in a way that doesn't cause her any problems.

'Come on, Zaki,' says Ali. 'We're just starting to talk honestly.'

The only thing he regrets is that he has exploited the memory of his father for the sake of the operation. His father was a lifelong pacifist. How could anyone who spent three years in a Syrian prison enjoy harming animals for sport? He didn't even eat meat that often.

'Maybe I should call the waiter over,' says Ali, 'talk to him instead.'

Zak wants to say something. It might be childish, but he wants to have the last word. But he can't think of anything.

He puts his napkin on the table, stands up and walks out.

~

Sir William Rentoul stands alone at the apartment door. Even though McQueen and the dentist are not inside, Ned insisted that best practice these days is to knock first, just in case a neighbour happens to have their eye glued to a spyhole at that very moment. You see, Ned explained, knocking on a door isn't the behaviour one expects of a burglar. Picking a lock is, unfortunately, said the other one, but there's not much we can do about that, is there? Sir William can't help but hear the *these* of 'these days' as italicised, as freighted with such patronising disdain that the word can't quite stand upright. He has begun to hear the same thing in *sir*, in *you see*. All these words toppling like so many dominoes of irony. What happens when there's more irony than non-irony in a sentence? he wonders – a realistic prospect if things continue. What happens if irony becomes the majority shareholder in a sentence? Irony belongs on the placards outside the boardroom, not in the boardroom itself. You can't run a team on irony, or an agent. You can't run an operation.

Or something like that.

He looks around. There's only one other door, across the landing.

If anyone's inside, he thinks, the sound of a knock might rouse them. He kneels down and sets to work.

Although Sir William was taught the rudiments of lock-picking as a junior officer, he has never come close to doing it in the field. You'd always hand a task like that off to an expert. *Click*, he hears. The only thing that's enabling him to make progress now is the locked box of correspondence that he found under his wife's bed in the weeks after her death. *Click*. He was unhurried then, alone with the box and a set of picks that he'd borrowed from the partially deaf locksmith who works in the sub-basement. Life had never felt less like a lock than it did that afternoon, living never less like a skill that could be learned from a set of handwritten instructions filled with so many misspellings like *tumblar* and *backplait* and *cilinder* that it felt like an ancient Druidic text. *Click*.

These days, he hears. *These* days. They're my days too, you bastards.

He turns the handle, steps through into the apartment, eases the door shut behind him. He slows his breathing in response to a rising heart rate. In through the nose, out through the mouth.

Once his eyes have adjusted to the gloom, he treads along a carpeted corridor towards three doors. The first is slightly ajar. Sir William removes a head torch from his backpack and puts it on. Stepping in, he switches on the torch and is momentarily dazzled by his reflection in a mirror. Once the glare has gone, he looks around an empty bathroom. The shower hasn't been used, the toilet hasn't been flushed. He raises the lid of the pedal bin by hand, knows better than to use his foot, the one at home clatters like he's Keith Moon. Empty. He steps back into the corridor.

He expected to feel exhilarated but instead this is all strangely familiar. He moves around his own house in the most appalling silence too. When his wife died, he found himself being unnaturally noisy every morning – banging the cupboard door, arguing with the radio. He took up whistling. But all that has stopped.

Now he moves around so quietly that he sometimes wonders whether he's really there. When he retires, when he has nowhere to go each day, what will life be like? The question terrifies him. He joined the Service at twenty-seven after a spell in the City, having briefly considered both policing and the army; he had a cousin who rose pretty steadily to become chief superintendent of somewhere up north. Sir William sees them as vastly inferior professions. Policemen and soldiers, you can spot them a mile off. They roll out their officers into pre-cut shapes. But spying is different. Spying is a partially deaf locksmith feeling his way by vibration, or that training exercise where they push you into a pitch-black room and expect you to assemble a piece of furniture by touch. Something happens in moments like that. It was the first time he felt it but he's felt it since, on perhaps half a dozen occasions over the years, the spirit of the profession entering him, exploring him, tracing his limits, expanding him, laying bare his inadequacies, inviting him to dissolve himself within its pitch-black whole.

Two doors, two bedrooms. They're both empty. He's not surprised. They haven't even spent a night here yet. Footage from the Eurostar indicates that the dentist travelled directly from work with just the clothes on his back. Aphra McQueen carried a small shoulder bag.

Sir William's purpose in coming here is to install eavesdropping devices in the living room. He adjusts the weight of his backpack and walks down the corridor.

~

'Is there any update on the assassin?' says Ned.

He and Robbie are leaning over a mobile phone they've just

purchased with cash. On the other end of the line is the head of the intelligence cell in London.

'We've just had another log-in to the Facebook account. This time from Venice.'

'Zagreb to Venice,' says Ned. 'He's heading directly west. Do we have any sense of his likely destination?'

'Literally none. It could be anywhere. South into Italy, north into Switzerland or Germany. We weren't aware of his previous targets before he killed them, so even an educated guess would be difficult.' The head of the cell goes on quickly, almost without any pause at all. 'Ned, Robbie, before you go any further, we've got Philip, Director of Establishments, here with us. There's some high-level concern about the way things are playing out over there in Paris, so Philip is here to represent the board.'

'Hello, Ned, hello, Robbie,' says Philip. 'I'm sorry you've been put in this very difficult position. To be stuck between Sir William and your own operational judgement can't be easy. The board recognises that and wishes to work directly with you to resolve this as quickly as possible.'

A brief silence. This is an unusual conversation for a mid-level officer to have with a superior. Clarity is needed.

'Directly with us?' says Ned. 'Does that mean . . .'

'We have tried to reach Sir William ourselves but he's no longer picking up our calls,' says Philip. 'In the conversations we have had with him, he has made it clear that he intends to stay in Paris and retain hands-on control of the operation, in direct opposition to our wishes. We will therefore need to work around him. Gents, allow me to steer us away from internal politics towards more pressing matters. We must inform HAARLEM that an Iranian assassin is on European soil as a matter of some urgency. We may have another twenty-four hours before CASPIAN commits a murder, but it's equally possible that his target is in Venice and he's preparing to strike imminently.'

'We are in total agreement,' says Ned. 'This is utter madness. Sir William has—'

'Yes,' says Philip. 'Thank you.'

It's a difficult line to tread. Philip needs to undermine Sir William's authority without undermining the idea of authority. Philip's most significant operational success has been the role he played in a certain West African coup, one of the successful ones, so in theory he is well placed to conduct such manoeuvres. In reality he was simply there when it happened, but in this building, in an organisation where the most important skills – persuasion, judgement, acuity, perseverance – are all unquantifiable and liable to inflation, that can be a sufficient foundation on which to build an entire career.

'If at all possible,' says Philip, 'we want to get Sir William out of France and back to the UK before we inform HAARLEM, but only if we can do that in the next hour or so. If it doesn't look possible, we will just have to tell the Europeans and weather any fallout. The clock is ticking very loudly.'

'Understood.'

'There is an additional complication you need to be aware of. French intelligence has learned that Sir William is in France.'

'How?' says Ned.

'There is a pan-European agreement in place according to which any intelligence chief travelling on holiday to another European country must inform them in advance,' says Philip. 'It's simply so they can ensure adequate protection is in place should something occur. We do the same in the UK. In support of this, the French must have placed a flag on Sir William's passport, which was obviously activated earlier today when he travelled.'

'Shit,' says Robbie.

'It gets worse. His French counterpart considers himself a personal friend. He attended the funeral of Sir William's wife. He is affronted that he was not notified that Sir William was planning to come to France.'

'What have we said?' asks Ned.

'The French have reached their own conclusion.'

'What do you mean?'

'Passport data will have shown them that Sir William travelled in the company of two men who are half his age. The French believe this to be *une liaison amoureuse*, or possibly even *dangereuse*. They are worried that the nature, the . . . ah . . . the purpose of Sir William's visit may expose him to unsavoury types, that drugs may be involved, that he may frequent establishments where he is at risk from predators.'

'Predators? Do you mean—'

'I am merely relaying their concerns, Robbie, as they expressed them to us.'

'They think he's come here for a dirty gay weekend?' says Robbie.

'Do they know where he is?' says Ned.

'We said that we understood he was in Paris but we didn't know his address. As you will appreciate, the vagueness of our answer served to confirm their suspicions. So, gents, all cards are face up and on the table. We need some ideas. How do we get Sir William back? If you tell him the French know he's in town, will that do it?'

'I'm not sure it will,' says Ned. 'My sense is that for him this is all about being back in the field. It's about agents, it's about surveillance, it's about the nostalgia of picking locks and installing bugs. Political and liaison sensitivities are the last thing on his mind.'

'So what do you suggest?' says Philip.

'We shatter his illusion,' says Ned. 'We make him look ridiculous.'

'Go on.'

Ned and Robbie exchange a glance.

'Yes?' says Philip.

'We may have . . .'

'Yes? You may have what?'

'We may have already put something in motion that will have the desired effect,' says Ned.

'What do you mean?'

'As we speak, Sir William is carrying out a covert entry of Aphra McQueen's rented apartment with the aim of installing eavesdropping equipment. We told him that the dentist was having dinner with his friend — with our agent — and that McQueen was in a nearby café waiting for him to finish.'

'Yes?'

'She's not.'

'She's not what?'

'She's not in a nearby café.'

'Where is she?'

'She's in the apartment.'

'She's in the apartment that he's just broken into?' says Philip.

'Yes. She left with the dentist and walked with him in the direction of the restaurant, but then she returned alone to the apartment.'

'Jesus Christ. You sent Sir William into a property that wasn't empty?'

'We didn't *send* him anywhere, Philip. In our defence, we would have sought authorisation if we could have got hold of you or anyone else today. But things are moving very fast.'

'I'm not saying that you've done the wrong thing.'

'This seems to us to be a fairly gentle way of achieving our aims. If Sir William knocks first, as we told him to do, McQueen will open the door. They will both be surprised. He will not know what to say and will look ridiculous. If he doesn't knock, he will pick the lock and enter the apartment. She will confront the intruder. They will both be surprised and he will look ridiculous. Either way, Sir

William will have shown McQueen that he's in Paris, meaning that he can no longer operate covertly against her. He is redundant, and will look like an old fool. It will be a more powerful message than any of us could deliver. All that will be left is for him to return to London with his tail between his legs.'

'And the others?'

'As soon as our agent finishes dinner with the dentist, we will whisk him away for an all expenses paid weekend in the south of France. McQueen and the dentist can do whatever the hell they like. I expect that they will also return to the UK, at which point you can have McQueen arrested for attempted theft of a secret file.'

'While HAARLEM members detain the assassin on the basis of intelligence provided by the British,' says Philip. 'It's ruthlessly neat, Ned, as long as McQueen doesn't brain Sir William with a vase. I must make a note never to get on your wrong side.'

He's lightening things with a joke. If there's one thing they all know, it's that there's no *right* side to anyone in this profession. Spies will stab anyone in the back, even one of their own, even the one at the very top.

'It's as neat as we can make it, sir. There may be loose ends: Sir William, Aphra McQueen, the dentist. But we can snip them off at our leisure once the pressure's lifted.'

~

There's something about a head torch that makes Sir William feel like a superhero. He opens the door to the living room. A leather sofa, two armchairs, a dining table. The curtains are drawn and there's a television on the wall. Three shelves in an alcove are filled with ornaments and a spray of dried lavender. There's nothing personal in sight, nothing that looks like it might have been left either by McQueen or the dentist. He places his backpack on the table.

Before coming here, Sir William spent more than an hour going through the equipment. He finally whittled his selection down to three things he thinks he'll be able to install, although 'whittled' feels like the wrong word since the selection process was entirely binary, basically coming down to whether or not he could work out what it was, and 'install' is also the wrong word, as two of the three come with bugs pre-concealed in the workshop by technicians.

He starts with the vase. He doesn't even bother looking for the bug, knows it'll be too well hidden. Its utility will depend on whether there is already a similar vase in the room. He crosses to the shelves, finds something more black than blue but of a similar height and circumference. He transfers the dried lavender to his vase, places it on the shelf and steps back, signalling his approval to no one with a brisk nod.

The second device is concealed inside a plug-in air freshener. It's the sort of thing that might be noticed, so Sir William looks for a wall socket that's out of the way, finding one behind the sofa.

He returns to the backpack to consider whether a third device is required. The last one is the most challenging to install, since he will be required to drill a tiny hole in the wall to conceal it, and the drill itself doesn't appear to work in the same way as an ordinary high street drill. But things are going so well that he doesn't want to discount it out of hand. Ned and the other one are too junior for Sir William to care about their opinion of him, but reporting that he has successfully deployed three bugs will be a useful way of keeping them in check, of uprighting some of those *sirs*, those *you sees*.

His backpack is not on the table.

He blames himself. This is confusing. This would be confusing for anyone in the dark, in someone else's apartment. He looks on the floor around the table, in case the backpack has fallen, and on the sofa and the armchairs, and beneath the shelves where he placed the new vase. Nothing. He tries to remember the precise order of events. Did he bring the backpack into the living room and *then* remove the vase and the air freshener? Or did he do that outside, in the corridor? Just asking the question seems to create a new memory, so to be sure he walks the length of the corridor to check. Nothing. The beam from the head torch leaps around the living room, an external projection of rising internal panic, as though he's lost that too, or lost *control* of it, the panic is so abundant within him that it's spilling out into the room. *Think*, he thinks. *Think*. It must be *some*where. He pats his back in case it's been there all along. They told me I shouldn't do this. They told me I wasn't qualified. He pulls the chairs from the table, examines the floor underneath, realises he didn't take note of the chairs' exact position before moving them. He hears a noise. The beam jumps. He's a lighthouse keeper gone mad, searching for safe passage through the rocks, for a glimpse of a backpack on a wild and uncontrollable sea, for a—

'Sir William?' says a voice. 'Are you looking for this?'

~

Sir William wheels around, sees Aphra McQueen standing in the doorway, holding his backpack. She recoils at the intensity of the beam.

'Do you think you could . . .?' she says, eyes averted, pointing at his forehead.

He briefly considers his options, rejects denial and violence. He switches off the head torch.

'Thank you,' she says.

The darkness offers a third option, of simply ignoring what has just happened. It seems strangely viable. He wonders how long he can stand there, if after an appropriate amount of time she will allow him to sidle out, gently lifting the backpack from her hands as he passes, closing the front door behind him with a soft click.

She switches on the light.

'Would you like to sit down?' she says.

They both know it's not a question. It's a question in the same way that an interrogator might ask a detainee if they're comfortable, having handcuffed them to a metal chair. Sir William's total humiliation has reduced him to nothing. In some odd way that he intuits but doesn't understand, leaving now would seal his humiliation, making it a permanent part of him.

He sits down in one of the armchairs.

'The landlord left a bottle of wine,' she says. 'Would you like a glass?'

'Red or white?'

'Red.'

'Ah,' he says, thinking: they betrayed me. Ned and the other one. They set me up. They said she was out of the apartment. They didn't say they weren't sure, they didn't say they'd lost sight of her. They said she was out. Is it possible they sent him a message to warn him? He takes his mobile from his pocket, sees there's no message, covers it up by pretending he's checking the time.

'I don't usually drink red after nine but tonight I'll make an exception,' he says.

Aphra brings two wine glasses and a bottle from the kitchen, opens it, thinking: men of Sir William's generation don't use their phone to check the time, not when they're wearing a perfectly good wristwatch. He was checking for a message, but the screen was blank, meaning that he didn't get one.

She hands him a glass. 'What shall we drink to?'

She's made no attempt to exploit Sir William's embarrassment, and now she's effectively conceding the floor to him, allowing him to set the tone for their conversation. She's not doing it out of kindness. The situation is layered, there may be angles she can play. Because it is simply inconceivable that the head of British intelligence should be breaking into an apartment in Paris with a backpack full of technical equipment and a torch strapped to his head. Aphra knows relatively little about how spies operate in the real world, but she does know that *this* isn't normal.

'*À la vôtre*,' he says, raising his glass.

If Ned and the other one set me up, he thinks, they're getting fired. It's beyond unprofessional, what they've done.

She raises her glass, has a sip.

The only alternative to *them* getting fired, thinks Sir William, is *me* getting fired. He knows that he's ignored calls from London. He even knows that he's been running the operation in an unorthodox fashion. But he never expected the axe to fall quite so quickly.

'Well, this *is* complex,' Aphra says with a smile that says there's nothing she enjoys more.

She swirls the glass, considers what she knows. Sir William is in Paris with the two case officers she met. They have been following her. Sir William came here to install bugs in the apartment. None of this is a normal thing for a spy chief to do. He is angry that his team didn't send him a message to warn him she was here, which they could have done, since she made no effort to evade surveillance.

'You mean the wine?' he says.

She inclines her head as though to say: go on.

'I would agree,' he says. 'More New World than Old World.' He dips his nose into the glass, breathes deeply. 'Some wines take a while to reveal themselves, but I detect an unexpected partnership of floral notes and . . .'

He swirls the wine, dips again.

'Dried fig.'

Aphra thinks: what the hell is he talking about?

Sir William empties his glass. If Ned and the other one's betrayal was sanctioned by the board, he thinks, I'm out. In which case, it may be sensible to keep all options on the table. It's not as though any of us know what Aphra's up to. It may turn out to be the case that our interests align.

He stands. Aphra stands too.

He unplugs the air freshener and collects his vase, returning them to his backpack while Aphra watches.

'We should do this again,' says Sir William. He writes his phone number on a piece of paper and places it on the table.

'Maybe not *exactly* this,' says Aphra.

~

Susan has pulled her chair closer to the gas engineer; it turns out she quite enjoys talking to him.

'What do you think of it?' she asks.

'It's like drinking a mug of Benson & Hedges,' he says, pulling a face. 'Are you sure you're supposed to put milk in it?'

'That's what the other lady did. You should have seen her collection.'

'A connoisseur.'

'More like an aficionado.'

'What's the difference?'

'She likes tea, I'm not sure she knows that much about it.' Susan takes a sip. 'This building's full of people like that. You know, a few years ago now they brought in some big firm of consultants to look at the way things were run. They concluded that at best we were a bunch of gifted amateurs.'

He puts the mug down and returns to his task. Funny how she

never knew it was here. He's got an ordinary wall panel open. She must have walked past it hundreds of times. Inside are pipes and valves and a digital display unit that he's connected to a tablet. Engineers used to carry screwdrivers, these days they carry computers.

'Gifted amateur's not so bad, is it?' he says. 'My dad would give anything to go back to the days when rugby was an amateur sport. More flair, he says. Flair and individuality. These days it's all spread-sheets and data.'

'Maybe you're right. Maybe I'm just having one of those days.'

'Why don't you give it up? You must be well past retirement age.'

'You cheeky little sod. Four years left, I'll have you know.'

'Your problem is that you've only ever worked here, Susan. We think you lot know what you're doing, you think the rest of us know what we're doing.'

'You *better* know what you're doing,' says Susan. 'Of all people. There better be a certificate hanging on your bedroom wall. Otherwise that leak's going to blow us to kingdom come.'

'Oh, I'm just a gifted amateur,' he says.

~

'I don't mind the spying-is-a-game-of-chess ones,' he says, 'there's a place for that. But there needs to be a bit of high-octane at some point, otherwise I'm definitely changing the channel.'

'You would say that.' Susan sips her tea. 'As a gas engineer, I mean.'

He looks up, past Susan, at something behind her.

'Hello, Susan,' says Elizabeth, the ethics counsellor. 'Can I have a quick word?'

They walk a few paces down the corridor.

'I've got some good news,' says Elizabeth. 'I've explained your situation to the Director of Establishments. Philip is very understanding about these things. He is willing to let the incident with the file pass without an official reprimand. It is regrettable that it happened, and you must never do anything like that again, but he is prepared to let it go this once.'

'I appreciate that, Elizabeth,' says Susan. 'Thank you for coming to tell me.'

Elizabeth rubs Susan's upper arm, smiles.

'I'm so glad I've been able to help.'

'What about the researcher?' says Susan. 'What about Aphra?'

'What about her?'

'I still want to apologise to her.'

'Philip is going to handle that via his channels.'

She mouths *channels*, rather than saying it aloud, as though to impress upon Susan just how secret and effective Philip's channels are.

'His what?' says Susan.

Elizabeth glances at the gas engineer, leans in, lowers her voice.

'We need to make sure that the right conversations are had with the right people at the right levels.'

'What does that mean?'

Seven professional grades lie between Susan and Philip. There's no leapfrogging in government service, so even if Susan woke up tomorrow with a brand new set of abilities, it would take her a minimum of twenty-one years to reach Philip's level in the organisation. Elizabeth assumed that this gulf would mean something. Now she's not so sure.

She smiles, decides to change tack.

'We think it's best if you don't have any further contact with the researcher,' she says. 'Your desire to apologise is admirable, it really is, but it doesn't need to be done face to face.'

'It needs to be done by me because I'm the one who did the thing.'

'It's a question of how the responsibility is handled. In agreeing to let this pass, Philip is taking the responsibility for what happened away from you. He is now responsible – or, rather, the *organisation* is now responsible. The organisation will decide how best to rectify the situation.'

'An organisation can't be responsible,' says Susan. 'It's not really a thing, is it. It's . . . It's an idea.'

'Mmm. A powerful idea.'

'An idea can't be responsible for something. Only a person can be responsible for something.'

'I see this organisation as a community.'

'Listen,' says Susan, taking a boxer's little half-step forward. 'I did it. I did the thing. I want to make it right. That doesn't sound so complicated to me.'

Elizabeth notices the small gold cross hanging around Susan's neck, decides to have one last go at this.

'I suppose in a way the Service is *absolving* you of responsibility, Susan. It's a wonderful, wonderful thing. You're being . . . forgiven. Now, if you choose for whatever reason to hold on to that thing you did, it's not going to make you happy. It can be quite destructive, in fact, to cling on to toxic elements from our past. Much better to take the first opportunity to hand it off. Does that make sense? We're thinking of *you*, really – your interests lie at the heart of this. Philip will find the best way to reach out and make it right. Please trust him.'

Susan shifts the weight off her bad leg. She's getting a bit fed up of this, to be honest.

'I don't know how to be any more clear, Elizabeth,' she says. 'There's no reason we can't wrap everything up today. A couple of phone calls and I'm sure we can get everyone back in the same room. I'd be happy to have her boss there as well, I think he's called Julian, and Sir William, even Philip if he's got nothing better to do.'

Susan rubs Elizabeth's upper arm, returns to her chair. She picks up her paper.

'Shit,' she says.

'What?' says the engineer.

'She's the tea woman. I should have asked her if you're really supposed to put milk in rooibos.'

~

It's barely been five minutes since Sir William left when Zak walks through the front door of the apartment. Aphra can't hide her surprise. He sits in an armchair, pours a large measure of wine into the same glass that Sir William used just moments earlier.

Aphra sits down opposite him.

'Tell me one good thing and one bad thing,' she says.

He laughs, lifts his small tortoiseshell glasses, rubs his face and his beard with a large hand. He's still wearing his long grey coat with the curiously feminine collar.

'He admitted smashing the eggs,' says Zak. 'When we were boys. He said he wanted to annoy me because he resented being dumped with us for the summer.'

Aphra nods.

'One bad thing?' he says. 'That's where it gets tricky. There's a few to choose from. I walked out on him, for a start. They'd just put the food on the table. Plus he smells a rat with the whole Narcotics Anonymous thing, the guy I put him in touch with. You've never told me what happened there but it must have made him suspicious. He also put a shot of something in my coffee earlier, without telling me, even though he apparently knows that I go to NA.'

'I'm sorry,' says Aphra. 'I didn't know. Is that what made you walk out?'

He smells the wine but doesn't drink, at least not yet.

'He was talking about my father in a way I didn't like.'

'Zak—'

He raises a warning finger.

'Don't tell me I've done a good job,' he says.

'I'm going to tell you that your parameters are wrongly aligned.'

He slumps back in the armchair, looks at the ceiling.

'As unpleasant as they were,' says Aphra, 'none of the things that went wrong are relevant to your task, strictly speaking. We agreed on two objectives. One for you, one for me. Firstly, resolve the egg question; secondly, find out his uncle's name.'

'I came so close to getting it. Your hunting idea worked, but he got so annoyed that my father had never taken him hunting that he stopped listening to me. In hindsight I should have just let him rant a bit, get it out of his system, and *then* asked the question. But I thought: if I can slip the question in while he's worked up, he may not even notice it.'

This is positive. It's part of the healing process, recasting events in a different light, imagining how things might have gone better. I assume Aphra's going to send him back to Ali – that she's got him to this stage already is a good sign.

'So you met the first objective, and came within a whisker of the second,' she says. 'Is that a fair summary of what happened?'

When he doesn't answer, she sits forward, looks intently at him even though he's still fixed on the ceiling.

'Zak, forget everything you've read or seen in films. This is not a pretty game. It's not ballet, it's a rugby scrum. Players throw punches, they stamp, they gouge their opponent's eyes. You mentioned the NA thing. We haven't just thrown you on the pitch with no training whatsoever, we've tilted the field in the other side's favour. You see, the colleague of mine you met at NA and introduced to Ali didn't do a great job, to be perfectly honest. Ali suspected something about the encounter and so we withdrew our officer. We thought that was it – we thought we'd blown our one shot at Ali. Then you wrote your letter and here we are. Ali was *always* going to question your motives in visiting him after what happened. We knew that you'd get knocked about a bit, that's what happened tonight, but we thought it was worth it on the off chance that you'd emerge from the fray with a point or two.'

Zak is quiet for a while. He knocks his knees together like two dusty doormats.

'Are you going to tell me it's a game of two halves?' he says.
She laughs.
'There are no easy matches at this level,' she says.
'On the subs bench with a glass of wine,' he says. 'Very nineteen seventies.'
'What did Ali say about your father?'
'He said that he'd read my father's diary.'
'And?'
'That my father had . . . mixed feelings about me.'
'According to Ali.'
'According to Ali, according to my father. Depends if you believe him.'
'Did you know your father kept a diary?'
'No.'
'So . . .'
'I know. Maybe he's lying. But maybe he's not.'
'It's a clever tactic,' she says. 'It sounds very like Ali to me. I suspect you could say to any husband or wife, your partner keeps a secret diary, and part of them would believe it. There are things I know about Ali that I can't share with you, but I can tell you that he lies a lot. For example, he hasn't been to China this year, and he's not actually running the family business in any meaningful way. His father's still

doing that.' She selects her own lies carefully, one general, one specific. 'His father owns that apartment, too,' she says, 'and when he comes to Paris, Ali has to move into one of the guest rooms.'

He's so slumped in the armchair that the coat has bunched up around his neck and his head.

'I'm like one of those kids who breaks a bone if they make the slightest contact with, I don't know, a chair,' he says. 'You try saying to them, it's just a chair. A chair can't hurt you.'

He swirls the wine glass. A drop splashes on his shirt.

'Are you married, Aphra?' he says.

'No.'

'Who are you closest to?'

'I've got a brother.'

'Does he keep a diary?'

'Not that I know of, but it's possible.'

'Do you?'

'Keep a diary?' she says. 'If I did, I'd have to keep it locked in a safe.'

'Too many secrets. Meet me halfway, tell me one of your secrets. One of your own ones, I mean.'

'I used to work at a university.'

'How's that a secret?'

'Hush now. I haven't finished. The last year that I was there, just before I left to come and do this job, I broke into my boss's computer and posted the exam questions on a student forum.'

'Did you get caught?' he says.

'I was accused of it but so was everyone else in the department, at one time or another. There was no evidence to link it to me.'

'Why did you do it?'

'It was a period of upheaval. I needed to do something to break out of the world I lived in, something that felt liberating.'

'You liberated the exam questions. You set them free.'

'That's exactly how it felt,' she says. 'Like I had gone round the zoo at night and unlocked all the cages. It can be a problem with teaching, that knowledge starts to feel like a commodity that you grant others access to according to a schedule. Penguins at eleven, dolphin show at three. I was tired of it all. More than that, I was tired of myself as zookeeper. It felt like the only way to leave was to do something that took even me by surprise.'

'Your new employers must have loved it.'

'How so?'

'I don't know. It sounds like quite a spy thing to do.'

'I would never have passed vetting if I'd told them. What I did was a criminal offence under the 1990 Computer Misuse Act.'

'You haven't told anyone? Not even your brother?'

'Even more than the fact it was illegal,' she says, 'I just don't want it to follow me around. "Look, there's the woman who let the tigers out."'

'The letter I wrote volunteering to you lot was my version of the same thing, I suppose. A bit less dramatic than what you did, but the same impulse, perhaps, the same feeling of wanting to break free from it all. Except I'm back where I started.'

'Who says you're back where you started?'

'I should have just gone on a yoga retreat.'

There's a muffled noise from his coat pocket. He takes out his phone.

'He's calling me,' he says.

'Who is?'

'Ali.'

'Don't answer,' says Aphra. 'Don't answer.'

～

Ali is still trying to phone Zak when his doorbell rings. He opens the door to find Ned standing there.

'This is a surprise,' says Ali, putting his phone away. He steps forward, gives Ned a hug. 'Where's your partner in crime?'

'Waiting for us downstairs behind the wheel of a 7 Series,' says Ned. 'Come on, pack an overnight bag. We've got a treat for you.'

'What are you talking about?'

'A reward for all your hard work, Ali. Two nights in a very exclusive château outside Épernay. Champagne tasting, a tour of the vineyards in a classic car, plenty of downtime for the three of us to catch up. All courtesy of His Majesty's government.'

Although this was conceived primarily as a way of untangling Ali from whatever it is Zak and Aphra are doing, it couldn't have come at a better time, given that CASPIAN is on European soil for the first time this year. There's every chance that Ali's uncle will be arrested while they're in Épernay. As his handlers, Ned and Robbie will want to manage Ali's reaction to the arrest. He has willingly cooperated with them, but it's likely he'll experience some guilt and remorse that they'll need to manage downwards to safe levels.

'The forecast is good so pack your trunks.'

'Right now?' says Ali.

'I'm sorry we couldn't give you any notice but we're having to be even more careful than usual with phones these days.'

It's about control, too. They're paying Ali a lot of money. It started at 3,200 euros a month, when it was just about his uncle, but is now at just under 5,000 since he's demonstrated access into dark corners of the Iranian government. Everyone expects it'll go higher before long. In return for that, they'll expect him to do as they say, even though it's never couched in those terms.

'You've already got your coat on,' says Ned. 'You must have had a sixth sense that we were coming.'

'I've just had dinner with an old friend.'

This is useful. They'll want to hear from Ali what Zak has been saying, as it may shed useful light on Aphra's murky intentions.

'Who's the friend?'

'Nobody important,' says Ali.

Presumably he'll loosen up on the drive.

'We need to get going,' says Ned. 'Robbie's parked on the equivalent of a double yellow line.'

'I'm sorry,' says Ali. 'It's out of the question.' He turns Ned by the shoulder towards the door. 'And please don't surprise me like this again. I really don't like it.'

~

'I don't know why,' says Zak, 'but it's so weird that you had another job before you became a spy. It's like bumping into your teacher at the cinema or something.'

'Are there some jobs a person should be born into?'

'Other than a spy? Priest or imam, definitely. Those are the obvious ones. Anything which comes with moral or spiritual authority, I guess. You can't drive a minicab and then get ordained.'

'Why not?' says Aphra.

'Because otherwise all the authority comes with the job. I'd find it easier to believe that a person was born with moral authority than that they had it, I don't know, inserted into them at a ceremony.'

They're in the same chairs. Aphra has made them both a cup of tea, cleared away the glasses. Running the tap to obscure the noise, she emptied the wine bottle down the sink.

'The sources are a little unclear, but Jesus may have worked as a carpenter first,' she says. 'Like his father.'

'That's different. I'm not sure it was ever his profession. More like something that he grew up doing.'

'What about Muhammad?'

'He was a shepherd and later a merchant. But Muhammad's a prophet, it's different. Prophets are given a message, it's not their own. It can happen to anyone at any age. I don't know if you've listened to a sermon recently, but priests are definitely making their own stuff up.'

'I'm not sure,' says Aphra. 'You're saying this applies to any profession that assumes some level of moral authority, that you can't just switch to it at some random point. What about a judge? You can't just start off as a judge. You have to work your way up. They've all been barristers or solicitors first.'

'Judges apply a man-made law,' says Zak. 'It's the literal opposite of what I'm talking about. They look at a person's actions, then they look at the law, then they match them up to see if there's any overlap. Look at it this way. Where does a priest's authority come from?'

He points at the ceiling.

'Right?' he says. 'Where does a spy's authority come from?'

He keeps his hand pointed at the ceiling.

'The spy's authority comes from God?' says Aphra.

'It comes from a mysterious source – that's what I'm saying. There's something divine, something *godlike* about spying. No one knows what you guys are doing, how you're doing it, *why* you're doing it. You're massively powerful yet totally unaccountable. We assume that God and spies have our best interests at heart but the evidence so far is mixed. You both work according to some sort of ethical yardstick that permits waterboarding and dead babies. Take this operation. I have no idea what Ali's done wrong. I have no idea which other members of your team are here, other than the guy in the football shirt and whoever you put that extra wine glass out for. I don't even know what we're trying to achieve. That sense of power emanating from an unseen place is definitely otherworldly, which is why you shouldn't be able to go from – I don't know – accountant or consultant to spy.'

'It's not in my interests to say this, but since we're drawing a line under this phase of the operation I'm going to say it,' says Aphra. 'You really, really shouldn't think about us like that, Ali. No one has all the answers. Priests don't and spies certainly don't. It worries me that in your head writing to us was like writing—'

'Writing to Father Christmas.'

'I was going to say "God".'

'That's another job you should be born into,' says Zak.

'God?'

'What do you call them? The lookalikes, the ones who turn up in department stores. They've got the same mysterious and magical authority as far as kids are concerned.'

'But that's all spies are, Zak. Chartered accountants and management consultants dressed up in a rented Santa costume. There's no more to it than that.'

'This is where you tell me that you don't know why my father went to prison for three years.'

'Did you think we would know?'

'What about me?' he says. 'Do you know why I was arrested?'

'I don't know that either.'

He laughs.

'The funny thing is, I thought this experience would be enlightening. I thought it would be one long slow immersion into a fizzing vat of self-knowledge. I thought I'd find out things about my story and my character. But it might be possible that I know less now than when I started. Now I have to worry about what my father thought of me. I thought I had that covered at least. I thought that was one of the few things I had covered. But now I get to be ignorant about that as well as everything else.'

'I am sorry to disappoint you. There's so much we don't know. We make mistakes all the time.'

'I know you make mistakes,' he says. 'But God does too.'

He lifts his glasses, rubs his eyes.

'How much of a mess is your life, Aphra?' he says. 'One to ten.'

'I wouldn't say it's a mess. I wouldn't use that word. I'm very clear in what I am trying to do. In that sense it's the opposite of a mess. But my life isn't . . . it's not a particularly happy place.'

'Give me a number.'

'It's low.'

'Sub-five?'

'Oh, for sure.'

'Really?'

'When you were talking about having the rug pulled out from under your feet?' she says. 'You put it better than that. But that sense that the world is not the place you thought it was: I know what that feels like.'

'How do you cope with it?'

'You've got to fix your eye on an objective. It's really the only way.'

'What's your objective?'

'Murder, mayhem,' she says. 'That kind of thing.'

'Come on.'

'Yours could be . . . I don't know, it's very presumptuous of me to suggest anything. But you've said that you were a keen weight-lifter when you were younger. Did you ever enter competitions?'

'You're looking at the recipient of the bronze medal in the 1998 Shepherd's Bush Powerlifting Club's annual under-21s tournament.'

'That's impressive.'

'There were five entrants in my category. One of them was trying it for the first time.'

'Did he get silver or gold?'

He laughs.

'Powerlifting is different to bodybuilding, is that right?' she says.

'I can't believe you asked me that.'

'I'm just clarifying.'

'I'd take the number 64 from the corner of Armstrong Road, past a hairdresser's called Scissors Palace and a gentleman's haberdasher that I literally never saw anyone going into. I had one of those Adidas bags in blue, and I'd rotate between three different tracksuits, depending on my mood and what my mum had washed. You didn't need much: a weightlifting belt, shoes, wrist straps, knee supports. I remember the sound of men clapping their chalky palms together. The wooden floor was sprung so you could feel the bend under your feet when you took hold of the barbell, like it was alive.'

'It was really called Armstrong Road?'

'I know. What was your sport?'

'Fell running,' she says.

'Were you any good?'

'When I wasn't sick with one thing or another.'

'I could never stand team sports,' he says. 'That whole twelfth man thing.'

'What's that?'

'To drum up support for matches, our coach at school would talk about a noisy crowd being the equivalent of a twelfth man on the field. Have you never heard that? It's obviously meant figuratively. But there's something that happens when a group comes together. A kind of super- or supra-identity, I don't know what you'd call it. Team spirit? It becomes a thing that feeds off the group but is separate from it. Anyway, that's the twelfth man. He's supposed to be invisible but I could hear him trotting up behind me, whispering in my ear, telling me to try harder, telling me what the others would say if I continued to be a useless fat shit. He was always hanging around the changing room and running up and down the sidelines. He never turned up to weightlifting, though, I can tell you that. If he had, I would have dropped a thirty-kilo dumbbell on his foot.'

'Did you do weightlifting with anyone else?' she says.

He shakes his head. 'That was what I liked about it.'

'Maybe friendship is a team sport.'

'What about you?'

'Friendship? Bronze medal at best. Depending on the size of the field. I had my brother, of course. He was all I needed. There was a girl called Sally-Anne who stuck around for a few years.'

'Do you stay in touch?'

'We did for a bit. Her parents sent her away to boarding school. I think she's a nanny or something in Singapore now.'

'I always loved the idea of having a best friend,' he says. 'That, and growing up in one place, maybe a village by the sea where everyone knows their neighbours. We'd solve mysteries, have a secret den that was impossible to find unless you knew which part of the old gnarly oak tree to push aside.'

'I've broken so many rules tonight,' she says. 'One more won't hurt. Can we stay in touch after this, Zak? I'd like to have you as a friend.'

'Does that mean we're done here? Are we going home?'

'I think so,' she says. 'There's a mid-morning train.'

He nods, absorbs the news.

'You've got a . . .' He points at her. 'You've got a tooth that looks a little grey to me. That one.'

He taps one of his own teeth.

'UL2. Come and see me after we're back. I'll fix it for you.'

~

The Director of Establishments, Philip, stands in the centre of the room occupied by the intelligence cell. Assuming control of the operation, his first decision was to task GCHQ with monitoring police radio transmissions in northern Italy, western Austria, southern Germany and Switzerland. He is terrified that the assassin will strike before European counterparts have been notified. Updates are tumbling onto a large wall-mounted screen so fast they are almost impossible to read.

Lucerne: vehicular manslaughter, nightclub queue, two dead
Padua: domestic violence, victim dead on arrival at hospital
Oberammergau: tourist mugging, victim in ICU
Zell am See: violence at Far Right rally, multiple arrests, one victim
    on life support

His initial request to GCHQ was for reports of murder or attempted murder only, but it seems clear that further filters will be required. He is not interested in nightclubs or tourists or domestic violence. What I am interested in, thinks Philip, picking up a pen and starting a list on a whiteboard, is:

- Victims of Iranian or Middle Eastern origin
- Any reference to religion or politics
- Evidence of extreme violence or mutilation

He knows that the assassin logged in to his operational Facebook account in Zagreb and then Venice, which leads Philip to believe that he is travelling westwards. That is the sum total of what he believes to be true. It's what the spies call a low evidence base. Philip stares at the map, picks out Innsbruck, Munich, Grindelwald, Bergamo. There's little he can do other than wait. He has already written the urgent communiqué to the HAARLEM group informing them than the Iranian operative is on European soil. Before he sends it, though, Philip wants confirmation of two things: that Ned and Robbie have spirited their agent out of Paris, and that a chastened Sir William is on his way back to London. That will leave just Aphra and the dentist executing their baffling manoeuvres across the chessboard, their loops and zigzags and runic runs. If required, Philip will rely on the spy's classic fallback: plausible deniability. If the pair come to the attention of French intelligence, their British counterparts will convincingly claim total ignorance. He's half Syrian, they'll say, and she's nothing more than a former low-level parliamentary researcher. They're nothing whatsoever to do with us.

Sir William, though? There's no plausible deniability when it comes to Sir William Rentoul.

Philip feels little surprise at the way events have unfolded. He and his eight fellow directors have been accommodating Sir William's memory lapses for months now. They have actively covered up numerous errors of judgement and fact. What Philip didn't expect, though, was that Sir William's exit would provide him with such a clear-cut opportunity for personal advancement. It would be unprecedented for Philip to be promoted to the top over the heads of Sir William's three deputies, but a route has opened up to the slot vacated by whichever one of those deputies succeeds Sir William. Philip has always assumed that next in line would be one of his fellow directors, either the Director of Russia or the Director of Counterterrorism: he's always thought 'Director of Establishments' sounds too much like the person who refills the vending machines and locks up at night.

But the trajectory of Sir William's fall from grace – he was too old, they'll say; he should have retired years ago – will lead to calls for the promotion of a moderniser, and Philip considers that he has all the hallmarks of a moderniser. He is the youngest director by several years, and everyone knows that modernisers are young. He is also frequently seen around the office without a jacket and tie. Speaking personally, I have no opinion about Philip and his suitability or otherwise for one of the top roles. He has no actual values, of course, but I don't hold that against him. May the best man or woman win. The whole thing will prove inconsequential. The lesson every single one of them will draw from the Sir William episode is that change is required, whereas the lesson they should draw is that change is irrelevant.

Someone calls his name. Philip turns to look at the screen.

Chamonix: stabbing, multiple wounds, Arab victim, no witnesses.

~

'How did it go?'

'Great. You?'

'We just . . . we just went for a walk.'

Sir William nods. These two, he thinks. They . . .

He can't quite put his finger on what they have done that has left him so angry. He knows his triggers. Fatigue, dehydration, stress and unfamiliar surroundings can all heighten his confusion. He may have fallen asleep in the armchair. He looks around to get his bearings, sees the interior of the safe house, remembers where he is. He doesn't remember them walking in, just opening his eyes and seeing them both standing there.

'Are you alright, Sir William?'

The facts may have retreated, but they have left behind an emotional residue that yields some clues. He feels betrayed, he knows that. Betrayed and patronised, although the latter is a permanent feeling these days, so it may not be anything they did. The betrayal, though, the betrayal. Betrayal rises off these two like a stench.

'Did the installation go smoothly?'

'Fine.'

'No technical problems?'

'None.'

'How many devices did you install?'

He remembers the vase, which was similar in colour but not shape to one his wife made in her pottery class, and the plug-in air freshener.

'Two,' he says.

Without thinking, his hand goes over the arm of his chair to touch the backpack. His hand remembers first, his head second. He didn't install the devices. They're in the backpack. Instead he had a glass of wine with Aphra McQueen. He is surprised all over again.

Their eyes follow his hand to the backpack, which looks full, although it's hard to be sure.

'Have we received any audio product from their apartment yet?'

He shakes his head.

A half-formed thought floats across Sir William's consciousness. Is there any way that he might draw operational benefit from his condition, from the breakdown in reality's walls that he is experiencing? You wouldn't want an accountant with dementia, or a lawyer. But the terrain occupied by a spy is permanently uneven, foggy, virgin. After all, none of this should be happening. It defies the natural order that these two subordinate officers should have betrayed him, yet they did.

'Are you sure you're okay, Sir William?'

It all comes back to him. They knew that Aphra McQueen was present in the apartment but sent him in nonetheless, possibly with the support of London.

He smiles at them, showing his teeth.

'Fine,' he says. 'You?'

~

'Is that Susan?'

'Speaking.'

'Hello, Susan. My name's Mary. I'm calling from the HR team to book you in for your exit interview.'

'My what?'

'Your exit interview.'

'What's one of them?'

'It says here that you've handed in your notice. We do an exit interview with everyone leaving the Service just to make sure that all the ts have been crossed.'

'I haven't handed in my bloody notice,' says Susan.

There's a pause. Down the line, Susan hears the sound of some-one tapping a keyboard.

'Are you sure?' says Mary from HR.

'Why would I hand in my notice? I've got four years until my pension kicks in. Who's going to pay my mortgage?'

'I'm so sorry, Susan. It must be a glitch in the system.' Mary makes an exasperated sound. 'We've had a few of these recently. They've designed a totally new IT system to handle all the HR stuff and' – she lowers her voice – 'between you and me it's really glitchy. Last month it promoted someone three grades overnight. We only knew it had happened when the officer brought us their pay cheque to ask why it had doubled. We would never have known otherwise.'

Susan wants to end the call, get back to what she was doing, which was filing her overtime claim for the past month. The dead-line is today. Then she plans to review the staff discussion pages, see whether any rows are blowing up. There's usually something enter-taining, even if it's just complaints about blocked toilets or mush-rooms disappearing off the breakfast menu. Susan likes a bit of conflict. Last week it was all about some book that's been written by a former officer. *Why can't we prosecute*, said one person. *It damages staff morale*, said another. This wobble with Aphra and the file doesn't mean that Susan has changed her view with regard to any of that. She's discovered her red line, that's all. She's as fierce as she always was about anything that crosses it. In fact, if she'd had more time, she would have weighed in, posted something punchy like—

'It's these wretched IT contractors,' says Mary, breathing noisily. Susan wonders if she's wedged the phone between her chin and shoulder. 'They promised us this new system would streamline things.'

'Fresh from their success at the Post Office, no doubt.'

'What we're going to have to do . . . Are you in front of your computer, Susan?'

'Yes.'

'Great. Log in to the HR portal, please. This won't take a minute. Unfortunately I can't override the system, it's one of the new features they promised us. These days it's all about giving users control over their own HR choices rather than having to go through some centralised system. Now, can you see the tab at the top marked Leaving the Service?'

'Yes,' says Susan.

'Wonderful. Click there, please. Most of the boxes on the next page are populated automatically, there's no need to read it, but if you look at the bottom you'll see a box marked Reason. Just put anything you like in there.'

'Wait, I told you that I didn't hand in my notice. Why are we doing this?'

'I can't reset your HR status as full-time employee without concluding this process,' says Mary. 'I know, it sounds daft, doesn't it? But at the moment the system has you as "resigned brackets pending close brackets". I'm not allowed to override that. But if we conclude the process, I'll be able to reassign you to the system as a full-time employee.'

'Won't that have me as someone who has joined today?'

'No, I can enter your real start date, which I see is . . . 16th March 1982. That'll stay the same. It's really just an administrative thing at my end. It won't make a difference to anything else.'

'What am I supposed to do?'

'Write anything you like in the box marked Reason.'

'I've put, *Crap IT*.'

'I'll tell you what,' Mary says, 'this is actually very useful for us as we'll be able to take it back to the contractors as another example of a fault. I know it's a pain for you, though.' She taps at her keyboard. 'Now at the very bottom there's a box to tick—'

'Found it—'

'Then right click with your mouse. Add Electronic Signature should pop up . . . You still with me? Click on that, then the purple Submit box at the very bottom.'

'Are you totally sure this won't—'

'I'll correct it straight away,' says Mary, 'don't worry. Here we are. I can see it's come through on my side. Brilliant. Thank you for your patience, Susan. Have a lovely evening.'

Elizabeth, the ethics counsellor, sips her aniseed and fennel tea and smiles with her eyes at Mary from HR.

～

'What's taken you so long?' says Philip.

'It's not good,' says Ned. 'Our agent refused to come.'

'He refused? Point-blank? Jesus Christ. Why?'

'I think it was the short notice. He said he had things to do.'

'Was there any shift in demeanour towards you?'

'A bit, yes. We gave him the opportunity to tell us that he's seen the dentist but he didn't mention it. He's normally very compliant.

But we haven't taken him by surprise like this before, so it's hard to be sure. Is there any news about—'

'We had another Facebook log-in about half an hour ago. Milan, this time. CASPIAN is still heading westwards. On reflection, I took the decision to inform the HAARLEM network that he's on European soil.'

Even down a phone line, Ned and Robbie spot the lie. They exchange a glance. 'On reflection'. It's like saying, I took a calm and measured decision to. 'On reflection' means that Philip panicked.

'Intelligence agencies and police forces in that part of Europe are now on high alert,' says Philip. 'The Italians are flooding the area between Milan and the Swiss border with bodies, and the Croatians have sent a team to the internet café he used in the hope they'll be able to get a workable CCTV image of him. The Italians are doing something similar. If he paid with a bank card, they'll know which name he's using, which may lead them to a car rental company. Most of Europe is covered by ANPR, so there's even a chance they'll be able to pluck him off the road.'

It's easy for these two to judge, to roll their eyes, but there was nothing wrong with Philip acting the way he did, apart, perhaps, from a leadership perspective. The way he acted didn't exactly inspire confidence in his subordinates. But the prospect of the assassin having murdered someone in Chamonix, despite turning out to be a false alarm, rattled him. Spies aren't used to violent death in the way that police officers are. Spies are a sensitive lot. Gains and losses in the spying game are usually marginal, a question of grams and micrograms. Philip saw the prospect of a ten-kilo weight dropping onto his finely calibrated scales and panicked. He's only human, at the end of the day, which is exactly when the crows come home to roost.

'The French are mobilising on their side of the Swiss border,' says

Philip. 'Hopefully, it'll keep the focus away from Paris until Sir William leaves.'

'There's more bad news,' says Ned. 'I'm afraid Sir William is not going to leave.'

'Why? What happened?'

'We just saw him. Apparently the installation of eavesdropping equipment in the targets' apartment went smoothly.'

'How is that possible? I thought you said Aphra McQueen was inside the apartment?'

'She was,' says Ned. 'She *is*. There's no way Sir William is telling us the truth. I think he ran into her and left but won't tell us because he wants to save face.'

'Which might still be enough to make him leave, no? If he's run out of operational road and made a fool of himself in the process, what's left to stay for? That's how you sold this to me, Ned. But now you seem to be saying that your plan isn't going to work.'

I think I've changed my mind. I did say *let the best man or woman win*, but now I actively want Philip to be promoted as a result of all this. Thin-skinned, prone to blaming others, quick to panic: this is a man with so many buttons, knobs, pedals and levers, it'll be like playing a cathedral organ.

'It's possible,' says Ned. 'He seemed really confused. But he gave the strong impression that he was staying.'

'So absolutely nothing has changed, that's what you're telling me. Except that we've put every intelligence agency and police force in western Europe on high alert.'

He thinks.

'Here's what we do,' he says finally. 'We leave your agent where he is. There's not much else we can do if he refuses to come with you. Our tradecraft has been solid so even if the French realise that he's CASPIAN's nephew, they shouldn't find anything to tell them that he's a British agent, which will keep our face free of egg. But let's review his status after this is finished. I don't like his refusal to come with you.'

He thinks some more.

'Aphra McQueen and the dentist: well, we leave them to it. They're both deniable. Nothing whatsoever to do with us. Which leaves Sir William. We can't do *nothing* there. The French know he's in town. I'm going to tell them where he is. I don't see any alternative. But I will appeal to their head of service to approach Sir William personally, as a friend, explaining that Sir William's health is faltering and – exactly as they have concluded themselves – there are aspects of his visit to Paris that would cause us some embarrassment if they became public knowledge.'

Philip walks to the window, lowers his voice.

'Place one or two items around the apartment that will support their assessment.'

'What assessment?' says Robbie.

'That the purpose of Sir William's visit to Paris was . . . romantic.'

'What kind of items would support that assessment?'

'Use your imagination,' says Philip. He raises his voice to normal levels. 'Once that's done, take the earliest possible train back to London. If there are no trains, cross into Belgium and fly back. But I want you both off French soil in the next two hours. Is that understood?'

'There is one more thing, sir,' says Ned.

Philip likes the 'sir', although he wonders whether it undermines his modernising credentials.

'Yes?'

'There's something I'd like to do before we leave.'

~

Zak opens the front door to the apartment block, breathes deeply of the cold night air, steps out. He starts walking. He needs a little time by himself. His cells feel as though they have been reorganised. He begins his inspection anticipating permanent damage but finds himself to be in reasonable shape. Not the *same* shape, but he would be the last to claim that the shape he was in when this started was reasonable. If anything, it was profoundly *un*reasonable. It made no sense. He wasn't the sum of his parts, or the product of his experiences, at least not in any way that he could decipher. He wonders what has changed. At the time he was convinced Ali was doing permanent damage, but in retrospect everything that's happened today feels, if not cosmetic, then almost therapeutic, as though he's endured a particularly vigorous massage, as though like a wrecking ball Ali has smashed loose a plastery crust of self-pity, nostalgia and sentimentality, leaving behind something almost unrecognisable. He takes a left, thinking that he'll do a wide loop back to the apartment, where Aphra is cooking them a late dinner. It's certainly helped to talk it through with her. She may be the key to this – in fact he suspects that she is – that the warm attentive press of her character has loosened some knot deep inside him. He mustn't replace one sentimentality with another, though: the cornicing and ceiling rose will be back up before you know it. But the thought crosses his mind that a friendship with Aphra might just be a richer prospect than any other he has encountered in recent years. Maybe you just need to find someone you like and who likes you, he thinks. Maybe that's the key to friendship. Maybe then it just happens.

Or something like that.

He sees a person sitting on the pavement. They look up as he approaches.

~

'I'm sorry,' says the man. 'You couldn't give me a hand, could you?'

He sits on the pavement with one hand pressed against the back of his head.

'Are you okay?' says Zak, bending down.

'He came out of nowhere,' the man says. He removes his hand from the back of his head, examines it for traces of blood. 'No permanent damage, thank goodness. I'm just a little shaken.'

He starts to get up, wobbles.

'Let me help you,' says Zak, gripping the man's upper arm. 'Take it slowly, don't try to rush.'

The man stands, breathes deeply, turns his face towards Zak.

'This is really very kind of you,' he says.

'Do you want me to call an ambulance?'

'No, I'm fine, really. Thank you, though.'

'Did he take anything?'

The man pats his pockets.

'My phone, I think that's it.'

'Did you get a look at him?'

'He was wearing a motorcycle helmet.'

'Which way did he go?'

The man points. 'That way, I think.' He looks up and down the road. 'The lighting is so bad that it's hard to be sure.'

'Do you want me to call the police?'

'Goodness, no. What are they going to do? I'll get tied up in red tape and they won't even bother looking for him. The phone's covered by travel insurance so it's not the end of the world.'

He looks both ways, attempts a smile that doesn't quite get there.

'Tell you what,' he says, 'do you think we could walk together to the metro? It's only a few minutes from here. Safety in numbers and all that.'

'Of course.'

They start walking.

'Are you here on holiday?' asks the man.

'A few days away from work, that's all. What about you?'

'It's my wife's birthday tomorrow. We're here for one night and then I'm taking her to Épernay for the weekend.'

'Thank goodness she wasn't with you,' says Zak.

'It would have been quite the start to a birthday weekend.'

'You've left her alone this evening?'

'I fancied some fresh air.'

'Aren't we going to the metro?' says Zak.

'That's a very good point. She may try to call my number and find she can't get through. Do you think there's any chance I could call her from your phone?'

Zak takes it from his pocket, holds it out.

'This is amazingly kind of you.' The man takes Zak's phone, keys in a number. 'Do you speak French?'

'Poorly.'

The man turns away, presses the dial button, speaks rapidly in French for about thirty seconds before hanging up.

'She says it's my fault for always being so absent-minded.'

'You spoke to her in French,' says Zak.

'She *is* French. Or half French. Her father's from a small town near Bordeaux.'

'Why did you speak to me in English?'

'What's that?'

'When you called out to me. You spoke in English.'

'Isn't that curious? Did you look English to me, perhaps, was that it?'

'It'd be the first time anyone's said that.'

'I wonder if I revert to English in perilous situations. What would a psychologist say, I wonder? That in some primordial way I'm calling out for my mother?'

'If you were delirious and on your deathbed, maybe.'

'Yes, it doesn't seem plausible in this scenario, I agree. What about head trauma? Haven't there been cases of people waking up from comas speaking an entirely different language? If that's a real thing, this wouldn't be all that odd, would it? A bump on the head and I revert to my mother tongue.' He points to a side street. 'The metro's down there.'

They turn.

'What made you choose Paris?' says the man. 'If you don't speak a word of French.'

'Do you only visit countries where you speak the language?'

'Good point. And I suppose Paris is one of those universal cities, isn't it? It belongs to the whole world, not just the French. Like London, like New York.'

'I might peel off here,' says Zak. 'I've got to get back.'

'Have you got someone waiting for you?'

'It's been a long day.'

'See me to the metro itself, will you? My nerves are a bit jangled.'

Zak stops walking.

'There's not much I can do,' he says. 'If he'd knocked out a tooth, it'd be a different matter altogether.'

'You're a dentist?'

'Yes,' says Zak. 'What about you? What do you do?'

'I'm a spy,' says Ned.

~

Zak is confused. It can't be a coincidence that he's here in Paris with Aphra, a spy, on a spying mission, and now he's speaking to a man who also claims to be a spy. That can't be a coincidence. And spies don't tell you they're spies unless they're up to something, he knows this, unless they want to recruit you, which has already happened in his case, or they want to warn you about something. He smiles foolishly at the man who's just told him that he's a spy. His own behaviour isn't normal, he knows that. A normal response would be to express surprise, to pull an expression that suggests the self-proclaimed spy is a fantasist, to walk away. By doing none of those things Zak is confirming that he is also up to something.

He has an idea. He wonders how much time has passed.

'Sorry?' he says. 'I didn't quite catch that.'

The man watches him, content to let Zak do whatever he wants for as long as he wants. Why would he hurry this on? It's almost as instructive as a conversation, the way that Zak stands pinned to the spot by his own culpability.

'I just need five minutes of your time,' says the man.

Zak needs to reach some sort of interim conclusion. To be binary about it, this man is either friendly or unfriendly. He sounds British, Aphra is British. He's one of Aphra's team. He was told to watch Zak on his walk to make sure he was okay, but then he was genuinely mugged, or maybe Aphra needs to get an urgent message to Zak, or maybe he just got bored and fancied a chat and this is how he goes about it, maybe a spy can't pop out to buy milk without looping the neighbourhood a dozen times first.

'I don't understand,' says Zak.

'What don't you understand?'

'Why we're doing this here, on the street, like this.'

'How would you prefer to do it?'

Zak's confusion deepens. Isn't this the most perfect setting for a conversation, the man seems to be saying, and Zak can see his point. It's a Paris night, the lamp posts are topped with a cottony orange glow, the air cracks to the touch.

'There's enough happening already without additional . . .

theatrics,' says Zak. In case that sounds unkind, he adds, 'I'm assuming you weren't really mugged, of course.'

'No, you're right,' says the man, nodding. 'It was a bit thoughtless. Why don't you tell me how we can do this in a way that would make you more comfortable?'

There's nothing in the man's manner to suggest his intention is hostile so Zak still favours friendly, although he feels a warm spurt of exasperation at how roundabout the man is being. Where does it come from, he wonders, this hostility to the straight line, to the direct statement, to the let's lay our cards on the table way of doing things?

'Well,' says Zak, 'shouldn't we involve . . .'

The man looks at him, smiling, nodding. There's a moment of silence.

'Aphra?' says the man.

'Aphra,' says Zak. He exhales, smiles, shakes his head. 'You had me worried for a moment.'

~

'It's even worse than I thought,' says the man. 'For you, I mean.'

A couple approaches, hand in hand, leaning deeply into each other as though beneath an umbrella. The spy smiles at them, his blue eyes crinkling. When they've passed out of earshot, he turns his eyes on Zak.

'You think Aphra's a spy,' he says, smiling at the gaiety of it all. The idea is so absurd that it's hard to keep hold of, it threatens to blow away into the Paris sky. 'You think that whatever it is you're doing here is on behalf of British intelligence. It makes sense, I suppose. We've been scratching our heads, trying to work out what's going on. Why would you close your surgery at the drop of a hat and rush to Paris? What on earth could she offer to make you do that? You wouldn't do it on behalf of a stranger. But you might do it on behalf of a stranger who said that she worked for British intelligence.'

Zak is still smiling, infected by the lightness of the man's mood, how close he seems to laughter. 'What are you talking about?' he says.

'There are three possibilities. The first is that she's a crackpot. The second is that she's co-opted you into some private agenda of hers. The third is that she's actually working on behalf of a hostile foreign state. Do you know the term "false flag"? It's when someone pretends to be the officer of another country's intelligence service in order to trick a person into doing something. If that's what is happening here then what you're doing may well be illegal under French law. I'm no lawyer, though. It's best if you discuss that with someone who knows the ins and outs.'

'What do you mean?'

'That's only if you plan to stay. My advice would be that you leave France immediately. On your way, I would throw that phone into the first bin that you see.'

'Why?'

'Have you heard of the DGSI? It's the French domestic intelligence agency. That call I made on your mobile was to their public hotline, informing them that the number I was calling on was being used by a foreign spy ring attempting to undermine French interests. Silly stuff. Why would someone call from the number of one of the bad guys? It makes no sense. But by law they have to look into every allegation that's made, so I would expect that around now someone will be running traces on your number, which will probably lead them to a contract in your name, and from that they'll see that you entered the country earlier today in the company of Aphra McQueen. What they'll do next, I don't know. It depends how busy they are. They might do nothing at all.'

Zak's in freefall. Every book he's read on the subject of spying has used the term 'smoke and mirrors' at some point, but he didn't appreciate until now how apt the phrase is, how it's possible to be confused about your confusion, to be unsure whether you're confused about the right things, to suspect that your confusion is a wispy simulacrum of some deeper confusion that you haven't yet experienced but lies just around the corner.

Or something like that. To be honest, I'm past caring with this guy. He needs to hear this.

'There's another aspect to this, Zak. You're a dual national. That makes you vulnerable. Unlike Aphra McQueen, I do actually work for British intelligence, and I can tell you that we are perfectly happy to deprive British nationals of their passports. It's very, very, very easy for us to do, and by and large the voting public either doesn't care or supports us.'

'You can't send me to Syria. I haven't done anything wrong.'

'That remains to be seen. Until this moment your defence has been that you simply didn't know. You were tricked. It's not a great defence, in fact ignorance is no defence at all under the law, but it's something. But if you stay here beyond this point, that defence crumbles. I need you to understand that, Zak. If you don't leave France now, you may well arrive back in the UK at some point in the future to find yourself in a heap of trouble.'

It's a masterclass. Not all medicine tastes sweet.

He looks at his watch.

'Our five minutes is up. I wish you well, Zak, I really do. We don't often throw people a lifeline, but that's what's just happened. Take it. Grab it. Start swimming.'

~

Sir William sits alone on a bench next to the Seine, thinking about his wife. Paris was the first stop on their honeymoon. They had dinner in a small restaurant in Montmartre and a heated argument about his admission that he was about to become an intelligence officer, something he'd never previously told her, something she wasn't nearly as impressed by as he'd expected. The next day they drove east to Baden-Baden and talked each other into stripping off for the spa. Turning their borrowed Land Rover north, they headed to Copenhagen, Oslo and finally a small cabin fifty miles outside Lillehammer, which came with a rack of cross-country skis, a wood-fired sauna, bedding made of reindeer hide and a dozen bottles of aquavit.

A man sits down on the bench. Sir William recognises his profile but can't immediately place him.

All of the following is true: that their marriage was at times unhappy; that sexual attraction kept them together through the most difficult patches; that she never forgave him for insisting their children be sent away to boarding school at the age of seven; that he loved her very much and misses her deeply. He was unfaithful to her seven times, and he's aware of one brief affair that she had, with the owner of the Land Rover, as well as a long emotional attachment, played out in the hundreds upon hundreds of letters that he found after her death, to a boy she grew up with who joined the merchant navy and settled in the Caribbean.

'One never tires of such a view,' says the man.

When she complained that he travelled too much for work, or that he was too secretive, they would talk about retirement and make plans to return to Lillehammer, where they would ski the forest trails by day and huddle beneath reindeer fur by night. After she died he was hurt to discover that the first letter to her child-hood sweetheart was dated the day after they returned from honey-moon. If it had been an unhappy trip, he wonders, why did she want to return? Sir William accepts complexity and contradiction in his professional life but struggles to do the same with matters of the heart.

'Are you not cold, William?' says the man.

Sir William looks at him. There's nothing wrong with his eyesight, he can see the white hair crimping at the neck, the proud nose, the network of blood vessels in the man's cheeks.

The man sees Sir William's confusion and frowns.

'Is everything alright?' he says. 'Do you not recognise me?'

He can even see an earlier image of the man in his mind's eye, which shows all the ways he's aged in the year or so since they last saw each other, at the funeral of his wife.

'Hello, Jacques,' says Sir William.

At any other stage of his career, this would be a disaster. To be caught doing undeclared operational work in another country is bad enough, but for that country to be an ally, for the head of that country's service to be a friend, for that friend to be the one who sits down to deliver the bad news, well, it's almost unthinkable. This will be escalated to the Élysée Palace and Downing Street. If Sir William's career wasn't over before this, it most certainly is now.

But although Sir William can appreciate the scale of the disaster unfolding before him, it has no real effect upon him. It's like being told the size of the national debt, or reading an article about climate change. He's already started to lift away from his previous life. These things are happening to someone else, someone far below him on the ground.

'I am not here to cause you any embarrassment, old friend,' says Jacques.

How spying has changed, thinks Sir William. That you can be caught red-handed in another man's capital and be forgiven on the spot.

'These things happen,' says Jacques. 'A late flurry of passion. We're only human. It's not the end of the world.'

You can rely on the French, thinks Sir William. Passion is precisely the word to describe how he feels about spying. He feels a surge of gratitude that he is being given an opportunity to talk it over with an old and dear friend.

'Your two . . . companions,' says Jacques. 'They have left?'

'I suspect so. They've been keen to leave since the moment we arrived.'

'Oh, really?'

'To be perfectly frank with you, it's all been so much more complicated than I imagined, so much more . . . messy. I'm not sure I'm cut out for it at my age.'

Jacques raises his eyebrows briefly, nods, looks to the Seine for something unchanged and unchangeable.

'It was a mistake, Jacques,' says Sir William. 'It was my mistake, no one else's. I hope you can forgive me.'

'It's not for me to forgive you, William. We are of the same generation, you and I. There is a temptation to see these things as black and white. But that is not the way the younger generation sees it, and I dare say they are probably right.'

At any other time, Sir William would have seized upon Jacques' revelation. That the new generation of French spies are relaxed about other countries operating on their territory without permission is a significant piece of intelligence. Friend or no friend, you make a note of such indiscretions, add them to the file the moment you're back in London.

'It's never too late to discover new things about ourselves,' says Jacques. 'I suppose in a way I am honoured that you chose my home town. I only wish you had called me first. We could have had dinner. Marie would have loved to see you.'

'Is it too late for that?'

'I think so. You should probably return to London. There will be many other opportunities for dinner. Besides, you will be returning to a Service basking in the glow of success.'

'What do you mean?'

'To have identified an Iranian operative in the act of moving from Zagreb to Venice to Milan is a real coup. Everyone has mobilised their resources. There is a good prospect that we will catch him before he strikes. Your tenure will end with European relationships at the strongest they have been for several years. This is a legacy to be proud of, William.'

Jacques stands, as does Sir William. He is a formal man, and so feels some embarrassment when Jacques unexpectedly takes him in a hug.

~

Aphra stirs a pan filled with what looks like spaghetti, garlic, chilli and garden peas. She looks at her watch, checks her phone for messages. She walks to the living room and the window overlooking the street. It's bolted shut so she presses her face to the glass to look one way and then the other. She goes to the front door and opens it, putting one foot into the hallway to lean out and listen for the sound of anyone climbing the stairs or the shudder of the old lift. I'm not even going to try to guess what she's thinking. One might surmise that she's worried about Zak, who's been gone for longer than she expected, but I really don't care. If he's got any sense, he'll be on his way back to London. She takes her phone, begins to type a message but then changes her mind, remembers that he's allowed her to access his location. She squints, peers at the screen, grabs her coat, runs for the door.

~

Zak arrives at the Gare du Nord. It's only now that he remembers the man's advice to throw the phone away, but immediately a problem presents itself. If he dismantles it, scattering the pieces among half a dozen bins, the loss of signal will indicate to French intelligence that Gare du Nord was his destination. They will conclude – correctly – that he dumped the phone before boarding a train to London. It will be the easiest thing for them to search the train and detain him, and that's the worst possible outcome here, that he goes back to prison. He can't do that. He really can't do that. The thought terrifies him. But if Aphra works for the Russians, which is possible, or the Chinese, then by logical extension he does too. Given that Ali is Iranian, it's possible that she's a Saudi agent, a prospect that opens up new dimensions of fear. Even if he is cleared by a French judge, these things can take months, *years* to resolve, and thousands of pounds that he doesn't have.

An idea comes to him. If he plants the phone on someone leaving the station on foot, the French will think he's changed his mind and gone elsewhere. They will throw their resources into following that person, and by the time they discover it's not Zak, he will have slipped onto a train and made his escape.

He looks around. Almost immediately he finds what he's looking for. An elderly woman embracing her grandson, who's in his late teens or early twenties. He's put on his best blazer for the journey, and carries his canvas holdall as though it's a backpack, with the handles looped around his shoulders. She kisses him on both cheeks, wipes tears from her eyes. A hessian shopping bag by her feet holds her weekly groceries. She's off back home to a Parisian suburb, thinks Zak, to turn those onions into soup, while her grandson returns to university, in Marseilles or Brussels or London.

Zak finds a discarded newspaper on a bench and rolls it into a tube. Gripping one end of it as though it's a natural extension of his coat sleeve, he walks towards them. Her bag of groceries is slightly off to one side. A step or two away, Zak takes his mobile phone in his left hand and lets it drop down the inside of the opposite coat sleeve. Straightening his elbow, he feels the mobile bumping down the lining and sticking slightly to his clammy palm before shooting through the rolled newspaper into the bag of groceries. The whole thing takes no more than a second or two, and the mobile is only visible for a few millimetres, if that. He continues walking until he reaches a café with red check tablecloths. Stopping to inspect the menu, he glances up to see the pair still locked in a tearful embrace.

Any pride he might otherwise take in his tradecraft is lost in the waves of panic that splash over him.

He looks at the departure board.

He feels a hand on his arm.

~

'Is everything alright?' Aphra says.

He doesn't want a scene. The last thing he wants is a scene.

'I'm totally fine,' he says. 'I'm sorry I didn't call you but my phone battery died. I just thought, if we've done what we can here, if we've reached the end of the road, why hang around?'

'I understand,' she says. 'That makes perfect sense.'

He doesn't need to, but he goes further.

'There's a leak at the surgery, too. Huma called. Part of the ceiling has fallen in. I need to deal with that.'

Part of the ceiling? Part of the *sky*.

'Thank you for everything, Aphra,' he says, extending his hand. 'Goodbye.'

She shakes it. He wishes that she'd just go. Standing in plain view of the world with a woman who might be a Russian spy, he doesn't know why his mind always turns to the Russians, it might be because they kill people, but so do the Saudis, and who knows what the Chinese or the Indians or the Emiratis do . . . Standing here is hardly the low-key, incognito departure that he had in mind. He wonders whether they're being watched at this very moment. He wonders whether their words are being recorded for use in his forthcoming trial.

'I'm sorry that I've been unable to help you do whatever it is that you wanted to do,' he says. That should help clarify the limits of his involvement, but no harm in underlining the point. 'In retrospect, I probably shouldn't have let you talk me into coming.'

'Didn't you volunteer?'

He opens his mouth, doesn't know what to say.

'It doesn't matter,' she says. 'I really appreciate the fact that you came. I know it hasn't always been an enjoyable experience, which makes your good humour and patience throughout all the more impressive.'

'I didn't really *do* anything, though.'

'Oh, that's not true, Zak, you did—'

'As I said, I didn't really *do* anything. I had dinner with an old friend who I would have seen anyway.'

He glances at the departure board.

'I'll walk with you,' she says.

He walks with his hands in his pockets, hunched over, his eyes on the ground.

'Has something happened, Zak?'

'No, why?'

'You're acting a little strange.'

'I'm just tired. It's been a stressful day. I didn't bring my prescriptions with me. I need to get home.'

They reach the back of the security queue. Zak glances down the line to see how long it'll be until he's free of Aphra, spots the young man in the blazer three places ahead. He turns to wave at his grandmother. She looks nice. Zak hopes the French authorities will be gentle with her.

'Is it still alright if I come to visit you in Birmingham sometime?' says Aphra.

'I've got a busy month but, yes, give the surgery a call, let's see what we can arrange.'

The young man unslings his canvas holdall and drops it onto the X-ray machine belt. Zak can't see any obviously heightened police presence, listens for the sound of sirens. He feels his anxiety drop a notch for the first time in the past hour. It looks as though he might make a clean getaway, and on the last train of the day.

'Goodbye, Aphra,' he says.

'Goodbye, Zak.'

He doesn't have a bag but takes his coat off, drapes it over his arm in readiness for the machine. He watches the young man's canvas holdall disappear into the X-ray machine, followed by a hessian shopping bag filled with groceries.

His first thought is: who takes onions from Paris to London? Haven't they heard—

'Are you alright, Zak?' says Aphra. 'You've turned pale.'

He can't be on the same train as his phone, the phone used to call French intelligence. It's the one thing that links him to Aphra.

The young man has been asked to unpack his groceries. He finds Zak's phone in the bottom of his bag, holds it aloft in puzzlement, turns around.

'Isn't that yours?' says Aphra.

She takes it from the young man and hands it to Zak.

'Thank you,' he says, putting it in his pocket.

He turns and looks for the nearest exit. He puts his coat back on, smiles awkwardly, runs for the street.

'I've just remembered that you're a fell runner,' he says, once he's able to speak.

'They told you, didn't they,' she says. 'On your walk. Someone told you that I'm not a spy.'

'Aphra, or whatever your name is, I would like you to leave me alone.'

Running from her will be exculpatory, he thinks, yet more evidence that he played no part in whatever it is she's doing, that if anything he's a victim. First the CCTV footage from the Gare du Nord, then eyewitness testimony from the tram driver, now the fact that a security guard outside Notre-Dame is watching him try to shake her off. He's clearly trying to get away. He wants nothing to do with her.

'I want to explain,' she says.

'I'm not interested.'

Big gestures, he thinks. It's night, the guard's eyesight might be poor, camera footage will be grainy.

'I don't want you to walk away with the wrong impression, Zak. From what you've already shared with me, I know that this news is likely to land badly. I can see it *has* landed badly. I want to make sure you have the context, in case that makes any difference.'

She's flustered. It's the first time he's seen her like this. It's a night of revelations.

'Nothing you say could make any difference.'

'It'll take a few minutes of your time,' she says. 'Then I swear I'll leave you alone.'

'I can't afford to be seen with you.'

'Why?'

'I'm in way over my head. I don't know how this is going to end, but it feels like it won't be good. For me, I mean. Even if I don't go to prison, there's still the Russians or the Chinese or the Saudis or whoever. I can't . . . I'm not . . .' He fumbles for the right word. 'I'm not equipped for this. It was a mistake to come.'

'What have any of those countries got to do with this?'

'You tell me,' he says, turning to look at her.

'What did they tell you?'

'It doesn't matter. I don't want to have anything to do with you.'

'I'm not doing this on behalf of any of those countries, Zak. Or any country at all, in fact. Did they say that? If they did, they were just trying to scare you into leaving.'

'So go back to London. Tell them that you're innocent.'

'I can't. There's a chance I'll be arrested.'

'There you go.'

He might have stopped running but he's still walking at quite a speed. She rewinds the red scarf around her neck and tucks its loose end out of sight.

'Until yesterday I was a parliamentary researcher,' she says. 'Someone planted a classified file in my bag, and a security guard found it. That's what they'll arrest me for, but I very much doubt they'll charge me with anything. They'll just use it as a pretext to seize my passport and stop me from travelling. But that's nothing to do with you. You've got no involvement with any of that. And neither of us has done anything remotely illegal on French soil. I know you're angry, but it's important you understand that you're not personally at any legal risk. I don't want you to go home with that additional anxiety on your plate.'

'It's a bit late to start worrying about that.'

'I get that.'

'The man warned me that as a dual national I run the risk of losing my British passport.'

'That will never happen,' she says. 'If it comes to it, I'll shout from the rooftops that I tricked you into all this by pretending to represent the British government.'

'A woman facing criminal charges is going to stand up for me. That'll swing things in my favour.'

'They won't take any action against you because it would embarrass them. Remember that they themselves used you to get close to Ali. The patient, first of all, the one who said he'd just moved from Paris, and then the man at the NA meeting. You were right on both counts. They were British agents. I've seen the file. It was their clumsiness that made you believe me when I turned up at your door. They laid the groundwork for this. The last thing they'll want is for their incompetence to see the light of day.'

'They're *spies*, Aphra. They can do whatever they want. You said it yourself, they planted a file in your bag to get rid of you. They'll just deny doing all that stuff and I'll be left in the dock like an idiot claiming that I met spy number one when I examined his teeth and spy number two at an NA meeting. What do you think a jury will make of that?'

'The man was warning you. He was saying, go back to the UK *or else*. Stop doing whatever it is you're doing in Paris *or else*. Well, you've stopped. Whatever unlikely penalty he was holding over you is not going to be necessary because we're parting company and you're going home.'

'It's easy for you to say that it's all over. You're not facing the prospect of being deported to Syria.'

'What did he actually say?'

'He said, we don't often throw people a lifeline. Grab it and start swimming, which is what—'

'Which is what you're doing, if you put to one side the fact that you generally *stop* swimming if someone throws you a lifeline, you don't *start* swimming.'

'Jesus, Aphra—'

'It'd be like the police checking in with a criminal to make sure he knows the possible legal penalties of what he's doing. It just doesn't happen. The man spoke to you because there's nothing else they can do, especially because you're on your way home.'

'If I even get there.'

'Why wouldn't you get there?'

'He called the French intelligence hotline from my phone and told them that it was being used in some conspiracy to . . . I don't know . . . To undermine French national security. It's not funny, Aphra.'

'It's a bit funny, Zak. Did you check the number? Did you look it up?'

'No—'

'He called his pal, that's who he called. Check it yourself. Calls to those numbers are recorded. There's no way a British spy would let himself be recorded by French intelligence making a false claim.'

'Who says it's a false claim? Did the spy lie, or did the person who lied about being a spy lie? As far as I know, you *are* involved in a plot to undermine French national security, and if you are, then I am too. Can you not see this, Aphra? The spies think you're up to something, the spies think I'm complicit, the spies—'

'Oh, damn the spies, Zak! Damn them! To tell you the truth, I'm sick and tired of pretending to be one of them. This is the grubbiest I've ever felt, and that's saying something. What's inside me might be ice-cold. How else could I have treated you so badly? But at least it's *clean*.'

She stops, stands still. He turns to look at her.

'The worst part of this is that I was starting to like you,' he says.

There are moments when Zak feels like something cobbled together yesterday, a rough, ill-judged prototype that will quickly prove pointless, its many flaws so evident to the world that it's a miracle it ever saw the light of day. It's part of what he liked about Aphra. There's something in her that's just as broken – he's always been able to see it – but in her the cracks glitter like seams of gold. For a day or two it gave him hope.

She starts to speak.

'Don't,' he says. 'Please. There's nothing you can tell me that would make any of this okay.'

He hears his own words but also their futility. Because there's something different about Aphra now that she's no longer pretending. She was never going to be deterred, *that* hasn't changed, but he sees now that the pace she was setting was responsive to him, she was maintaining a forward pressure but one that yielded to him and his anxieties. That's no longer the case. Now there's no stopping her. She looks exhausted, electric, ancient.

'We used to go up Dollar Hill the first sign of a thaw,' she says, 'take our shoes and socks off and stand in the rushing water. The challenge was to outlast the other one. My brother used to say it was cold enough to freeze his wee boaby off. Being a boy put him at a disadvantage. We'd argue that one for hours. No wonder he became a lawyer, he was that good at taking an unreasonable position and arguing you into the ground, and no wonder I went on to become an academic, seeing as how he was my first specialist subject, along with the secret paths through the bracken and the woods where a huge hollowed-out fallen tree was so warm and soft with decay that it was like crawling inside your bed at night. If you were still for long enough, the wee bugs and creepy-crawlies would come out to eyeball you. "Can you imagine putting this tree in a box and burying it underground," he said one time. "We should do this with dead people. Let them fall like trees, let them rot like trees. It's as crowded with life in here as any city." I tried to find it last year. Our parents aren't around so it was just me and him. The tree was long gone, but I carried him for hours trying to find another one, and of course I didn't want to leave him in the woods on his own, I didn't want to say goodbye, but it got so cold and so dark. In the end I crawled inside with him cradled in my arms and we lay there until morning.'

He says something but I don't think she hears him. There are tears in her eyes.

'It was in Germany,' she says. 'There was a noise in his neighbour's house and he went to investigate. His wife went to look for him after he didn't come back. She found the body of the neighbour first, and then she found my brother. He'd been stabbed thirty-six times with a bread knife. The killer had made a botched attempt to cut his head off. The neighbour got it worse, if you can believe that. He was a former Iranian journalist who produced a monthly podcast with twenty-two subscribers. The police did what they could but didn't turn up anything of note, beyond concluding that my brother was only murdered because he interrupted the killer in the act. Their first theory was that it was a burglary gone wrong, which was ridiculous given the level of violence, but the Iranian was a widower in his sixties and so a crime of passion seemed equally implausible. They soon gave up. It took a journalist to identify a string of murders of Iranian exiles across Europe, but even that didn't lead to the identification of a suspect. Everyone assumed it was an Iranian government operative, but as soon as the file passed to the spies, everything went silent. "We don't comment on intelligence matters", that's everyone's party line.'

Zak opens his mouth to speak but nothing comes out.

'I applied for a job as a researcher for the parliamentary committee that oversees the spies,' she says. 'After two years I saw an opportunity to get access to the file. I'm talking about things that happened yesterday, but it feels a lot longer ago than that. I found out that Ali's uncle is the person who murdered my brother. But before I could dig any further, they planted a file in my bag and got me fired. I didn't know what to do next. I didn't even know your name, just that you ran a dental surgery next to a shop that sells discount fireworks.'

Where does a story end? There's a rain so light that it only exists in the orange glow of the lamp posts. The life's gone out of her.

'It's only just occurred to me how dangerous that sounds,' says Zak.

'What?'

'Discount fireworks. What was my part in all this? Why did you come to me?'

'Because I don't know the uncle's name. In the file he's always referred to by a codename. I know he's a chemistry professor, but there are twelve professors in the department. He's Ali's maternal uncle so his surname will be different. Four of the twelve are women, three of them are too old, none of them looks enough like Ali to make it obvious. I've no idea how to narrow that list down any further.'

Zak absorbs this, shakes his head.

'That was it?' he says. 'Just his name? I thought that was a warm-up exercise.'

The rain is so light, the walls of Notre-Dame are so wet. You'd be forgiven for thinking that all the water in the world was being held inside, that it was slowly leaking through the stones.

'That was it. I'm sorry, Zak. I don't know if I've said that already. I can't say I wouldn't do it all over again, so you're doing the right thing by leaving. I'm in no fit state to be anyone's friend.'

'What's your plan? After you get his name?'

'I'm going to write him a letter on St Andrews university note-paper asking if I can visit him in Tehran.'

He waits, expecting more.

'That's it? It seems a little . . . thin,' he says. 'Why would he want you to visit him?'

'Abu Rayhan al-Biruni. He was an eleventh-century Persian scholar whose work encompassed the sciences. I'm looking at him from the perspective of a historian and need the help of an Iranian scientist. I'll make it clear that funding is in place and he'll be paid handsomely for his time. All he needs to do is spon-sor my visa.'

'And then? How are you going to get him out?'

'I think it's probably best if I don't tell you everything.'

'It really is just a name you need.'

'I'll come up with something.'

'Let's think about this.'

'I've put you through the wringer, Zak. I can't begin to apologise properly for that. There's no way I'm going to ask you to do anything else for me.'

'We could develop a computer virus, send it through the university's firewall to the chemistry department, have it extract the HR files.'

'I'll look into that. Now——'

'He'll have had to put his mother's maiden name on his application for residency in France, no? Can we bribe someone in the Interior Ministry to have a look for us?'

'You know what,' she says, 'maybe I'll wait a year or so and then try with Ali myself. Pretend to be a genealogist, or wait for his parents to visit him in Paris and try to find out from his mother. She might even look like her brother.'

'I wish I could have another go. Now that I know the context, I really think I could do it. Not that I want you to go to Iran. That sounds like a suicide mission.'

He takes a step towards her, is unsure what to do.

'I think we should both go home, Aphra.'

The rain's really falling now.

'This is the way home,' she says.

PART THREE

Maybe it takes a monster to protect the bells of Notre-Dame. There are ten of them in the main towers, the oldest of which was recast in 1683 at the request of King Louis XIV. It rings in F-sharp. Nine of the ten were melted down and turned into ammunition by revolutionaries during the French Revolution. These information boards are fascinating. Quasimodo was lured away from his duties in the belfry by a sentimental attachment to a young dancer called Esmeralda. There's a surprising amount of story that follows from that, involving a lustful archdeacon, false accusations of murder, a cathedral under siege and Esmeralda's discovery of her long-lost mother. There's even a pet goat who can spell out a name with letters written on pieces of card. Needless to say, it ends badly for all involved. It's difficult to avoid the conclusion that Quasimodo would have been well advised to focus on his responsibilities and harden his heart against the sob story *du jour*. The bells were what really mattered; he should have been there to protect them. One was named after the mother of Christ, another after Maurice de Sully, the bishop of Paris who laid the first stone of the cathedral in 1163, but that didn't stop the authorities replacing them in 2013 because of what they called 'harmonic discrepancies'.

~

Zak has lain awake in the apartment on Boulevard du Général Koenig for the last three hours so hears his phone when it softly vibrates on his bedside table. He gets up, puts on his clothes. Aphra is in the living room. He has every intention of running this past her. From one angle it might seem inconceivable, given his state of mind just a few hours ago, that he is even contemplating this, but life is a sum whose answer changes by the minute, or so he is learning, and at this very moment he can't imagine any other solution than the one that has just offered itself across the screen of his mobile phone.

Aphra sits in a puddle of lamplight. Her head rests against the side of the armchair. She's still wearing her black raincoat, and her red scarf has been put to good use as a pillow. It might be the only concession to comfort Zak has seen her make in their short acquaintance.

He is aware that it would be an option, a *reasonable* option, for him to doubt the story she has told him. Her bag sits on the floor by her feet. He could easily rummage around, at the very least confirm her name. If she's lying about that, he can probably safely discard the rest of it. He allows himself to indulge his suspicion momentarily, but prior experience of such things leads him to recognise that in his case it would be a gateway to the heavier rush of paranoia, already beckoning him with its promise of never-ending excitement, of threats that never materialise, of life as one long spy novel.

Nah, he thinks. Not interested.

He intends to return from his visit to the land of spies with empty pockets.

Or something like that.

He gets a blanket from the bedroom, drapes it over her knees and closes the front door behind him with a click that is barely audible.

～

Aphra wakes shortly before dawn with a crick in her neck. I suppose you'd call it yoga, what she does on the floor, but it's remarkably brisk and lacking in self-reverence, more like a kind of human origami performed by someone who hates paper. She goes into the small kitchenette, boils some water in a pan, makes a cup of black tea. Her immediate plan is to buy Zak breakfast in a little café around the corner and then see him onto the first train to London, which departs at 7.22. This has been discussed and agreed, so she is surprised by what happens next.

'Zak,' she says, knocking on the bedroom door. 'Zak.'

She knocks again, harder this time.

'Zak?'

She pushes the door open and sees that the room is empty.

It's only when she returns to the living room that she notices the blanket on the floor by the armchair. She says his name aloud in the empty apartment. His first attempt at flight she can understand. He had just learned that she'd lied to him on an epic scale; it would have been odd if he'd done anything *other* than run. But they talked about that and much more until well past midnight, and it really seemed that in an extraordinary display of generosity he had forgiven her.

She tries to access his location on her phone but it doesn't work.

An answer pushes its way loudly to the front of the crowd. Just last night the British tried to persuade Zak to leave. The officer who approached Zak on the street would have followed him to the station, believing his intervention had worked, but then watched in dismay as Aphra arrived and caused it all to unravel. They would have no way of knowing that Aphra intended to take him to Gare du Nord this morning. In fact, they would assume she'd redouble her efforts to do whatever it was she was doing in Paris.

Why would they give up? Why would they *not* try again?

She goes down to the street. It takes ten minutes to find a taxi.

They called him, she thinks – it's too easy to ignore a message. In her mind's eye she assigns Ned the task, and it's his side of the phone call she sees. *What do you think you're doing, Zak?* he would have said. *The French are on their way to arrest you. National security offences trigger an initial detention of up to twenty-eight days.* What would Zak do? He'd panic, he'd leave – again. If that's what he's doing then she has no desire to stop him, but she would like to make sure he's alright.

Gare du Nord is so large that it's hard to feel she's searched every corner, but she goes into all the cafés, all the passenger lounges, all the shops. She walks the concourse several times. When she's stopped by a cleaner coming out of the men's toilets, she tells him that she's looking for her teenage son. A vantage point on a mezzanine floor allows her to study the crowds below. He's not there, she's fairly sure of it, and she's equally convinced that he wasn't on the first train to London, which has just left the station. She gives a few coins to a homeless man wrapped in cardboard. Their exchange prompts a new thought.

Is it conceivable that Zak would place a blanket across her knees *and* leave her to face the wrath of the French authorities on her own? Is the universe a place where those two things can coexist?

As someone who prides herself on staring down hard truths, Aphra is dismayed to realise that she has ignored a second possibility.

~

She rings Ali's buzzer but there's no answer. The blanket tells her everything she needs to know. The blanket says: I'm going to do something for you, Aphra. I'm going to get the name you've been looking for. But she woke up this morning with a fresh idea of her own: find a Tehran University student online, perhaps one already in the faculty of science, hire them as a field researcher and after a suitable period ask them to profile the chemistry professors so she can select the right one to collaborate on a project. It's not perfect but it's a good start. The point is, she doesn't *need* Zak to go back to Ali. She doesn't need him to try again. He probably won't succeed, and there's an increasing chance that Ali will relay this whole episode to his uncle, putting him on alert. Then there's the question of the emotional distress that Zak has already incurred. Aphra's grief is so enormous that she imagined there would be no room for guilt, but it turns out she is wrong. It takes her by surprise, just how wrong she is.

Or something like that.

She presses the buzzer again. She only has one idea left. She takes her phone and dials a number, turning away from the sounds of the street when the other side picks up, causing her to miss the midnight-blue BMW saloon that glides up the ramp from the building's underground car park, turns left without indicating and drives right past her before disappearing from sight.

~

'Is this your car?'

'Who else's would it be?' says Ali.

'It feels like an older man's car, that's all. I thought it might belong to your father.'

'He'd never buy a hybrid.'

'An old-school oilman,' says Zak. The car pulls off the ramp and turns onto the street. 'I suspect my father would have loved the idea of electric cars. For a while he was the technology correspondent for a Syrian newspaper. He wrote pieces about fax machines and mobile phones. He came back from one visit to England with a Teasmade. Do you remember those? Umm Saida was horrified, utterly horrified. Not that she would be replaced by a contraption, just that you don't make tea like that, you make it in a pan on the stove with tea leaves.'

'I remember her tea,' Ali says. As he drives he makes adjustments to the air flow, to the angle of his seat. 'She insisted that the water had to be freshly drawn from the well.'

'She looked at almost any piece of technology as a regression. As though it came from the past rather than the future. It took years before she was happy to switch on the radio he bought for her and listen to music while cooking.'

'I've forgotten what car your father drove.'

'A 1968 VW Beetle,' says Zak. 'Gunmetal blue.'

'Oh yes.'

The BMW glides like nothing he has ever experienced.

'He taught me to drive in it the summer before I turned seventeen,' says Zak. 'I picked up so many bad habits that I failed my first three tests in London.'

'That's your excuse.'

'That's my excuse and I'm sticking to it.'

'I remember the hot plastic seats,' says Ali.

'And that smell. There was nothing better than the smell of that car on a summer's day.'

'It was all bashed up at the front, wasn't it?'

'He was showing me how to do something, it might have been a three-point turn, when we were clipped by a pickup truck filled with crates of chickens. It was somewhere in the countryside. The other driver couldn't get his truck to start so we filled my father's car with the chickens and ferried them to a market a mile or so down the road. The farmer let us keep the last crate because the accident had been his fault. That's how things worked back then.'

'We're back to chickens.'

'I'm not going to ask about any of that again.'

'I'll tell you anything you want to know, Zaki, I really will.'

'Tell me how you learned to drive, then.'

'My father had an old Mercedes he let me use,' says Ali.

'Of course he did.'

'Listen, I would have preferred a 1968 Beetle with my father in the seat next to me. Instead I had this cranky old man who had taught my dad to drive too, if you can believe that. He'd once been a police driving instructor. We couldn't pass a checkpoint without him wanting to stop and tell them who he was. Literally half of every lesson was wasted with him telling some bored conscript about the time he drove past the Shah in a national police day parade, or some rubbish like that. He was incredibly strict about things. When you were changing gear, for example, you had to place your hand around the gearstick and not on top of it. I never understood why. After I got it wrong a few times he started taping a drawing pin to the top of the gearstick so if I put my hand there without thinking I'd jab myself in the palm.'

'What do you think he would have made of electric cars?'

Ali laughs.

'Like driving a Teasmade,' he says.

'Well, you seem to have learned something.'

Ali watches the mirror, at the last minute pulls the car to the right and down a slip road that swoops around to join an arterial road leading out of the city.

'It's an automatic, Zaki,' he says. 'Why don't you settle in, have a nap. We've still got a way to go.'

~

Sir William Rentoul stands in front of a 1982 Land Rover. He's removed the price card from its position on the bonnet, as though he's already decided to buy it.

'What do you think?' he says.

'This may be a difficult question for you to answer, Sir William,' says Aphra. She considered asking him on the phone but thought she'd stand a better chance in person. 'I want to know where Zak is. I want to know that he's alright.'

'Zak?'

'The dentist from Birmingham.'

He nods.

'The agent,' he says.

'No, not the agent. It's the Iranian who's your agent. He's called Ali. But they might be together.'

Sir William circles the Land Rover.

'What do you think of the colour?'

'Zak has either been taken back to London by your officers, or he's with Ali, your agent. Either way, I expect you will know.'

He looks at her, thinking: this might be the last time someone says those words. *I expect you will know.* He won't hear them if he returns to London, that's for sure. He won't hear them from his children, none of whom like him very much, or so he suspects. He invited them all round for lunch a few weeks back, and the vigilant silence that fell whenever he spoke thickened his tongue and turned him reticent. Looking from one to the other, he saw in their eyes a kind of thrill, as though it was a game of pass the parcel, with each wanting to be the one whose question tore off the wrapping paper to reveal his inadequacy. He feigned a headache to get rid of them as soon as lunch had been cleared away.

'Why did you tell me where you were if you're not prepared to say anything?' says Aphra.

'The price seems high, I know, but old Land Rovers tend to hold their value.'

'You might not be allowed to tell me anything.'

It's a small needle, but a good one.

224

'*Allowed* is not a word that applies when you're in charge of an organisation,' he says.

'We're all just puppets on a string at the end of the—'

'Nobody pulls my strings, miss . . .'

Reality tugs him back into its gnarly embrace.

'The truth is,' he says, 'I'm out of the game now.'

And not just in his own mind. He made it official about half an hour ago. He'd once imagined he would depart with a fanfare: a reception at Downing Street, tea with the king, a party for key global allies. The Americans would no doubt fly him over to Washington for something. In the end he sent a text message and that was it done.

'Sir William? Are you alright?'

A text message to *Ned*, of all people, someone humiliatingly junior in official rankings, but he didn't have anyone else's number. The reply was just as hard to swallow. *The board accepts your resignation, effective immediately. You are expected at the office at 9 a.m. tomorrow morning to formalise proceedings.*

He discovered this thing called 'voice notes' on his phone.

Oh do fuck off, he sent back.

'Sir William?'

'I'm afraid I don't know anything at all,' he says. 'I would gladly help you if I could, Aphra. But the truth is that I don't know where any of these people are, or what they're doing, or what the intentions of my former colleagues might be. I'm sorry. I really am very sorry.'

~

'Look at all these cars,' says Zak. 'BMW, BMW, Mercedes, Audi, Audi, VW, Volvo, VW, Audi, BMW. They all basically look the same, or at least as though they all came from the same mind. One of the things I miss about Syria is the way that the streets look like a classic car parade.'

'It might look nice but it's a sign of stagnation. That people had money for fancy foreign cars in the sixties and seventies – when the oil boom was happening – but haven't been able to upgrade since.'

'I never thought of it that way.'

'In the nineteen seventies Iran was the second-largest oil exporter in the world,' says Ali.

'Then 1979 came and the country shut its doors. The classic cars are a kind of high-water mark.'

'High, low.'

Zak picks up his mobile phone, sees that the battery is dead.

'I didn't mean that it's all been downhill since then,' he says.

'Of course it has.'

'You're not a fan?' says Zak.

'What, of theocracy? Of clerics running the country? Of police beating young women? No, Zaki, I'm not a fan. I just meant that old cars aren't better than new ones. Putting nostalgia to one side, don't you prefer this to your father's Beetle?'

'I suppose one of the attractions of old cars is that they have engines that an ordinary person can fix, unlike something like this.'

'That's true,' says Ali. 'Did your father know how to repair his Beetle?'

'I'm not sure he knew much beyond the basics, but he would pull up his little wooden stool and sit with the neighbour – who *did* know – when he came over to fix something. Abu Maryam, he was called. I saw him at my father's funeral. Even when he went under the car to fix something he'd never get dirt on that little white hat that Druze men wear. My father, though, he would always get a bit of oil on his clothes or his face, just from sitting there drinking tea and chatting.'

They're on the autoroute now. Ali moves into the outside lane, takes the car up to 140 kilometres per hour.

'Can your father fix a car?' says Zak.

'Same as yours. He's got a driver now who takes care of all that. But even when I was growing up, before he made a lot of money, he'd call someone else to come and fix it.'

'What about you?'

'My father wanted me to learn,' says Ali. 'He'd say, go outside and sit with Zeeshan, see how he does it. I didn't mind because he would let me smoke one of his cigarettes. And then once he'd fixed whatever the problem was, he'd let me drive the car in the streets around our house.'

'That's taking quite a liberty for a mechanic.'

'He wasn't a mechanic, he's family, it's different. Although once I hit a neighbour's wall and scraped the paintwork. My father wasn't very happy about that. My mother had to step in, smooth it all over.'

They slow for a toll gate. There's only one car ahead in their lane, another BMW, but it's not going fast enough for Ali's liking, and he swings across to the neighbouring lane and drives through the gate at speed.

'What's the fanciest gadget in this thing?' says Zak.

'I don't know. The reversing camera is HD, that's pretty cool.'

'I don't think my TV is HD.'

He lightly touches the mahogany-effect dashboard, investigates the cupholders.

'What's this thing?' says Zak.

'It's a battery pad. Put your phone there.'

The charging symbol appears on the screen of Zak's phone.

'Whoa.'

'That technology's, like, three years old now. I hate to see what instruments you're using on your patients.'

He glances across at Zak, still wrapped in his long grey-checked overcoat.

'Are you converted to new cars now?' he says.

Zak smiles.

'You're really going out of your way for me,' he says.

The needle climbs to 150, 160.

'It's actually a good opportunity to check on the chalet,' says Ali. 'My father is always pestering me to go there.'

~

Aphra is still at the used-car dealership with Sir William when she receives a text message from Zak.

Zeeshan? He's got an older relative called Zeeshan.

One of the Tehran University professors on her shortlist is called Zeeshan. Is that what he means? She checks his location again, this time is able to see that he's south-east of Paris, not far from Chablis. It's the last thing she expected.

Where are you going? she types.

I'll be back in town later this evening, he replies immediately.

Are you ok?

Totally fine.

Are you going somewhere with a friend?

Yes.

Keep your phone charged and switched on.

Ok.

Look forward to seeing you when you're back.

He sends a strong-arm emoji and goes offline.

She thinks: he's with Ali, he must be. The map suggests they're driving in a car rather than passengers on a train. She doesn't like not knowing where they're going or why, but there are plenty of harmless explanations. Ali's on a work visit of some kind and has invited Zak to tag along, or he feels bad about how rude he's been and is making it up to Zak with a day trip to wine country, lunch in the countryside, that sort of thing. It's even possible that Zak said he wanted to go somewhere and simply asked Ali to drive him. None of those things are inconceivable.

'I think I'm going to make an offer,' says Sir William, looking around for the salesman. 'These people never expect to get the price on the card.'

She hates the thought that all she can do is wait. She looks at Sir William.

'It's so strange to think that the day before yesterday we were talking in your office in London,' she says. 'Both our careers have come to an abrupt end, it seems.'

'Let's not indulge in self-pity,' he says. 'We brought it upon ourselves, each in our own way.'

'One of your officers planted a file in my bag. So, no, I wouldn't say I brought things upon myself.'

'What about writing a complaint and then pretending it came from within my organisation? Whose responsibility was that?'

'That isn't why I was fired.'

He waves a hand as though to dismiss her quibbles.

'We can reflect on events in our respective retirements,' he says.

'I'm not going anywhere.'

'You can do what you like, that goes without saying, but you'll need to find a new windmill to tilt at.'

'Why's that?'

'The file is closing as we speak.'

'Which file?'

'The one you were caught with.'

'What do you mean, Sir William? Why is it closing?'

Secrecy, he thinks. It's been there his whole adult life. It's remarkable that this thought has never before occurred to him, that secrecy might have driven his wife away, or at least kept her at a distance, created a cavity wall between them stuffed with operations that didn't quite come off, old files no one's going to revisit, the half-dozen or so alias identities that he used in the field. No wonder they couldn't feel each other's warmth. His work provided cover for six of his seven affairs. Late nights, last-minute trips, but also a telltale furtiveness, a distance that he could attribute to a mind preoccupied with matters of national security.

'Why is the file closing, Sir William?'

He lowers his voice.

'Because he's here.'

'Who's here?'

'The assassin.'

She hears only the sibilants, steps forward to make sure she doesn't misunderstand him. He repeats himself.

'The assassin. The Iranian assassin. As we speak.'

'When you say *here*.'

'In Europe.'

'Do you know where exactly?'

'He's heading west. Zagreb, Venice, Milan.'

Can it be a coincidence, she thinks, that if the two lines – one heading due west from Zagreb, the other heading south-east from Paris – continue on the same path, they will at some point converge?

'Who's trying to catch him?' she says.

'Everyone.'

Another possible reason for leaving Paris presents itself, one that barely makes any sense yet empties her lungs of air.

'But they haven't yet,' she says. 'Caught him. As far as you know.'

'It's just a matter of time,' he says.

Aphra turns away from Sir William, takes out her phone.

Be careful, she types.

Can you call me, she types.

We need to talk, she types.

She looks around for the salesman, she looks around for a car she can afford.

~

Philip, the Director of Establishments, stands in the middle of a crowded room. It's crowded with people not actively involved in the operation. They are here because word has spread that a significant success is about to be had, and people quite understandably want to be there when it happens. He could clear the room of everyone except for himself and two officers and things would proceed just as effectively. He could even leave the room himself, truth be told, take himself down to the canteen to do the crossword over a fry-up and it would make no difference at all, but that's not an idea he's prepared to countenance. One of the officers is monitoring the Facebook account being used by the Iranian operative, the other is drafting updates to the HAARLEM group. Philip is theoretically approving those messages before they are sent, but the changes he has made are purely stylistic, a question of replacing—

'There's been another log-in,' says one of the officers.

Philip holds up a hand to silence the room.

'Zermatt, Switzerland,' says the officer. 'Eleven minutes ago.'

Philip approaches the bank of desks to stand behind his two officers. He's removed his jacket and tie, although now he wonders whether a loosened tie would have been better than no tie at all.

'I'll draft a message with the coordinates,' says the other officer.

On the wall-mounted screen there is a map of Europe with each log-in location marked alongside a grainy photograph of a man walking across a car park. The Italians pulled it from a CCTV camera outside Milan. They also seized the computer the man used in the internet café. Work is underway to analyse traffic moving across

Europe and identify any vehicles that have appeared in the proximity of all four log-in locations.

Philip approaches the screen, stands directly in front of it with hands on hips, narrows his eyes as though running a complex analytical algorithm that will at any moment spit out a ream of insights.

The room watches, waits.

~

'Who were you texting?'

'The dental nurse who works for me,' says Zak. 'There's a leak from the flat above the surgery. She's getting some painters in to redo the ceiling.'

'It's a good time for you to be away, if the surgery's out of action.'

'I wouldn't have had to close it, if I'd been there. The damage is mostly cosmetic.'

Zak has taken off his long grey coat, folded it on the back seat. He fumbles for the handle, slides his seat back as far as it'll go, stretches his legs out.

'Have you skied in Iran?' he says.

'A few times, yes. There are some pretty good resorts to the north of Tehran, near the Caspian Sea. Darbandsar, Dizin. It's nothing like skiing in Europe, of course, but it's better than people would expect. They call it the Switzerland of the Middle East.'

'Come on, no one has *ever* called Iran the Switzerland of the Middle East,' says Zak, turning to smile at Ali. 'Except maybe the Iranian tourist board, but even then they would have had the Lebanese tourist board calling up to complain about copyright infringement.'

'I'm just saying I've heard people call it that,' says Ali.

'It would be a tough job, working for the Iranian tourist board. I can see why they would feel the need to be . . . creative.'

'I don't know. They're working with good raw materials. Plenty of UNESCO World Heritage sites, beautiful countryside, rich history, low prices. Tourist numbers are definitely increasing.'

They've been in the outside lane the whole way. Ali does this thing of driving right up behind cars, to within what feels like a few metres, and flashing his lights until they move out of the way.

'This may be too nosy of me,' says Zak, 'in which case tell me to mind my own business, but how does it work, doing business in Iran? Does your father have to make some sort of compromise with the government?'

'He is careful to stay away from politics. He goes to dinners organised by the Minister of Trade, this sort of thing, and I expect he makes some political contributions as well. You need to have allies. But he's not such a rich businessman that they will notice him, to be honest. I think he makes sure to keep most of his money outside the country.'

'Nowhere safer than Switzerland. The Switzerland of Europe, that is, not the Switzerland of the Middle East. Is that why he bought a place there? As an investment?'

'Probably.'

'Does he rent it out?'

'Sometimes.'

'What's it like?'

'If you've seen one chalet, you've seen them all.'

'I've never seen a chalet,' says Zak. 'I mean, I've seen a picture of a chalet, but I've never been inside one.'

'It's your lucky day.'

'How often would you go there as a kid?'

'Not that often.'

'But you keep things there,' says Zak. 'You keep my father's diary there.'

'One year I brought a whole load of boxes over from Iran and needed somewhere to store them, so I put them in the attic,' says Ali. 'I'll be glad to give it back to you. My father's always asking me to get rid of the stuff up there.'

'Who looks after it when you're not there?'

Ali shrugs, shakes his head, as though exasperated by all the questions.

'I have no idea,' he says. 'A local woman.'

Zak is still looking at him, as though considering a question like *what's her name?* or *does she know we're coming?* or *which websites is it listed on?* but he doesn't say anything, he just turns to watch the world flashing by at a speed which makes everything feel out of control.

～

It's been a while since Aphra drove an automatic. She keeps on reaching for a gearstick, for a clutch, for a different idea to explain why Zak and Ali are driving at high speed towards the last known location of an Iranian operative who has killed at least ten people on European soil. Her phone is clipped to the dashboard. She chases the blue dot. Every other idea that presents itself is a slip road off the inevitable. There's no need for exploratory diversions if it's obvious where you're going, and it *is* obvious, or at least it's obvious that it's somewhere bad, somewhere Aphra really doesn't want him to go. He hasn't read any of her messages. She's thought of calling him, but it might put him in a difficult position if he's not ready with an explanation of who she is. She's thought of calling the police, but she's not sure what she would say, and according to Sir William it sounds as though they're already involved. How things can change in a matter of days. A week ago all her energies would have been directed at the man who killed her brother, but now he exists on the margin of her thoughts, he exists in relation to Zak, who stands in the centre, dressed in his long grey coat with the curiously feminine collar, his ears turned out like wing mirrors, a half-smile on his tired face.

~

'The diary has travelled much further than my father ever imagined,' says Zak. 'Aleppo to Tehran and then to Lausanne.'

'And now it'll go back with you to Birmingham.'

They've crossed the Swiss border. The road started climbing about an hour ago, and twisting violently. Ali fights with the car to prevent any of that slowing their onward progress.

'I'm still confused, if I'm honest,' says Zak. 'If his diary went missing all those years ago, why didn't he ask us if we'd seen it? Why did he never mention it?'

'I think he assumed that you'd taken it, Zaki.'

'Why would he assume that?'

'I'm not saying it's rational. His worst fear was that you would read the diary's contents. Once he'd had that thought he just couldn't put it to one side,' says Ali.

'But he never said anything.'

'That's my point. He assumed that you'd read the contents. The last thing he would have wanted was to have to explain all that to you. Much better to pretend nothing had happened.'

Zak looks out of the window at fields filled with cows the colour of caramel.

'If he was an Englishman, maybe,' he says. 'I was awake last night thinking about this. It's just not how we communicated with each other.' He lifts his glasses, rubs his eyes. 'What does it look like?'

'What do you mean?'

'What does the diary look like?'

'It's a notebook,' says Ali.

'What did you do with it?'

'I read it, then stuffed it at the bottom of my bag and forgot about it. At some point I was going to put it back. It was only when I got back to Tehran that I realised I still had it.'

'It seems incredible to me that he would never suspect you. Especially as you were obviously so unhappy staying with us. What date did you take it?'

'How should I know?' says Ali.

'From the last entry.'

'I don't remember.'

'Was it after all that stuff happened with the broken eggs and the dead chickens?'

'I knew you'd go back there at some point.'

'You said you were happy to talk about all that.'

'It's just boring, Zaki. Really boring.'

'You've admitted that you smashed the eggs, will you also admit that you let the neighbour's dog into the chicken coop?'

'I will admit that I never expected we would be talking about that summer thirty years later.'

'We're only talking about that summer because it's when you stole my father's diary. Can't you see that it's difficult for me to hear that he felt that way about me? Can't you imagine how you would feel if I'd read your father's diary and told you that he never really liked you?'

'I know exactly how my father felt about me, Zaki. I don't need a diary to tell me that. Most days he would tell me himself. That I am an embarrassment, that I bring shame upon the family, that I am inadequate, that I deserve every single slap and kick, that he wishes I was more like Zaki with his good grades and strong physique and respectful behaviour that makes a father so proud.'

He turns the car off the main road and onto a track that coils upwards into the hills.

'I'm sorry, Ali.'

They drive through a forest of mountain pine and silver birch.

'Is that why you've made this story up, because you were jealous?'

'I haven't made anything up, Zaki. It's only a little bit further. You'll have the diary in your hands soon enough.'

~

The car is so heavy that Zak imagines he can hear stones cracking open under the weight of its tyres.

'Where are we?' he says.

Ali opens his door, walks briskly to the boot, retrieves a small backpack.

'What is this place?' says Zak.

'The chalet is up there,' says Ali, looking up to the thickly wooded hills. 'It overlooks Lausanne. The views are really spectacular.'

'You've seen one chalet, you've seen them all. Remember saying that?'

'I didn't want to spoil the surprise.'

'There's no road? How did the builders get their trucks up?'

'There's a road from the other side but we've been sitting in the car for so long I thought it would be nicer to approach on foot.'

'Is there anyone else up there?'

'No.'

'What about the local woman who cleans?'

'She doesn't work today, but I asked her to leave some supplies in the fridge for us. We can have lunch on the balcony and then head back to Paris.'

'With my father's diary.'

'With your father's diary,' says Ali. 'Come on, let's go.'

~

Ali leads the way along a narrow path that quickly enters a wood. The air turns cool. Zak pulls on his coat. They walk in silence for a half-mile, saving their breath for the steep incline. The birds call out their warnings. Zak lifts his head to listen.

'Let me catch my breath,' he says.

'Have some water,' says Ali, offering him a metal flask.

Zak drinks deeply. He feels the cold water on his beard.

'You didn't need to go all the way to Iran to hunt, with this on your doorstep,' he says. 'You should have brought your uncle here.'

He drinks again, hands the bottle back.

'Is he the same one who would come over to fix your father's car? The mechanic?'

'Why do you say that?' says Ali.

Zak shrugs.

'You said he was family.'

Ali puts the flask in his backpack.

'Are you closer to him than your father?' says Zak. 'I'm curious because I don't have any uncles or aunts. I've always wondered what it would feel like.'

'He doesn't have any children of his own,' says Ali. He swings the backpack over his shoulder. 'Come on, let's go.'

'How much further?'

'Not long now, Zaki.'

'I think I'll let you go ahead.'

'What?'

'I'm out of shape. Not like you. I'll see you down at the car.'

'What about the diary?'

'Can you bring it down?'

Ali looks at him. After a while he nods.

~

Zak's about halfway down to the car when he stops for a rest. Sitting with his back against a tree, he stretches out his legs and breathes deeply. The climb has really taken it out of him. His father has been so much in his thoughts these last few days that it's little wonder his mind turns there once again. It's a place of comfort. The quality of the sunlight, the colour of the tangerines. The birds have gone quiet, he thinks. He remembers that weightless feeling when you reach the top of your swing and nothing but the air holds you up.

He fights to keep his eyes open.

There are other thoughts that crowd in – how could they not, with such little time left? He knows what the water has done to him. He would have wanted to have children, but is glad in this moment that it never happened. The puff of chalk, the sudden give in the floor before a big lift. He's happy to have known the precise weight of his mother's hand. The way that Aphra makes him laugh. A teenage Ali, feathers stuck to his clothes, blood so deep under his fingernails that he'll never be free of it.

Zak knows with certainty that there is no diary yet is able to feel grateful for the journey that briefly led him down that path, for the way it has returned him with a new sense of joy to a place he should never have left. He smiles at his father. He holds aloft the tangerine he has picked. And at just the right moment he launches himself off the swing and floats through the air towards his father's embrace.

He barely hears the footsteps on the forest floor.

~

There's no struggle. Zak is already unconscious when the knife sets to its task, and death comes quickly, not through any feeling of mercy, there's none of that on display, but because for him the most meaningful part is what happens after death, that's the part he doesn't like to hurry. There are tools, some of which have been adapted. The odd thing is, for all the savagery, it is evidently a work of creation, at least in his mind, the way he sets about meeting such an extraordinarily precise need. He's done this before. Every artist paints the same picture over and over again, I suppose, every sculptor casts and recasts the same image. In the one act there's both deep familiarity, as though he's encountering himself, and a look of astonishment and wonder at the way life can surprise us with joy. His hunger is so fierce that it imposes an efficiency on each action. Everything has its place, everything has its turn. The order he brings to his work is like a raft that carries him out onto a violent sea, and as the raft begins to break into pieces, as it was always meant to do, the birds watch in silence as Ali finally abandons himself to its wild frenzies, to the endless pleasures of its black-tentacled depths.

~

The celebrations in London start in the early afternoon, shortly after the arrival of an incoming message informing members of the HAARLEM group that the suspected Iranian operative has been detained on the road between Zermatt and Lausanne. Swiss police found four large bottles of hydrofluoric acid concealed in the boot of his rental car, along with a box of thick rubber gloves. The man, aged somewhere in his late fifties, claimed that the items were not his and requested consular assistance from the nearest Iranian embassy, despite carrying a passport that purports to be that of a Turkish national.

Plaudits are flooding in, mostly marked for the attention of Sir William Rentoul. Among them is a personal note from his French counterpart, congratulating Sir William for 'rightly repositioning the UK at the heart of Europe's security' and inviting him to return to Paris at the first opportunity to attend a retirement dinner held in his honour.

Philip, the Director of Establishments, basks in the glow of operational success. Several members of the board, as well as two of Sir William's deputies, come down to congratulate him and his team. 'We don't yet know the identity of the intended victim,' Philip says to the crowds spilling out into the corridor. He spots one or two of his rivals. 'What we do know is that the people in this room have saved a life today, and in my book that goes down as a day well spent.'

~

Aphra has lost the signal from Zak's phone. She's tried to call him dozens of times but it goes straight to voicemail. The only thing she can think to do is find the general area where it was last active, arriving several hours later when the light among the trees is already thickening into a blue-grey mist. There can't be more than an hour or two of visibility left. She looks around, sees that other tyre tracks are visible, has no way of knowing when they were made or by which kind of vehicle. She locks the car and sets off along the path.

She walks quickly for almost an hour, looking around her for anything that seems out of place. At times, in the absence of anything better to do, she lies down on the forest floor and listens. At other times she calls his name. It's so quiet that even minutes later she can still hear the frayed edge of her screams.

In the end it's the darkness that delivers her to what she is looking for. She can barely see well enough to follow the path back down the hill, stumbling over rocks and roots, but in the sensory blackout forced upon her she detects the faintest smell of smoke. Pushing her way through the trees, she walks into the wood, pausing every minute or so to stop and breathe and adjust her direction. She's so afraid of breaking the spell that she doesn't use the torch on her phone until she can't go any further. The smell of smoke around here is strong. The torch reveals only a forest floor of pine needles and damp earth, much as she would have expected. She drops to her knees and spreads her hands and runs them lightly over the ground, expanding the circles until she burns her skin on the edge of something smouldering. It's a piece of material, no more than an inch across, the grey check pattern of Zak's overcoat briefly visible, but in the instant she turns her torch on it the wool crackles and flares and it's gone for ever.

~

I'm just going to say it: life goes on. It *must*.

~

Sir William drives his Land Rover into Germany, stopping in Cologne and Leipzig before arriving in Berlin late one rain-sodden evening. He spends an entire day in the Spy Museum, and is awake early the next morning, having signed up for a walking tour of Cold War sights that includes a Stasi prison, the Bridge of Spies and Checkpoint Charlie. He gets lost on his way to the meeting point and has to phone the tour guide to come and get him. Lunch is a paper plate of Kaiserschmarren from a street vendor operating out of an Airstream near the Reichstag. The guide is a softly spoken PhD student. Sir William tries to engage him in conversation, wanting to give voice to an increasing sense that the profession he loved was in fact bad for him, but the young man has his eye on a Canadian student with pink hair and walks away from Sir William mid-sentence on the pretext of checking that everyone is happy with their lunch. He sends postcards to each of his nine grandchildren.

~

One of Sir William's two deputies is temporarily promoted to lead the Service pending a recruitment campaign to find a permanent replacement. Number Ten announces that it will be inviting applications from candidates outside the intelligence community in an attempt to inject bold new ideas at a time when the UK faces an unprecedented level of threat. Two front-runners emerge, both from the private sector, but their campaigns are scuttled when stories appear in the press suggesting one made a series of now deleted social media posts praising Chinese innovation while the other was once subject to an HMRC fine.

Many inside the organisation are surprised when Philip, the Director of Establishments, is asked to cover the vacant position of deputy. Forgetting that such a thing is premature when the promotion is temporary, Philip gathers together the staff working directly to him and pledges to bring 'the zeal of a moderniser' to his new role.

The most urgent task facing Philip is to formulate three communications strategies – for staff, for Whitehall and for the Five Eyes community – that will explain Sir William's sudden disappearance from view.

~

A few days after she formally resigned via the office's automated HR system, Susan receives an email with details of her exit date. When she protests that she didn't mean to resign, that she was instructed to submit the form by someone from HR, that she has worked in the Service since 1982 and has no intention of going anywhere, she is told that HR is aware of this but unfortunately the software cannot be manually overridden. She will therefore have to leave but is assured that she will be rehired the next day, receiving in the process the very competitive joiners' bonus being paid to all new entrants.

When Susan asks to have this put in writing, she is told that there is absolutely no need to worry as a record of the conversation will be kept in her HR file.

~

Aphra McQueen is arrested by police at St Pancras Station for an alleged breach of the Official Secrets Act. She makes no comment throughout her interview, which focusses on the alleged theft of a top secret file from a government building several days earlier. She is released within twenty-four hours under strict bail conditions.

It is a universal truth that sailing in the right direction requires some sailing in the wrong direction. A sailboat in a choppy sea makes an infinite number of tiny adjustments. The best judge of navigational accuracy is not the hapless deckhand, it is the gull many hundreds of feet above the waves. This is perhaps a lesson that Philip has been promoted too quickly to absorb, because instead of accepting that recent events were regrettable but unavoidable, like a strong headwind or a devilish current, he concludes that they need to be neatly closed off, and so he decides to invite Aphra McQueen to attend a meeting.

~

This first thing he thinks is, there was no need to do this. Look at her. Just look at her.

'Thank you for coming in, Miss McQueen,' he says.

He had thought to sit behind his desk but comes around to take a seat directly opposite her. He crosses his legs and leans back, studying her for a full thirty seconds. He has not smiled yet and does not intend to do so until she leaves.

'There is some value, I hope, in spelling out a few home truths,' he says. 'You were arrested on a very serious charge that carries a prison sentence. The police will have made you aware that the evidence against you is strong. It even includes CCTV footage from our own cameras of the moment the stolen file was discovered in your bag.'

He gives it another ten seconds.

'It gets worse.'

He gestures towards a stack of papers, face down on his desk.

'We have here additional evidence, not yet handed to the police, that you used classified information in the stolen file to contact a vulnerable individual in Birmingham, masquerade as a British intelligence officer and persuade him to accompany you to France.'

He shakes his head in dismay at her actions.

'I'm not going to ask you to comment on any of this. It's for you to discuss with the police and with your lawyer, if it comes to that.'

He sips from his cup of coffee. She has not been offered anything.

'The situation facing you is dire indeed, Miss McQueen. A conviction is something you will carry with you for the rest of your days. You don't need me to spell out what you will lose, in terms of your home, your career and your reputation, not to mention your liberty. Entirely against my better judgement, however, I have been persuaded that it would be judicious to at least explore whether there is a way to avoid the publicity a prosecution would inevitably bring.'

He sighs audibly to signal his frustration at those invisible forces that have corralled his impulses.

'For us to set aside our best interests in this matter, we would need the strongest possible guarantee from you that you will not discuss recent events nor the material in that file with anyone at all, with absolutely no exception.'

Philip knows that Susan has admitted to planting the file in Aphra's bag, which will preclude any charges *actually* being brought. The Service would have to admit this to the CPS. Her arrest was therefore no more than an intimidatory piece of theatre, but Philip intends to use it as a means of cowing her into a permanent and binding silence. He has already drafted a non-disclosure agreement to that effect.

'Well?' he says, handing her the piece of paper. 'What do you say?'

~

Sir William somehow manages to find the cabin fifty miles outside Lillehammer where he and his wife stayed on their honeymoon. It's off-season and the cabin is unoccupied. His attempts to track down the owners by knocking on the door of a nearby farmhouse prove fruitless. He returns to the cabin as dusk is settling and breaks a window to gain entry. Climbing through, he catches his hand on a shard of glass and bleeds over the kitchen floor. There's plenty of firewood and an old tin of tuna. He boards up the window using four tacks and a square of material cut from his waxed jacket. In the place where his memory tells him the sauna was located, he can only find a narrow cupboard, stacked high with board games and children's toys, and in that moment he realises that he may have broken into the wrong cabin.

The first snow of the season falls that night. At dawn he fills an envelope with a thousand pounds worth of Norwegian kroner and leaves it on the kitchen table, along with the keys to the jeep. The clothes in the wardrobe are mostly too big but he finds salopettes and a brightly patterned sweater that will do if he rolls up the sleeves. The fresh snow is dazzling. He doesn't know if he's ever seen anything quite so beautiful, apart from his wife, apart from his wife.

Strapping on a pair of cross-country skis, he sets off, his heart full and happy, an old hunting rifle slung across his back.

∼

'Some of what happened was reported in the press,' Aphra says.

'That's correct. A suspected Iranian operative with alleged links to a string of murders across Europe was detained by Swiss police. He was released due to insufficient evidence and deported.'

Philip senses it's not enough and so adds:

'The strongest possible representations have been made to Iranian embassies across Europe.'

She looks at him.

'It's a success, Aphra. That so many murders were allowed to happen is tragic, but the way he was finally caught was a triumph of modern intelligence work.'

He feels as though he's the one under pressure.

'They had to let him go. No one doubts that he was on his way to commit a murder, but that means that at the point of his arrest there was no forensic evidence. No blood, no bone, no foreign DNA. They examined every inch of his car. And of course there was no body.'

She still hasn't taken the piece of paper from him.

'Now you know what happened, Aphra. Look over the terms of this agreement and sign at the bottom.'

'*I* know what happened,' she says, taking the piece of paper but not looking at it. 'The question is, do *you* know what happened? Where's your agent? Where's Ali?'

'We don't discuss our agents.'

'He's moved out of his apartment in Paris.'

'It's a long-standing principle and one that is not up for negotiation.'

'It all happened very quickly, according to his neighbours. A dozen men packed his belongings into a truck with a British licence plate.'

'There is no point pursuing this line of questioning.'

'Have you relocated him to the UK?'

'I think you've forgotten why you are here.'

'Did you bring him to the UK to prevent him being caught up in the French investigation?'

'Listen—'

'I assume you've only just realised the truth, that *he* killed all those people. The alternative, that you've known all along, is too horrific to consider. His uncle was the handler, the clean-up man. He made sure there was no forensic evidence. The perfect job for a chemist, when you think about it.'

'If you repeat a single one of these lies outside this room, you will go straight to prison.'

'You have decided that keeping him as an agent is more important than handing him to the French to be charged,' she says.

'You have no idea how these things work.'

'Do you know what he is?'

'I've had enough of—'

Aphra stands up, throws the piece of paper back at him, her voice so loud that the staff in Philip's outer office are able to hear.

'I asked you a fucking question! Do you know what that man really is?'

~

The house they've given him is unimaginable. He's learned all these new terms: pebble-dash, two-up two-down, stipple. His neighbours invited him around for a barbeque at the weekend, and when he said no, they stood there expectantly, smiling and nodding, waiting for something that never came, something that never comes with him, an apology or an explanation or a promise to be different next time.

Ned gets the train up from Liverpool Street twice a week. On his most recent visit, he tried to suggest that Ali had brought it upon himself, that this house was the best that could be done in tight circumstances and at short notice. You need to stay out of the lime-light for a while, he said. Let's see how things go. After a year or two we may be able to move you to London. There's an implicit threat buried in there. He should know – he knows about threats, he knows about burials. Get better or stay here, that's what Ned is telling him.

At least he's still able to use his own name, that's something. He's not hiding from the Iranian government, he's just getting away from legal repercussions that might arise from recent events, as Ned puts it. It's the closest he gets to discussing what happened. Ned much prefers to talk about Ali's next trip to Iran and all the things he can find out for them. The other stuff he leaves to the psychiatrists, who come in a pair, spending several hours with him every afternoon.

He's feeling a lot better, he really is. At night he stands at the window and looks out for hours at a time.

~

I keep half an eye on Aphra, but to be honest it's a dispiriting task, and there's so much else happening that requires my undivided attention. That's a joke, by the way. I feel we know each other well enough for such things by now. My attention is always divided, of course it is. Wherever two or three are gathered in my name, or whatever the line is, that's where you'll find me. There's new recruits to spend time with, and some of the proposals being generated by the board are simply dangerous, and one or two members of the social media team seem to have forgotten where they work. The new ethics counsellor has completely misunderstood their purpose. Philip is requiring considerable mentoring as he grows into his new, now permanent role. Julian Redruth and his parliamentary committee might have been tamed, but that still leaves affairs, fights, rivalries, ambitions and resentments that snag at the fabric of this place, requiring patient and skilful repair.

Aphra does nothing anyway, at least for six months. She takes her hiking boots to the Dolomites for a long while, and upon her return she joins the London Library. She has a letter published in the *Historical Journal*. She sends a card to Julian Redruth when he steps down from Parliament. He invites her to the Members' Tea Rooms in the House of Commons, where she apologises for her actions, attributing them to a slow psychological breakdown, triggered by grief, for which she has been receiving treatment. Julian finds himself moved by her words. He makes a note of the conversation and passes it to his successor as chair of the Intelligence and Security Committee, who passes it in turn to Sir William's successor, now in post, to be added to the file.

She cuts her hair short and lets it grow back some of the way, experimenting briefly with a silvery-grey colour. As part of the healing process, she takes to returning to this building and its environs, sitting for hours in local coffee shops until something happens inside her and she rushes off for no apparent reason. She must cover at least ten miles a day on foot. There's neither rhyme nor reason to the places she haunts: the National Gallery, Liverpool Street Station, the New Covent Garden Flower Market, Victoria Park. She often attends the morning service at the Crown Court Church of Scotland on Russell Street.

I do wish she'd eat more. I'm glad she's getting better, but I'd like it even more if she got a job or started dating or took up a hobby. What happened was awful, but I can't imagine that the calculation made by Philip and Ned and others was a straightforward one. It would take a moral bookkeeper of preternatural ability to tally the columns, and even then I suspect the difference would be marginal. I can understand how difficult that is to hear. I really can. It's just a sad fact of life that what might be a marginal difference to the spies is large enough to have swallowed up the lives of two people she cared for.

~

There's a night-time walk that takes him outside the town to a gap in an overgrown hedge, a footpath and a small wooden bridge. Beyond it are the marshes and then the sea. The reeds are already scratching at his trousers when he realises that someone is standing on the path a little way ahead of him.

'Hello?' he says.

A bone-white tree stands pale against the dark sky. There's enough light from the moon to make out her features.

'I've seen you before,' he says. 'In Paris. You were on the street outside my apartment.'

She doesn't say anything.

'How did you find me?' he says.

'It wasn't difficult. Some of your visitors have grown a little careless.'

He feels the wind on his face, smells deeply of the sea.

'I'm getting better,' he says. 'I really am.'

She nods.

'I'm doing a lot of work,' he says. 'Two of them come every day. Well, you probably know this already. We talk for hours about everything that happened.'

She waits.

'I should go,' he says, but something keeps him there.

'How many were there?' she says.

He shakes his head.

'Do you remember them all?' she says.

'I remember some things. Other things I've forgotten.'

'Tell me.'

'Was Zaki your friend? I'm sorry. I really am.'

The tree is an upended bolt of lightning stabbed into the marshland.

'It was like being chained to a heavy weight dragging me under-water,' he says. 'That's the only way I can describe it. I used to think there was no way of fighting it. I had to get to the bottom before I could begin to resurface.'

'Did it matter that they were people? People with lives, with families?'

'It sounds terrible but I didn't really think of any of that. I wasn't in control of myself or my thoughts.'

'Do you think about what it was like for them?'

'I think about it all the time. It's probably the thing we talk about most.' He hangs his head. 'It's awful to admit this but at the beginning I was pretending. I said what they wanted to hear. This hasn't been a gradual process. It was sudden. One day I was still being controlled by that thing, the next day I wasn't. I look back on the person I was with disgust. I simply don't recognise him.'

She's gone back to how she was on day one. The same hair, the same seal-black coat, the same red scarf.

'I've never lived in a place like this,' he says. 'The first few weeks I was desperate to get away. Now I can't imagine leaving. I don't pretend that my life here is normal, but I pass the time of day with the lady in the post office, and I'm looking after my neighbours' dog next week while they're away.'

He looks out beyond the marsh.

'There's something about the sea,' he says.

'You walk a lot.'

'Yes.'

'Especially at night.'

'Maybe it's the sense of shame,' he says. 'It's easier not to be seen by people, given the things I've done.'

He bends to pick up a stone from the path, throws it, glinting like a coin, high over the marsh.

'There's a house you go to,' she says. 'You stand at the bottom of the garden.'

'I've talked about it with the psychiatrists,' he says. 'The road not taken, that's what one of them calls it. A loving family, a domestic scene. They suggested that I use it as a way of exploring difficult aspects of my own childhood.'

'Do you tell them that you go right up to the window?'

He looks at her.

'Do you tell them that you climb over the fence, walk up the garden and watch them through the window?'

He bends to pick up another stone. He smiles at her.

'Do you tell them that you go inside the house when they're sleeping?'

He steps towards her and swings his arm at her head, the stone making contact just above the hairline. She falls to the path. He stands over her and swings for the bone next to her left eye. He throws it away, looks around for something heavier. There's a piece of driftwood next to the path. He staggers towards it, breathing heavily. His hand leaves a glistening red palm print on its flayed white surface. It slips away from him. He blinks, tries to take hold of it again. A sharp pain begins in his right armpit and crashes through his body. He slumps to the ground.

Aphra McQueen stands over him. There's a knife in her hand. The bloom of a rose clots her hair.

'No,' he says. 'No.'

As they were walking back from Notre-Dame, she recalls, Zak took out a piece of brioche wrapped in a paper napkin and tore it into two wildly uneven pieces, giving one to her and quickly putting the other in his mouth so she wouldn't see how small it was.

Ali tries to drag himself backwards, away from her.

'Please,' he says.

She remembers lying inside the fallen tree. Although she couldn't always see her brother, she knew he was there from the warmth of his breath, from the occasional scampering of his fingers across the rotting wood, from his intake of delight when he spotted a beetle or a grub. Sometimes the two of them would sing to each other, to the life that surrounded them.

Isn't it amazing, he once whispered through the darkness. This tree is as full of life as it ever was. Why is anyone scared of dying?

In death there is life, he taught her that. And in life there is death. She only has to look into Ali's eyes to know that.

If the smaller piece was enough for Zak, it's enough for her too. She drops the knife.

Nothing ever ends.

Acknowledgements

Plotted in private, executed under conditions of the utmost secrecy, subject to endless adjustments and reimaginings – it turns out there's more than one similarity between spying and novel writing. You return from another day of mixed results at the office to face the usual questions. 'Oh, it was okay, I suppose,' you find yourself saying, or 'It could have been worse. How was your day?' Then the unthinkable happens: it goes public. In such circumstances, standard authorial jitters would be more than enough without the additional anxiety that a top-secret operation has just been blown sky high.

In my case, the process has been made so much easier by those who have helped along the way. Yassine Belkacemi, Zulekhá Afzal and Jade Chandler at Baskerville have been unfailingly supportive and enthusiastic, and Georgina Capel, Simon Shaps, Irene Baldoni, Rachel Conway and Polly Halladay continue to be allies of the most steadfast kind. T. and D. told me what a pair of spies might make of the manuscript, and Lauren pointed out the flaws in my attempt to sound like a dentist. I would also like to thank my wife, who revealed far-reaching reserves of love and support during the writing of this book, and my two children, who are not satisfied in the slightest with my explanation for why their father's real name isn't on the front.

About the Author

James Wolff grew up in Beirut and has lived in Damascus, Cairo and Istanbul. He worked as a British intelligence officer for over ten years. He lives in England.

RAISING READERS
Books Build Bright Futures

Dear Reader,

We'd love your attention for one more page to tell you about the crisis in children's reading, and what we can all do.

Studies have shown that reading for fun is the **single biggest predictor of a child's future life chances** – more than family circumstance, parents' educational background or income. It improves academic results, mental health, wealth, communication skills, ambition and happiness.[1]

The number of children reading for fun is in rapid decline. Young people have a lot of competition for their time. In 2024, 1 in 10 children and young people in the UK aged 5 to 18 did not own a single book at home.[2]

Hachette works extensively with schools, libraries and literacy charities, but here are some ways we can all raise more readers:

- Reading to children for just 10 minutes a day makes a difference
- Don't give up if children aren't regular readers – there will be books for them!
- Visit bookshops and libraries to get recommendations
- Encourage them to listen to audiobooks
- Support school libraries
- Give books as gifts

There's a lot more information about how to encourage children to read on our website: **www.RaisingReaders.co.uk**

Thank you for reading.

---

[1] National Literacy Trust, Book Ownership in 2024, November 2024
https://nlt.cdn.ngo/media/documents/Book_ownership_in_2024

[2] OECD. 2021. 21st-century readers: developing literacy skills in a digital world. Paris, France: OECD Publishing.
https://www.oecd.org/en/publications/21st-century-readers_a83d84cb-en.html